Ramsey Campbell was born in Liverpool in 1946. He lived in Liverpool for many years before moving to Wallasey, Merseyside. His first book was published when he was 18, and he worked as a tax officer and in libraries before becoming a full-time writer in 1973. He is the author of the novels *The Doll Who Ate His Mother*, *The Face That Must Die*, *The Parasite*, *Incarnate* and *Obsession* as well as five collections of short stories: *The Inhabitant of the Lake*, *Demons by Daylight*, *The Height of the Scream*, *Dark Companions* and *Cold Print*. He has won the World Fantasy Award twice (for best short story of the year) and the British Fantasy Award twice (once for best short story, once for best novel) – more than any other writer in the field. Ramsey Campbell has also edited several anthologies of horror fiction, broadcasts frequently on Radio Merseyside as a film critic, and is President of the British Fantasy Society.

By the same author

Novels

The Parasite (I Wake the Dead)
The Doll Who Ate His Mother
The Face That Must Die
Incarnate
Obsession

Short Stories

Inhabitant of the Lake
Demons by Daylight
The Height of the Scream
Dark Companions
Cold Print

Anthologies

Superhorror (The Far Reaches of Fear)
New Terrors
New Tales of the Cthulhu Mythos
The Gruesome Book

RAMSEY CAMPBELL

The Nameless

PANTHER
Granada Publishing

Panther Books
Granada Publishing Ltd
8 Grafton Street, London W1X 3LA

This revised edition published by Panther Books 1985

First published in Great Britain by
Fontana Paperbacks 1981

Copyright © Ramsey Campbell 1981, 1985

ISBN 0-586-06367-6

Printed and bound in Great Britain by
Clays Ltd, St Ives plc

Set in Plantin

for Tamsin
(who helped without even knowing)
with my love

Acknowledgements

I am especially grateful for help and advice while writing this novel to Robert Aickman, Tony Beck, Arthur Cullimore, Phil Edwards, Kay McCauley, Christine Ruth, Tim Shackleton, Bob Shaw (the Glasgow science fiction fan rather than the Lakeland science fiction writer), Carol Smith, and John Thompson. I owe even more to Barry Forshaw, Peter and Susie Straub, and Thom and Alice Tessier, for their impeccable hospitality during my field trips to London, and I have a special thank you to Harlan Ellison and his feats of total recall.

It goes without saying that the Otford nursery school is my invention. Up to the time of writing there is no Barclaybank machine in Glasgow.

Prologue: 1940

The yard was larger than a football field, but it felt much smaller. As he stepped into the yard, the walls closed in. The summer sky and the hills were bright as posters, and gulls glided screaming over San Francisco Bay, but once you were inside the walls it was impossible to be aware of anything but them. Perhaps it was only the hundreds of faces staring down, the voices shouting propositions like desperate whores, yet it felt as if the walls were leaning over you, as if they'd grown senile with immeasurable misery and bitterness. Sometimes it seemed you could feel the stones aching.

But the tall man reacted to none of this. As he stalked across the yard, following his shadow which was thin as his limbs and black as his clothes, his long sharp face was expressionless. Only his eyes were bright and purposeful. He reached the north cell block and strode in as if he had no time to waste. Nevertheless, when he came to the green door he paused and peered through the window.

There wasn't much to see: just a room nine feet across, whose walls glared the same sickly green as the door. You couldn't tell by looking that the steel walls alone weighed over two tons. The two empty chairs that stood in the room might have belonged to a dentist or a barber who had gone out for lunch – except that nobody who had to sit in one of those chairs ever got up again.

After a while he strode along to the elevator and stepped in. If anything, his eyes were brighter now. But they were expressionless by the time the guard at the top of the shaft unlocked the elevator to let him through, and the next guard, who searched him in the outer cubicle, hardly glanced at his face. In a minute the cubicle door was locked behind him, and he was on Death Row.

It was much quieter than the yard, but the silence felt as though it was locked in. There was an atmosphere of men on edge with waiting while pretending not to wait at all. It hung in the air like gas, invisible but suffocating. Eyes that looked baggy with shadow stared at him from cells narrower than the stretch of a man's arms and little more than twice the length. Behind each man, beneath a caged light-bulb, was nothing but a stool and a bunk and a seatless toilet. Perhaps the eyes were dark with more than shadows.

The tall man ignored all this. He strode up to Santini, who stood rattling his keys and tasting last night's meatballs, and wondering what the sharp-faced guy looked like. Maybe if he could figure that he wouldn't feel so tense. Or maybe that came with the job. Whenever they brought a con into the Row Santini grew nervous, in case the sight of the place he was going to spend the rest of his life drove the guy berserk. Santini always breathed easier when the new one was locked up.

'I am Doctor Ganz,' the tall man said briskly. 'I am here to see Frank Bannon.'

Santini might have been a specimen in a laboratory, the way the guy was looking at him. No doubt Ganz was here to find things to bitch about. Psychiatrists and attorneys, they ought to be locked up in here for a while; they'd soon see how necessary everything was. Only they never looked so cool as this guy. Anyone who looked as cool as that after a walk past the gas chamber, there had to be something wrong with him.

When Santini unlocked the interrogation-room, which was scarcely larger than a pay toilet, Ganz sat down at the far side of the table. His elbows rested on it, his fingertips touched his bony cheeks, and Santini almost realized what he looked like. As Santini turned to join the other line-man, who was waiting to unlock the cell, he noticed that Ganz's eyes were gleaming.

Bannon glanced up with a faint vague smile when they opened his cell, and Santini felt sick to his stomach. Of all the animals they kept locked up in San Quentin, Bannon was the worst. Santini couldn't think of what he had done to that girl without wanting to puke. Somehow the way Bannon looked made it worse: always neat and clean, face scrubbed and so untroubled you couldn't even tell how old he was. Now Governor Olson had got up off his ass in Sacramento and was bitching about prison reform, about the dungeons and the rest of it – but by God, Bannon deserved to be left down there without a blanket if anyone did. Santini would have helped the guards with the rubber hoses if Bannon looked like getting out of hand. Maybe a taste of the lime and water treatment might make him cry a few tears for the girl.

The line-men escorted Bannon across the corridor, his slippers flapping. 'Thank you, Mr Santini,' he said, and Santini could have knocked him down. The son of a bitch observed the rules so carefully you'd think he enjoyed them. Santini slammed the door of the windowless room and locked it, but that didn't lessen his anger or the stale taste of meatballs. He was turning away when he heard Ganz say 'Good afternoon.'

You could forget the time of day in here, but that wasn't why Santini turned back. 'Maybe I'll stick around here for a while in case he gets through quickly,' he said.

The other line-man moved away, shrugging. No doubt he realized that Santini meant to eavesdrop, but Santini didn't care. It wasn't only that he wanted to hear what Bannon had to say about himself, the son of a bitch – it was more that he wanted to know what made the man in black so eager to talk to him.

9

At first Ganz sounded like any do-gooder with the usual assholed questions. Did Bannon ever feel depressed? Did they give him books if he wanted to read? Had he seen his wife since he was brought here? Would he like to see her? 'Sure, I'd like to see her if she wants to come,' Bannon said.

'How would you describe your married life? Satisfactory on the whole?'

'I'd say we had a pretty good life. She didn't complain much, and I never had any reason to. I was picking up good money as a senior engineer. We lived as well as any of our friends.' Santini's fists were clenching: the son of a bitch probably had a better marriage than he did – he didn't look forward to home leave any longer, not when she'd start chattering like a monkey as soon as he came in the door, not when greasy pasta came with every meal. No wonder she was twice the size she'd been when he had married her.

He made himself stop listening to himself, for Ganz was asking 'Do you remember what you did that brought you here?'

'Sure I do. I'm not crazy, you know. They said I wasn't at the trial.'

'And how do you feel now about what you did?'

'I feel all right. I can talk about it if you want.'

His indifference was appalling. Santini wasn't sure if he could bear to listen. He could understand some violence – a man hitting on his wife now and then, you couldn't blame a guy for that – but not what this animal had done.

'Yes, I'd like you to talk about it,' Ganz said. 'I want you to tell me everything you did and how it felt. Will you do that?' His tone had been professionally neutral, but now Santini thought he heard a hint of eagerness. He risked a glance through the small window in the door, and realized instantly what Ganz looked like. With his gleaming eyes, his elbows propping his thin arms, his long hands framing his sharp ageless face, he looked very much like a praying mantis.

'Well, where do you want me to start?' Bannon said. 'I just saw this woman in the street one day and followed her.'

'Why did you follow her?'

'Because she was so good-looking, I guess. It turned out she was going home, so I found out where she lived, in an apartment building. Only I didn't think I could do anything in there, in case someone overheard.'

'What did you have in mind to do? You were thinking of rape at that time?'

'Not at all.' Bannon sounded offended. 'I told you, I had a pretty good marriage. I never thought of being unfaithful, ever. All I knew was I had to get this woman alone somewhere we wouldn't be interrupted. The more I followed her, the more I knew I had to do that.'

'You followed her over several weeks. Did your wife notice anything unusual about your behaviour, do you think?'

'She said in court she never did. I just told her I was out on jobs. She had no reason to disbelieve me.'

'So eventually you got to the woman you were following. Tell me about that.'

'Well, I knew by now she worked in a factory, so I decided one morning to see if I could get in there. There were hundreds of people going in, nobody noticed me. Nobody questioned me or anything, even when I followed her to the section where she worked. I was just wondering if I could get her alone when I found an old pair of overalls someone must have used for mopping up. Well, I went behind a machine and put them on, and once I'd smeared oil on my face my own wife wouldn't have known me. I didn't like getting dirty and looking like some kind of junior employee, but I knew I had to. I went straight to the woman and made her understand I needed her to unlock the storeroom just across the way. I guess you know she was a supervisor. Well, she couldn't question me because of all the noise. She unlocked the door and I went in after her.'

11

Ganz sat forward. 'And then you – '

'Well, first I grabbed her keys and locked us in. That only took a few moments. Then I threw her on the floor and sat on her chest. She had her right arm free and I was kneeling on the other. I guess you know what I did then. I took the fingers off her right hand with a pair of pliers.'

'That must have taken some time,' Ganz said conversationally, and Santini had to bite hard on his knuckles to control himself. 'Did her screams bother you?'

'No, not really. I knew nobody could hear them for the noise outside.'

'Then how were you feeling?'

'I don't think I felt anything much, except maybe as if I was dreaming. I remember it all seemed to be happening a long way from me. Wait, I did feel one thing – sort of disappointed there wasn't more to it, somehow.'

'And why did you think you were doing this to her?'

'I didn't think about it much. I just felt it was something that had to be done.'

'As soon as you'd finished, you left her.'

'That's right. I locked her in and walked straight through the factory gates. They must have thought she was somewhere else in the factory, because they didn't find her for a while. I dumped the overalls as soon as nobody could see me and washed up in a public toilet, then I went in to work. I mean, nobody was going to ask why I was a little late. The only thing was, I had to buy a suit to match the one I'd dirtied up. Once I got rid of the dirty suit in the furnace, everything was fine.'

'How did you feel when you learned your victim wasn't dead?'

'Well, I was hoping she wasn't. I was afraid she might have died from loss of blood. For a while there I felt pretty bad when I thought about it. If she'd died I don't know what I would have done. When I read that the doctors had managed to save her I felt so good I had to tell my wife I'd landed an important contract, so she wouldn't wonder why I was laughing.'

'Then there is a gap of a few months. Were you ever afraid the police might trace you?'

'To tell the truth, I never thought about it. I kind of felt as if what had happened to her was someone else's responsibility.'

'But you were waiting for her, weren't you?'

'Oh, sure. I mean, I couldn't have got to her while she was in the hospital. It didn't bother me to wait, I just put it out of my mind. I knew I had to finish what I'd started.'

'Tell me about that.'

Son of a bitch, Santini was muttering through teeth that were clenched so hard that they ached, goddamn sadistic son of a bitch. He couldn't have said which of them he meant. 'Well,' Bannon said, 'I kept watching her apartment, so I knew when she came home. Her mother had moved in there already to look after her. I went up there one morning, when I figured most of the neighbours would be out of the building. I wasn't sure what I had to do this time, so I took along a box of tools.'

'Her mother answered the door.'

'That's right, and she let me in when I said the caretaker had sent me up to check the wiring. Then I guess she decided she ought to have called him first, because she went for the phone. I knocked her cold before she could do anything, then I went to her daughter.'

'What did you feel when you saw her?'

'Sort of disappointed. She wasn't nearly as good-looking. I mean, she must have been in her thirties and yet she looked older than her mother. She had something on her right hand, a kind of surgical mitten, I guess. I remember I was uncomfortable, the way freaks make you feel. I guess I felt disgusted with her for looking that way. She was sitting

13

up in bed, listening to Count Basie on the radio. She sort of woke up from dozing when I came in. She saw the toolbox, and then she looked at my face, and I could see she recognized me right away.'

'And what did you do then?'

'Well, first I had to stop her screaming in case anyone could hear,' Bannon said, and that was when Santini blocked his ears. He knew enough of what had happened to convince him that he couldn't bear to hear any more. He could imagine Bannon's victim, home at last and feeling as safe as she would ever be able to feel, looking up to see him in her bedroom. He swallowed the sour taste of meatballs and watched Ganz, whose eyes were even brighter now. He was supposed to be a psychiatrist, but Santini thought he should be locked up himself.

It must have been five minutes before he saw Ganz relax and felt he could risk listening. 'When her mother saw what I was doing she ran straight down the hall,' Bannon was saying. 'I could hear her screaming and banging at all the doors, even though I'd turned the radio all the way up.'

'But you were still there when the police arrived.'

'Well, the woman wasn't dead then. I wanted to finish if I could.'

'How did you feel when you were arrested?'

'Frustrated, I guess. I felt I hadn't finished. And then I felt that well, they'd caught me, there was nothing else I could do.'

'Is that how you feel now?'

'To tell you the truth, I just feel kind of exhausted, deep down inside myself. I mean, I did all those things to her, I guess they have to punish me for that. It doesn't seem to matter, somehow. Only I don't know, when I try to think about what I did, why I did it – '

Ganz's long hands reached out towards him. 'What? What are you trying to say?'

14

'Well, I feel somehow I was doing it for someone else.'

Santini felt restless and furious – it was just the usual psychiatric bullshit, even if he hadn't heard it put that way before – but Ganz was nodding. 'Yes. Yes, I see. Well, you have been very patient in answering my questions. Is there a question you would like to ask me?'

'Sure,' Bannon said at once, 'if you can tell me why I did all that to her.'

Something like a smile dawned on Ganz's face. 'You are not the first to ask me such a question. You understand what I am saying? You are not alone. If it is a consolation, there are others driven by the same forces as you.'

Santini saw Bannon's hand strike the table. It looked like a claw, ready to scratch. Maybe he would attack the psychiatrist, that might be a kind of justice. For the first time Bannon's voice was ragged. 'But can you tell me what the forces are?'

'Yes, I believe I can,' Ganz said, just as Santini heard the unlocking of the door at the end of the corridor. He turned to see his fellow line-man, two uniformed policemen, and the warden. 'He's in there,' the line-man said. 'Where Santini's standing.'

Santini strained to hear what Ganz was saying, but he could hear nothing over the approach of the four men. 'The nerve of that guy,' the other line-man said to him. 'He's no more a psychiatrist than I am. He's been giving them that line from here to Alcatraz. He'd never have got by here except for all the trouble with the Governor.' He lowered his voice as they converged on the interrogation-room, and hissed quickly to Santini: 'You could make out you waited because you suspected something. Might look good for you.'

Things were happening too fast for Santini to think of scheming. He could only watch bewildered as they un-locked the interrogation-room, then step forward belatedly in case there was trouble. It was obvious at once that there wouldn't be any from Bannon, who looked stunned by whatever Ganz had told him. He looked as if he would rather not have heard.

The tall man rose to his full height as the policemen closed in on him. 'Kaspar Ganz,' one said, 'also known as Jasper Gance – '

The policeman was met by a look of contempt so intense that he faltered. 'Arrest me if you think you have to,' Ganz said indifferently. 'It won't change anything. You can't stop what's happening, you don't even know what it is. You wouldn't be capable of understanding.' His eyes glittered so brightly that Santini's stomach churned. 'You won't know what it is,' Ganz said, 'until it's too late.'

1: 1979

At ten to five he began to gnaw the rim of his glass, and she was afraid it would break. 'It's too late,' he said. 'They've had second thoughts.'

'Not at all. It's early yet, believe me. They like to take their time.'

'I wouldn't blame them if they did have second thoughts.' He sat down again, but not for long. He'd been wandering between the chairs and the couch all afternoon, as if he was trapped in a lonely game of musical chairs. 'I tried to read the books myself last night, and I couldn't get into them. They just seemed self-conscious and tedious.'

'Paul, they're the best thing you've ever done. If they weren't bestseller material we wouldn't be sitting here waiting for bids.'

'I don't know, Barbara. I'm not so sure. You liked my other books, and look what happened to them. I saw the last one selling for pennies just the other day in the remainders, and still nobody wanted to know.'

'Never mind your other books. Mario Puzo wrote two commercial failures before *The Godfather*.'

'Maybe, but that's Mario Puzo. Who the hell am I?'

'You're Paul Gregory, and *A Torrent of Lives* is going to be a bestseller.' We know it is, she told the photograph of Arthur in front of her on her desk. Nevertheless Paul's restlessness was making her edgy, less able to ignore the stagnant July heat, the grumbling of traffic which dodged in from Piccadilly and Bond Street only to wrangle beneath her window, the singing of the Jewish demonstrators outside the office of Soviet Airlines. Whenever he

17

went to the open window his shape loomed on the high white ceiling.

Now he was lifting a book from her shelves, only to find that the pages were blank. He stared at that as if it were a novel he was forced to write. 'I couldn't get past the Civil War scenes in *Torrent*,' he said. 'They just go on and on. They never come alive.'

'Just listen, Paul. Sit down for a moment and listen to me. I only sent the first volume to Pan and Futura and Penguin, and each of them rang up the following day for a look at the other two volumes. That's how enthusiastic they are.'

'Well, I didn't think the first one was too bad overall. It's the others that lumber along like dinosaurs that won't die. I mean, I quite like some of the writing, but I just can't write the kind of thing that people want to read. Suppose I wasted two years of my life?' He was picking through the magazines beneath the glass-topped table, *Publishers Weekly* and *Bookseller*, in search of distraction. 'My life and Sybil's and the children's,' he said dismally.

She was growing exasperated, though she'd had some of these doubts herself until he had shown her the books at last. He'd gambled everything on them, he'd given up his job in advertising, only to find that they took considerably more than a year to write. By then he and his family were besieged by bills and bank loans. When he had typed out the books and brought them to her office he'd looked almost ashamed of them, but they were a revelation, an astonishingly complex structure interweaving the fortunes of several families, ending as a kind of science fiction set one hundred years ahead. Perhaps it fell short of his ambitions for it, perhaps that was all he could see.

When the phone rang he glanced up too quickly, then tried to pretend he wasn't nervous. She gave him a smile that was meant to calm him down as she said 'Barbara Waugh Literary Agency.' Her instincts had told her not to

18

expect too much, and it was only one of her authors calling to say that he'd finished his new novel. No doubt he was suffering from the novelist's usual post-natal depression. When she told him that she was conducting an auction, he rang off.

'Jesus, who'd choose to make a living this way?' Paul was rubbing the top of his head above his wrap-around hair as if to warm up his thoughts. 'Writing must be a form of madness.'

He gulped his scotch and poured himself another. He'd found last week's Sunday supplement among her magazines and was trying to read the article about her. 'If they did have second thoughts,' he muttered, 'would they call to tell you so?'

'They don't have second thoughts at this stage. That isn't the way things are done.' Of course there was always a first time but not, she told herself, for *A Torrent of Lives*. Paul was trying to watch the clock without her noticing. She knew it was twenty past five, that was still quite early. Arthur continued to smile at her; he could hardly do anything else. Everything would be all right, his smile said, and the phone was ringing. 'Barbara Waugh Literary Agency,' she said, cool as a recorded message.

When she sat forward and reached for her pen Paul sat up, crumpling the supplement. She listened and nodded and said 'Thank you' neutrally as she scribbled on her pad. She tore off the page and pushed it across her desk as she began to call the other bidders. Paul gaped at the page and looked afraid to smile in case he was reading it wrong. 'I have a floor price of thirty thousand pounds,' she said for the second time, and nodded at him.

'Good Lord. That's pretty good, isn't it?' He seemed not to know where to look.

'We can do a lot better.' She was confident now. 'Just wait,' she told him.

They waited. Perhaps time seemed even slower now to him. He went back to reading the article about her. She could tell when his face changed that he'd reached the paragraph about Angela. She wished they hadn't found out about that – but here was another bid, and she could lose herself in making the calls, lose herself in her work and forget about Angela, as if she could ever forget. 'We are now up to forty thousand,' she said.

Beneath her window commuters were streaming towards the Underground, footsteps and voices merging into a blur. The traffic had grown intermittent before she received another bid. She read *Publishers Weekly,* she drafted a few letters, she checked her diary – lunch on Cape tomorrow, lunch with an author on Friday, Ted's birthday dinner on Sunday. The last scrap of sunlight crept off the ceiling, leaving behind all the heat. Paul was mopping his forehead. Auctions were slower than the slowest poker game.

Mayfair was quiet except for a few strolling tourists before the auction finished. She called the bidder of the floor price. 'I have a final bid of one hundred thousand pounds.'

She was so certain he would exercise his topping rights that she had already scribbled down the amount: the final bid plus ten per cent. When he did so she tore off the page and handed it to Paul. 'That's yours,' she said.

He seemed limp with shock or scotch. 'Thank you, Barbara. That's wonderful,' he said, kissing her awkwardly. All at once he grew anxious. 'I must call Sybil,' he said.

Had his wife been waiting by the phone? Certainly she answered at once. He told her the amount of the advance and said 'I don't believe it yet. I feel unreal.' In a moment Barbara learned why he had been anxious. 'I hope I haven't spoiled dinner,' he said. 'I didn't expect this to take so long.'

She watched him as he hurried towards Piccadilly. He

was halfway there before he noticed that he was still clutching the page and stuffed it into his pocket. She closed the window, smiling to herself. How many readers realized that half the bestsellers were written by people like him, ordinary domesticated men and women, perhaps more nervous and insecure than average, who happened to be able to tell stories? No wonder they needed agents to look after them.

She emerged through the empty outer office. Louise would be back tomorrow, having survived hay fever. Barbara lingered for a moment in the entrance porch, whose stone pillars felt warm as flesh. Everyone in Dover Street seemed to have gone home but her: Christie's art dealers, Longman & Strongi'th'arm the jewellers, the Oxford University Press, its windows set in crusty piebald arches that looked barnacled. She strolled down to Piccadilly and crossed into Green Park.

Now that the auction was over she felt drained, oddly depressed. Perhaps that was caused by her feeling that the whole thing was a game in which expert play could bring enormous success while poor play with the same stakes led to abject failure. Or perhaps the cause was the business of agenting, where as well as negotiating on behalf of your authors you had to mother them, sympathize with their domestic problems if you couldn't solve them, build and rebuild their confidence, calm their nerves, sometimes act as midwife to their books – and those were only the easy authors. Still, it was the most satisfying career she knew.

In the park she walked beneath the trees. The whitish sky held down the heat, but it was cooler beneath the mat of leaves. Deck-chairs striped like butchers' aprons lay back on the green; silvery pigeons polished as shells ransacked the grass. Soon she felt in gear again, and hungry. Pausing only to direct a couple of tourists across the park to Buckingham Palace, she returned to her office for a manuscript to read.

As she reached the porch, a phone began to ring. It was late for a business call, but it might well be Paul, apologizing for not inviting her to a celebratory meal; certainly the phone was ringing in her office. She had to slow down on the stairs, for all at once the heat seemed to focus on her: her body was sprinkled with hot sparks, the edges of her vision charred. No wonder, when she had been rushing on a day like this.

She unlocked her door and grabbed Louise's phone. 'Barbara Waugh Literary Agency,' she said breathlessly.

Was that an indrawn breath, or a hiss of static? She heard someone dialling on another line, a stray twang of electricity, the microscopic ringing of a phone; a voice chattering in Arabic drifted by in the distance. Otherwise there was silence. She was about to replace the receiver when a voice said 'Mummy.'

So it was a wrong number. 'Barbara Waugh Literary Agency,' she said patiently for the umpteenth time today.

This time the girl's voice didn't pause, though it sounded rejected. 'Mummy,' it pleaded.

It must be Louise's daughter, however odd it seemed that she would mistake Barbara for her mother – or, for that matter, that she would think Louise was here. Barbara spoke more sharply than she meant to, but she wanted to be rid of the lump of apprehension in her belly. 'This is Barbara Waugh herself speaking.'

Then she grabbed the back of Louise's chair and lowered herself to the seat for fear of falling, for the girl's voice had said 'Yes, Mummy, I know.'

'No, it can't be,' Barbara said, but she wasn't as sure of herself as she tried to sound, which was why everything – her office, the phone in her hand, her hand itself – was dwindling away from her, and a charred blackness was rushing in.

2: 1966

She woke convinced that Angela was in danger. Perhaps that was what she had been dreaming. She struggled to waken fully, for Arthur was home at last, and she wanted to watch him when he saw their baby, the absolutely peaceful sleeping face, the plump microscopic fists held above her head as if Angela was playing cops and robbers in her dreams.

Barbara lay there for at least a minute before she realized what she was thinking, and then she was near to collapsing into grief. She mustn't, for Angela's sake. She got up quickly, to waken herself. In any case, Angela was stirring in the cot at the foot of the bed.

As soon as she saw her mother Angela began to make her sounds of greeting, squeals and delighted growls. She flipped herself over on her front and began to crawl back and forth, shouting at her confinement. Barbara hugged her for a while, to make herself peaceful. Then she changed her, no mean feat when Angela was determined to turn herself over now that she was able to. Barbara could hardly recall the minute sticky helpless creature that had squeezed out of herself.

She'd slept longer than she had intended. The wedge of sunlight from Arthur's workroom was halfway across the landing now. Latterly, on his infrequent visits home, Arthur would retreat in there with wads of paperwork in order to pretend he had no problems, which only meant that even when he was at home he would seem distant, sometimes hardly there at all. Perhaps he'd hoped to get closer to her by agreeing without question that they ought to have a baby before they were too set in their ways, or perhaps he had wanted to make sure that she wouldn't be lonely: how far could he anticipate? Her eyes were blurring moistly, but she couldn't allow that, not when she was carrying Angela downstairs. She strapped her into the buggy and wheeled her out into the August afternoon.

Beneath a Wedgwood sky the Kentish hills looked mossy with trees. Outside her house the Palace Field led to the ruined gatehouse and tower of the Archbishop's palace, where a terrace of cottages was wedged between the ruins; people sat reading or sewing in their gardens. Angela laughed at the glittering stream in the field. Everything was still new to her, but Barbara had taken this walk so often it had grown tedious as a television commercial.

Further into Otford the trees outnumbered the houses. Beside the pond on the roundabout, ducks sat like oval stones, introverted as tortoises. The inn was a block of white light, the police station – a two-storey red-brick building exactly like a suburban house – was ablaze. The dazzle made her grasp the handles of the buggy more firmly. Whenever she crossed a road with the buggy she was afraid that the handles would slip out of her hands.

In the village a giant razor-blade dangled outside the hairdresser's, rifles the colour of stormclouds gleamed ominously in the gunsmith's window. People stooped to admire Angela. 'Doesn't she look like you,' they said. She left her outside the greengrocer's, and had to keep glancing back. Whenever anyone stopped to look at Angela outside a shop Barbara would tense, ready to spring for the door.

Now someone was looking, but it was only Jan, in a T-shirt so misshapen it was large enough even for her. 'Ba ba ba,' Angela was shouting at her, clapping her hands inexpertly and laughing. Jan waited with her children until Barbara emerged. 'The Gripewater Kid is lively today,' Jan said.

'Active and demanding. Still, I'd rather have her than a dumpling baby.'

'So would anyone with sense. Don't run ahead, Jason, help me wheel the buggy, there's a good boy.'

For a moment Barbara was poignantly aware of three-year-old Jason; once they'd known that she was pregnant Arthur had played with him, bounced him and flown him, laughed when he made Jason laugh. For that moment she could hear Arthur's voice more clearly than Jason's. 'Dust,' the little boy said impatiently. 'Dusk.'

'That's right, Jason,' Jan said as she glanced at the headlines outside the newsagent's, 'ducks.' The ducks were unfolding beneath the willows by the pond, shaking themselves out like cloths. 'At least the Moors Murderers are locked up safely,' she said fiercely to Barbara. 'So now we all have to pay to keep them alive. I'd like to see anyone do something to a child while I was around.'

Barbara had glimpsed a headline about Saudi Arabia. She turned away, eyes blurring. Jan clasped her arm moistly with one big mannish hand. 'Don't worry about it. I'm sure we're safer living here.'

'Things like that were just news items to me before I had Angela.' That was true, but it wasn't the reason she had been momentarily upset. Still, she didn't want to be overwhelmed by Jan's large loose emotions, however kindly meant. 'Things like that student in Texas who shot twelve people the other day for no reason at all,' she said.

'Sometimes I think the world's going mad. All these people on drugs, as well. What in God's name do they think they're looking for?'

'Maybe they won't know until they find it, if they ever do.' They pushed the buggies side by side across the field; Angela and baby Nigel kept holding hands. 'By the way,' she remembered, 'there was something else I had to ask you.'

'Expert advice on all problems of child care. Just *look* at the stream, Jason, it isn't for paddling.'

'It's hardly what you'd call a problem. I was wondering if children of Angela's age ever have imaginary playmates.'

'Eight months is a bit young, I should think. Why?'

'Oh, just that she makes her greeting sounds sometimes when I'm not in the room.'

'Jason used to talk to the sunlight. I expect you'll find it's something like that with her.'

At their houses they parted. Through the wall Barbara heard Jason stampeding up and down the stairs. She played for a while with Angela, who was finding out that her plastic mirror had two sides, shouting at the blank side, shouting louder as she rediscovered herself.

At bathtime Angela, glowing pink and wriggling, lay in her towel. As she kissed the birthmark, a purple clover-leaf on Angela's left shoulder, Barbara felt her milk start, a spontaneous outpouring like love made tangible. She fed the baby beside the cot. Angela fell asleep in her arms, milk spilling from the corners of her mouth.

She was tucking Angela into her cot when she heard Jan's husband Keith arrive home. Jason went thundering downstairs, shouting 'Daddy, Daddy.' That was something Angela would never be able to do.

She collected Angela's toys and put them away beneath the stairs. Beyond Palace Field the sky was growing milky, cooling; clouds like ropes of dough rested above the hills. It had been as peaceful the night she had told Arthur she was pregnant, or had she felt peaceful because of the way he'd held her, quietly and protectively as she had known he would hold their child? He'd managed to seem not at all anxious or tense, and yet his problems must have been very bad – bad enough to keep him away from home for the rest of the pregnancy, bad enough that he almost forgot to phone her at Christmas. She'd kept hoping he would return for the birth, and when the phone rang one sagging day between Christmas and New Year she had thought he was calling to say that he would; who else would be calling from Saudi Arabia? But muffled and incomprehensible as it was, she could tell that the voice wasn't Arthur's. It had called again almost at once, but she'd had to run back to the phone from the bathroom, for there was a new movement in her belly, violent and unnerving. Yes, the voice said, it had just called her, but it had thought she couldn't hear it. Could she hear it now? Yes, it had been calling about her husband. Arthur Waugh, that was correct. Yes, he was dead.

It had seemed completely unreal, for she was already in labour. Her body had given her no time to think or feel. Arthur was even more distant, that was all, and she was so far from taking in the fact of his death that she hadn't even mentioned it to Jan as she had driven her to the hospital. In the labour room the truth had begun to seep through to her, when after hours of work she'd reached a stage where she had hung suspended in a limbo of futility, beyond comforting or help. She'd hated the student nurses in their masks like yashmaks, the Arabian doctors who hadn't saved Arthur. Suppose the shock of Arthur's heart attack killed her baby as well? Then, quite independent of her, her pelvic muscles had begun to heave. Though it seemed almost too glib a compensation, Angela was coming to save her from despair.

Angela was breathing in the intercom, loud as a spaceman in a Kubrick film. Barbara ate dinner, then she set out her work in the living-room. She couldn't work in Arthur's room, which felt oppressive, cramped by worries. She had nearly finished copy-editing the latest *Invisible Spy* novel. To think she'd expected to have time to write a novel herself! She wasn't forced to do the copy-editing – Arthur had left more than enough in his will to keep them until she could return full-time to publishing – but it helped her feel that she wasn't stagnating, that she hadn't been swallowed by motherhood. Or was the job welcome because it gave her less time to succumb to grief? Sometimes she wished she could succumb fully, for as long as it might take; since the news of Arthur's death she had never had the chance. The loss itself seemed distant now.

'You vill not be fuckink much ze ladies any more,' Hilde Braun sneered, brandishing a scalpel, but four-letter words were not for the popular genres, and so Barbara made her say 'You will have no longer much to offer the ladies.' With an output of ten books a year it was hardly surprising that the author didn't polish his work, but someone had to.

She had edited one chapter when Angela began muttering and squirming, amplified sounds that filled the room. She hoped the baby wouldn't have another restless night; she wanted to deliver the book by the end of the week. A man's indistinct voice was muttering – one of the many stray broadcasts the intercom picked up. The first time Barbara had heard a man's voice in the intercom she had almost panicked.

She crept upstairs. The first three stairs were noisy, and she couldn't stride over them all. The empty house magnified the creak. But Angela was asleep, wrapped in a tangle of her blankets and the twilight of the room. She'd plugged her dummy into herself without waking.

Barbara tiptoed back on to the landing and had just eased the door closed when she heard the indistinct voice again, inside the room with Angela. She was turning away, having told herself that the microphone beside the cot was picking up the transmission, when she realized that a microphone could do nothing of the kind. Someone was muttering at Angela beyond the door.

She jerked the door open so clumsily that she might have woken Angela. The room was empty and silent, except for Angela's regular breathing. Barbara had to creep in and

28

make sure, for dimness crawled on everything, changing familiar shapes. Even when she had checked the room twice, her heart felt unsteady. Perhaps she was hearing things because she'd had so many broken nights with Angela, but she left the bedroom door open when she made herself go back to her work. Whenever static passed through the intercom, it sounded like whispering.

3: 1968

'Not too far,' Jan called. 'Don't go out of sight.'

She and Barbara were sitting in Jan's garden, amid an assortment of toys that had spilled out of the house. Jason was leading Angela and his little brother about the field, to show how grown-up he was. Beneath the pale still April sky, the day was warm and absolutely clear. Bare glossy trees were tipped with new colours, the hills and the field were greener than yesterday, the first bees were clambering into flowers.

Angela had halted on the concrete path and was pointing excitedly if haphazardly towards the road. Barbara couldn't hear what she was saying over the hoofbeats of two horses which teenagers were riding around the field, and Jason only said 'Come on.' He was too old to listen to baby talk. Barbara watched her daughter in her bright blue overalls as she stumbled impatiently about the path, and could hardly imagine her as a newborn baby. 'God, I do love her,' she said laughing to Jan.

Angela had despaired of Jason. She stumped towards the women. 'Man flying,' she said urgently, pointing at the road.

The women stood up to look, ice jingling in their glasses. A funeral was gliding by, towards the church. In the first of the passenger limousines the widow dabbed at her eyes. 'Man above her,' Angela said.

'Really, Angela? That's nice.' Jan sat down quickly, in case the funeral party saw her staring. 'Children say some funny things,' she said to Barbara. 'I shouldn't tell her what it really is.'

Perhaps she knows more about it than we do, Barbara thought. Did we know when we were her age? She thought not. 'Do you remember what she said the day we passed the crematorium?' she said impulsively.

'Something about golden people, wasn't it? Something strange.'

'Golden people streaming up, to be exact.'

'Yes, she's got a good vocabulary. I expect it's because you read to her so much. It certainly was a peculiar thing to say.'

The momentary clatter of hooves on concrete drew her attention to the field, where Jason had forgotten he was looking after Nigel and was fighting with him on the path. 'Stop that, Jason,' she shouted, but perhaps he couldn't hear.

Before she could reach the boys, Angela had done so. They stopped fighting at once and escorted her rather solemnly towards the stream, across which the horses were leaping. 'They mustn't want to look bad in front of their girl friend,' Jan said.

'Do you think that's all it is?'

'What else could it be? What are you trying to say?'

Perhaps it was best not to share the secret. 'Probably just that I love her,' Barbara said.

'So you keep saying. Are you trying to tell me or yourself?' When Barbara's face changed, uncertain how to look, Jan said, 'How do you really feel?'

'Do you love Jason and Nigel all the time?'

'All the time? You're joking. I'd kill anyone who laid a finger on them but believe me, there are times I could cheerfully dump them both in the pond.' She glanced at the horses, which were kicking up turf as they raced around the field. 'But I think you mean something else. You're frustrated, aren't you?'

'It's just that sometimes I feel so cooped up. I start feeling

31

I've seen nothing but the inside of the house for years.' Barbara shook the ice-cubes in her glass as though she might throw sixes. 'And I really hate the work I'm doing, carving up books and calling it plastic surgery. No doubt they need the work, in some ways they're terrible books, but I don't want to be the one to do it any more.' She threw the melting dice on the lawn, where they glittered and then vanished. 'When I was working in London I could work with books I enjoyed.'

The sound of ice had roused Keith from his doze beneath sections of the *Observer*. 'Do I get the impression you're beginning to resent Angela for hindering your career?'

'Yes,' Barbara said miserably, 'I suppose I am.'

'You'd be abnormal if you didn't feel that way. Why don't you go back to work?' Jan suggested. 'I could look after her during the day.'

'Oh, Jan, would you really?'

'I'm sure it would be good for her and Nigel. Get them ready for nursery school next year.'

Jason had brought the little ones back from the field. 'Angela says she's tired,' he said gravely.

'I'll come in with you, Barbara. Keep an eye on the boys, Keith.' As they went up to the small bedroom she asked Angela, 'Would you like to play in my house in future while your mummy goes out to work?'

'Yes.' Nevertheless the little girl's smile looked fragile. 'Come home sometimes,' she bade her mother.

'Of course I will, darling.' Barbara hugged her and put her down for her afternoon nap. Downstairs she said ruefully to Jan, 'Now I'll feel guilty for wanting to leave her.'

'That's better than resenting her, isn't it?'

'I suppose it must be.' She switched on the intercom and heard a train of bleeps, the censored side of a police call fading away into the hills. All at once, amid her sounds of settling in the cot, Angela said, 'Daddy.'

32

Jan turned quickly to the window, in case Barbara wanted to keep her feelings private. 'Are you coming back outside?' Jan said.

'I think I'll stay in now. I have to finish butchering a chapter.'

When Jan had left, she set out the work. This chapter didn't seem too bad, except for the struggles the characters had to say anything plainly. 'No,' one barked, snapped, rapped and clipped off while his partner in the conversation uttered, breathed, husked and croaked. Someone was trying to interrupt by jawing, clacking, maundering and blathering, but they ignored him. Barbara couldn't help grinning to herself, partly because of Jan.

Still, that was unfair. Jan had thought that Angela was feeling her lack of a father and was calling an imaginary playmate Daddy. No doubt she had left so that Barbara could have a quiet weep, but Barbara was sure by now that Angela knew exactly what she was saying, and to whom.

Of course she had wept when she had first overheard Angela, yet she had often felt they were not alone in the house. She hadn't heard the voice again – perhaps it had been at least partly an hallucination – and the sense of an invisible presence had been much easier for Barbara to take. Once she'd grown used to it, it had seemed comforting, and she had come to believe that was because it meant to be.

She had hoped that she knew who it was long before Angela could form the words, for she kept making her greeting sounds when Barbara left her alone, yet once she'd begun saying 'Daddy' Barbara dared not believe. Perhaps Angela had picked up the word from Nigel and Jason.

One day she had left her album open at a photograph of Arthur before she brought Angela downstairs. Angela had never seen a photograph of him, since Barbara had thought it best to wait until she asked where he was. On the stairs she had been tempted to run down ahead of Angela and hide the album; her heart had felt like a small fist trying to punch through her chest, her breath had grown harsh as smoke. But as soon as Angela saw the photograph of her father, smiling widely but a little shyly as if he thought he wasn't really worth photographing, she'd said, 'Daddy.'

That was enough for Barbara. Perhaps Arthur had shared their child after all – Angela squeaking at her month-old hands as if to persuade them to reach her mouth, her first smile that was intentional rather than a colicky grimace, the first time she had managed to roll over and had burst out laughing at herself, her first words. In labour, Barbara had been haunted by an image of Arthur's face which crumbled like sand and blew away. So that had been nothing but a waking nightmare.

Sometimes she wondered if his presence had anything to do with Angela's aura of peace. It wasn't only Jan's children: nobody could stay angry for long near her. Perhaps the calm which Barbara felt while watching her was more than maternal. She didn't want to examine what was happening too closely; it was too delicate, it might be spoiled. She was almost used to it by now.

She finished work on the chapter quickly. He said, she said, said, said. Barbara left the man blathering and twaddling and rattling at them, for she'd grown too fond of him to cramp his style. For the first time in months she was enjoying her work, because she knew it was nearly finished. Soon she would be back at her desk. Angela ought to be safe with anyone, let alone Jan.

4: 1970

As Barbara reached Tottenham Court Road a man with a handful of pamphlets tried to grab her, muttering 'Apollo 13 was doomed from the start. We've got to watch out for the numbers.' He was darting at people beneath Centre Point, an empty cage of concrete and hundreds of windows. Earlier today a Scientologist had accosted her in Piccadilly; bald young men were dancing and chanting along Oxford Street like the tail end of a party, several youths were meditating cross-legged by the Gents in Leicester Square. At least the Apollo man's theme was relatively topical.

Close to the Post Office Tower, fifteen storeys of greenish windows like a stem of cheap cut glass, the Melwood-Nuttall office resembled a small bookshop. Football fans were tramping past from Euston, kicking parched litter, reeling into shops, cursing pubs for being shut. Outside Melwood-Nuttall a pneumatic drill juddered in rubble, a particle of the interminable rebuilding of London.

Ted Crichton was sitting behind a confusion of letters and dog-eared typescripts. His large round face beamed at her, his small nose wrinkled in greeting. When he stood up, knocking his jacket from the back of his chair, his desk appeared to shrink to classroom size. 'This is it,' he said, handing her the novel he was soon to publish.

'You think we could do the paperback, do you?'

'I think you could do very well. Let me know as soon as you can – some of the others are sniffing around.'

She slipped the typescript into her briefcase, alongside books for Angela. 'What else is new?'

'Would you believe a novel with Hitler as the hero? That

35

would put Melwood-Nuttall on the map – right out of the country, in fact. I told the author I thought it was somewhat ahead of its time,' he said laughing. 'Have you had anything unputdownable lately?'

'I thought so, yes. I thought I had the best first novel I've read for years, by a man called Paul Gregory. He can say more in a sentence than most writers can say in a paragraph. But The Pontiff said it was "of limited appeal", and I had to send it back.'

'Well, that's the price you pay for working for a large house. You ought to be like me, just me and my list of safe bets. At least then you'd know you couldn't afford to take chances.' When she didn't laugh he grew serious. 'You were really disappointed, were you?'

'I thought it deserved to be published. I'm sure it would have done well, handled properly. I just felt bad about discouraging such a talented writer. You could see his book had been the rounds.'

'Let me have his address and I'll take a look at it. Maybe if I can promise a hardback you can persuade your boss. You know,' he said, tugging at his greying beard, 'I've heard you talk like this before. At Frankfurt, wasn't it? That was the time of our mutual unburdening.'

He'd looked after her at her first Frankfurt Book Fair: he'd introduced her around, made sure she didn't have to eat alone, towered over lecherous editors if she seemed to need help. 'Maybe you should be an agent,' he said now. 'You've certainly got the energy. It might give you more freedom, not to mention a damn sight more money.'

He headed for the outer office to rescue his secretary from an invasion of football fans. 'You can take the books if you want them,' one was saying. 'There's nowhere to pay.' When Ted appeared, six foot three of him, they left at once.

'It's a good job I look daunting,' he told Barbara. 'I've

never laid a finger on anyone in my life. No future at all as a heavy father. How's the family?'

'Oh, fine. You say I'm energetic, but you should see her. Even though she's at nursery school she's raring to go when I get home. She's into snakes and ladders now.'

'That's pretty advanced for four years old, isn't it?'

'I believe so.' Yet she was by no means insufferably precocious. Everyone took to her at once – everyone except the lopsided woman, and more than her face had been wrong with her. However special Angela might be, she never behaved as if she knew she was. Once, when Barbara had tried to ask her about the times she talked to her father, she was suddenly just a child with a secret, unsure if she ought to tell. Barbara had changed the subject rather than risk making Angela feel that anything was wrong. Sometimes she was tempted to listen through the intercom, which was still in position though rarely used, but she felt that would be worse than eavesdropping.

Ted had noticed his fallen jacket at last and was trying to beat out the dust, though it hardly mattered: however impeccably he began the day, at lunchtime he was tousled; by now he looked as if he'd slept on a park bench. 'And she's made no difference to your career,' he said.

'I was lucky. My friend who lives next door looks after her, picks her up from nursery school and so forth. I feel quite guilty sometimes – I'm sure I have it easier at work than looking after her. Why,' she said, noticing how interested he looked, 'is your wife going to have a baby?'

'It looks that way. Helen came off the Pill, with all these rumours about cancer. Well, I suppose I can work on my famous unwritten novel after the bratling's gone to bed.'

'You're pleased that you're going to be a father, aren't you?'

'I'm sure I will be once it's born.' He was scratching his

eyebrows, which were thick enough to hide a frown. 'Helen wants it, that's the main thing.'

'I'm sure you do as well, really. Look, I must be going. My friend's little boy is ill – I said I'd try to be home early and take Angela off her hands. Pressures of parenthood. It's worth it, though, believe me.'

Outside, the September day seemed even hotter. The Post Office Tower looked jagged with light; Centre Point was a white-hot fire within a concrete mesh. Her briefcase was growing heavier. Should she leave the books with Ted? But she'd promised Angela that she would bring them home today.

The Underground was crammed with football fans, shoving one another to the edge of the platform, throwing empty beer-cans on to the track, scrawling on the walls, converging on solitary women; a pack of them closed in on Barbara, until she stared them away. The atmosphere was thick as sweat, which the winds that rushed ahead of the trains seemed unable to move.

On the train it was worse. Even though she'd reached a seat, Barbara felt in danger of fainting. Football fans dangled like meat from the handholds, the rest of the crowd was wedged between them; beery scarves swayed into her face. The tunnel closed tight around the train, which rocked back and forth to its shrill monotonous clattering. The train had been as crowded on the day the lopsided woman had sat next to Angela.

They'd been to Hamley's in Regent Street, buying toys. At Oxford Circus the crowd had rushed them on to the train and into seats. Barbara had been about to tell Angela to sit on her knee when the woman had sat next to the little girl, pinning her against the window.

At first, once she'd glanced at the woman, Barbara hadn't taken much notice of her, in case she had seemed to stare. Though her skin had looked worn out, the woman couldn't

38

have been more than twenty. Above a large nose red and porous as a strawberry, one eye had been lower than the other. She'd looked as if each time she came face to face with a mirror it sent her deeper into despair.

Then Barbara had seen how the woman was looking at Angela. Perhaps she was on drugs – London seemed full of people who behaved as if everything around them was shifting – but the reason didn't matter: she was staring at Angela as though she couldn't look away, and her eyes were full of fear and loathing.

Barbara had been poised to intervene – she had never felt so violently protective since Angela's first weeks – when the train stopped at Green Park and the woman had noticed her staring. At once she'd struggled through the crowd and off the train. Or had she dodged into another carriage? In the crowd at Victoria Station, and all the way home on the train, Barbara had felt pursued.

Here was Victoria, and she could leave the football fans behind. While she waited for the Otford train she scanned the headlines: Manson trial continuing, submachine-guns in the left luggage at the London Hilton Hotel. Perhaps she had needed to be shown that not everyone had to like Angela, yet when she remembered how the little girl had shrunk into herself, had hardly spoken until they'd reached home, she was furious again.

On the Otford train she dumped her briefcase next to her and settled back with a gasp of relief. A nearby train looked like a hatter's shop; men were raising their bowlers to mop their foreheads, one was even fanning himself with the brim, before fitting them back into place. Soon her train had passed the Battersea Dogs' Home, the Battered Dogs' Home according to Angela. At Peckham Rye the tower blocks went trooping away over the horizon, leaving the hills clear for villages. Over Kent the sky was growing stormy, the colour of twilight and rain.

As she reached Otford she heard distant thunder, the sound of the hills shifting forward, pushed by the leaden sky. The train shrank, a toy that dwindled to a speck, and then nothing moved on the deserted station, on the lurid neon hills. It was as if the air had turned into transparent resin.

She was halfway across the footbridge when she saw that the station was not quite deserted. A woman was standing on the London platform. She moved beneath the bridge as Barbara crossed, almost as though she were trying to hide.

Though she couldn't define her reason for doing so, though she told herself she was being neurotic, Barbara hurried so that she could see the woman's face. She was nearly at the foot of the steps from the bridge before she saw that it was Jan.

She had never seen her look so worried – Jan looked actually shrunken, no longer tall – yet this morning Nigel had seemed to have nothing worse than a cold. Who was looking after Angela? She ran down, the last few steps. 'What's the matter, Jan? Is Nigel worse?'

She faltered, for Jan was backing away from her, her crossed hands gripping her breasts. She must be bruising herself, yet she appeared to feel nothing. 'Oh, Barbara, I'm so sorry,' she said.

5

Barbara woke hearing thunder, and couldn't recall what was wrong. At least the thunder wasn't ominous, for it was Angela's footsteps overhead. Still, Barbara should wake up – she hadn't meant to doze off in the chair – so that the little girl wasn't left upstairs by herself too long.

Then the footsteps stopped, and she heard Jan muttering. The footsteps had been Nigel's, next door. Jan's hushed voice made her nerves feel raw, and at once she remembered why. Though it was weeks later she was still running from the station – but now she knew what she would find when she reached home.

She'd started running before Jan could explain. The houses stood back from her beyond their long gardens, the leaves of the trees looked shiny with oil. Everything seemed oppressively close to her yet unreal, flat as the dark sky. No birds were singing. Nothing moved except her, everything was trying to drag her back.

Jan was panting beside her and babbling. 'Someone went to the nursery school. He said he'd come because I was looking after Nigel. I was only a couple of minutes late,' she said desperately, but Barbara scarcely heard her; there would be time enough for explanations when she was home, when she saw for herself what had happened to Angela. She stumbled across the Palace Field, along the path that was choppy with hoofmarks; the briefcase full of books for Angela bruised her thigh. The sky had filled in windows of the ruined tower with slate, had turned the stream grey as mud, no longer sparkling.

Faces were watching her from Jan's house. There was

Miss Clarke who ran the nursery school, a dumpy middle-aged woman who preached purgatory to the children but whom they loved. There was Keith, bending down to speak to Angela – to some child, at any rate, below the level of the window – and there was the large fatherly sergeant from the cosy police station. The sight of him made Barbara's heart lurch, but at least he was in charge. Surely everything would be all right now.

He emerged from the house as she squeezed through her hedge. His face smoothed out, grew professionally solemn and reassuring, as she ran across the large shared garden. 'You mustn't worry, Mrs Waugh. The county police have been alerted. They'll be checking all the cars.'

The dark sky seemed to rush at her, to flood her brain. 'I don't know what you're talking about.'

'I tried to tell her. She wouldn't listen,' Jan said to him, almost pleading. 'Barbara, someone went to Miss Clarke's and took Angela away.'

Barbara was sitting on a garden chair and unable to recall how she had got there; the garden was wavering. 'Who let him take her?' she demanded.

'You mustn't blame Miss Clarke,' Jan said anxiously. 'There was no reason for her to be suspicious.'

She must be unemotional, she must learn everything to make sure they had overlooked nothing, she must talk so that she wouldn't be alone with her feelings. 'How long was it before you told the police?'

'I didn't know what had happened at first. Miss Clarke had gone by the time I arrived. She left as soon as the children went home. I had to look all over the village for her, and I had to keep coming back here in case Angela had turned up. Nobody had seen either of them. I thought perhaps they were together.' She looked afraid to go on. 'I found Miss Clarke after about an hour, and we went straight to the police.'

42

Beside her the sergeant looked perfect for comforting people and telling children off for stealing apples, but could he bring back Angela? 'You said they would be checking the cars,' Barbara said. 'Have you got the number?'

'I never thought to look.' Miss Clarke had come out, pushing her spectacles higher on her nose. 'I don't think even you would have, Mrs Waugh.'

'Did you see the car?' When the woman nodded Barbara turned to the sergeant, who was at least not so nerve-racking. 'Then you know the make, at any rate.'

'Well, no, they don't really.' Miss Clarke's frown dislodged her spectacles again; one finger shoved them back. 'I'm afraid I can't tell one make from another.'

'We know it's black or dark blue,' the sergeant said, 'and we think it's a saloon.'

When Miss Clarke nodded defiantly, Barbara could have knocked her down. 'How could you let him take her?' she demanded.

'I think you might have done so if you have been in my shoes, Mrs Waugh. He was very nicely dressed and beautifully spoken. But if he really was a thug as you all say, how do you think I could have stopped him? I'm only one woman, you know, and I had all the other children in my care as well. In any case,' she said almost triumphantly, 'it wasn't like that at all. Angela went to him quite freely.'

She must be able to hear Barbara's nails clawing the canvas seat. 'What did he say to her?'

'I can tell you that exactly. "Hello, Angela, I'm staying with your Auntie Jan. Be quick, or you'll have me done for parking." Well, you know yourself how narrow the road is.'

Barbara's teeth had begun to chatter. 'It didn't strike you as at all strange,' she said shakily, 'that he needed a car to take her halfway across the village?'

'I've never needed a car at all. Besides, it's easy to be wise after the event.' Miss Clarke was growing angry with her spectacles. 'I've seen you drive quite short distances,' she said.

If Barbara replied it might be by screaming, but the sergeant was pointing at a car that had just left the roundabout. 'Here are the county police, I think.'

Barbara managed to lever herself to her feet, though her arms were trembling. But the new policeman was alone, and had nothing to report. He was young and sharply efficient, and he seemed to disapprove of the way everyone had been allowed to scatter untidily outside the house. He took the sergeant down the garden to question him, then he came to Barbara. 'Can we go inside your house, please.'

Once there he began to interrogate her. He didn't seem especially sympathetic, but perhaps he felt there was no time. She mustn't waste time by resenting him. Did she live alone? Where was her husband? What had been his job? Had he left her a substantial legacy? What was her job? How much did she make? Was there anyone who might feel he had a title to her child? Could she think of anyone who fitted the description of the kidnapper? 'Nobody,' she said. 'How could he know all the names, my little girl's name and my neighbour's?'

'Presumably you call your daughter by name in the street. The names of adults are in the voters' list. It looks like a professional job. Maybe they reckoned that living in a place like this you could afford a ransom, or maybe they knew you could.'

Could he be envious? Now he was telling her about the kinds of phone call she might receive. He wouldn't have her phone tapped for the moment, but she must call the police at once if the kidnapper made contact. He left to interview the others, and there was nothing for her to do but wait, nothing to prevent her from demanding of herself how she could have cared so little for Angela, nothing to hold back the shudder that was spreading through her entire body.

The shudder had faded at last, leaving her fragile and hollow as shell, in constant danger of shattering. Perhaps she would have felt like that when Arthur died if she had had the time, but now there was guilt as well, guilt that pervaded her and everything around her, made them feel shabby, grimy, worthless. She was still waiting, and the worst thing was that she couldn't go driving in search of Angela; she dared not leave the house. For weeks she'd grown tense whenever she heard a car, she'd started violently the few times the phone had rung. Beyond the windows the sunlit days looked fake. Nothing but the unbearable silence of the house was real.

When the newspaper slipped from her lap to the floor she picked it up absently. She'd become obsessed with the idea that the kidnapper might not contact her by phone, that he might place an advertisement in one of the local newspapers instead. Suppose he referred to a memory which only she and Angela shared? Then the police couldn't tell that it was his message. She was terrified that he might harm Angela if he knew the police were involved.

There was nothing she could recognize in the Personal column. Suppose it was hidden in one of the other columns, the better to fool the police? She searched among the houses and second-hand cars until she realized that the only one to be fooled was herself. *The Railway Children, The Trouble with Girls, Heart of a Mother* – she folded the newspaper quickly, before she could see more of the entertainments page.

She stared at the headlines until they began to writhe as if they were burning. She felt as though her eyes were charring their way into her head. Sometimes she thought she saw Arthur trying to reassure her, in doorways or at the top of the stairs. No doubt he was a dream that her insomnia had forced into her waking hours, an hallucination like the child's distant voice that called 'Mummy'. Perhaps he always had been, she thought bitterly.

She went upstairs to the bathroom, to wake herself up if

45

she could. The first three stairs creaked, proclaiming that she no longer had anyone to waken. She wished the boys next door would make more noise – at least that might convince her there was someone near her – but Jan had kept them quiet all these weeks. Jan had been so helpful and considerate that before long Barbara had felt scarcely able to breathe.

At first Jan and Keith had tried to get her out of the house, exhorting her at least to come next door and eat with them, until they'd seen how stubborn she could be. Then they'd kept visiting her with the relentless cheerfulness of visitors to a death-bed. Eventually she managed to convince them that she wanted to be alone, though Jan insisted on shopping for her. She could see how anxious Jan was to be forgiven, but if Angela came home safely, *when* she came home safely, there would be nothing to forgive Jan for.

In the bathroom she splashed cold water in her eyes. Water trickled down her reflection, but she had no time for tears. Everyone's sympathy seemed so final, because she sensed that everyone was trying to prepare her for something which was assumed to have already happened – but she wouldn't be prepared, for that was almost as bad as wishing the worst to happen, to put her out of her misery. So long as Angela came back to her, nothing else mattered. She would give everything she had. As if that thought had started time moving again, she heard a knocking at the front door.

At once her stomach, and then her whole body, felt raw as her eyes. She grew dizzy and afraid that she would be sick. Then she realized that she hadn't heard a car. It must be another dose of sympathy from next door: don't worry, try and take your mind off things, you won't help Angela by getting yourself into a state. Only when the knocking was repeated did she notice that it didn't sound like Jan or Keith or the boys, and by the time she reached the stairs she was running.

6

When she opened the door she found Miss Clarke. Beside her was a woman who looked like an actress: make-up caked cracks in her face below a shock of hair red as a setter's, silk protruded from her sleeves, layers of scarves formed a ruff at her throat, bracelets tumbled down her wrists as she raised her hands in a gesture of instant sympathy. Perhaps sympathy was her job.

'I understand you aren't receiving visitors, Mrs Waugh, but I felt I had a duty to help.' Miss Clarke sounded as though she would listen to no arguments. 'This lady can help you,' she said.

'Oh bugger off, you bloody old fool,' Barbara just managed not to say, and realized how unpleasant she was growing. Wasn't she using Jan and Miss Clarke as scapegoats for her own sense of guilt? Could she afford to refuse any offer of help, when she would be refusing for Angela? 'That's very kind of you,' she said. 'Please come in.'

The scarved woman strode past her, overwhelming her with her perfume, and went straight into the living-room, whose picture window overlooked the field. 'There she is,' she cried.

When Barbara caught up with her, heart stumbling and mouth agonizingly dry, she found that the woman was gazing at the photograph of Angela that stood on the mantlepiece. 'Oh, my dear, what a beautiful child. Calm yourself now, if you can. I'm here to find her for you.'

All at once Barbara was suspicious. 'What exactly is your friend supposed to do?'

'She practises psychometry,' Miss Clarke said as though the word was long enough to silence all objections.

'You mean,' Barbara said, close to fury, 'she claims she can locate people by handling something of theirs.'

'It's more than a claim, Mrs Waugh. I've seen her do things I can't explain, and you wouldn't call me easily fooled, would you? You must give Angela this chance.'

The psychometer had pressed the photograph against her forehead; the glass was smeared with make-up. 'Is there an article of clothing which your little girl particularly likes to wear?'

'Yes,' Barbara admitted wearily, 'there are one or two things.'

'Bring me her favourite, quickly.' The psychometer, or the actress – Barbara was by no means convinced there was a difference – sat down at Barbara's work table, fists pressed against her temples. 'And an atlas of the world,' she murmured.

'I haven't one.'

The woman seemed to emerge from a light trance. 'Well, I'm sure she must still be in this country. An atlas of Britain will do.'

Keith had Barbara's road atlas, and he wouldn't be home for hours. 'I haven't one of those, either.'

'But Miss Clarke said you were a publisher. Otherwise I would have brought an atlas with me.' She seemed to be saying that she couldn't do her job if other people didn't do theirs. 'Never mind,' she said magnanimously, 'we shall see how much the article of clothing tells us.'

On the stairs Barbara grew short of breath. It wasn't only the smouldering October day; she felt clammily resentful, for could this really be anything but a farce? She faltered in Angela's room, which she had tidied for distraction, shutting everything away, in the first week she had been left alone. She wished now she had left it as it was, waiting for

48

Angela to come home – and then she realized that the psychometer kept speaking of Angela in the present tense, whereas she was sure that Jan and the rest of them thought of her in the past. She found Angela's favourite dungarees and took them downstairs.

The woman seemed not to have stirred. She was gazing at the photograph before her on the table as though she needed to fix every detail in her mind, though the photograph was out of date: Angela's blonde hair was no longer curly but poured straight down over her shoulders, her eyes were an even more piercing blue; the picture couldn't show how long her legs were, how graceful she already was. But the woman was too intent on it even to look away when Barbara handed her the dungarees. 'Yes,' she said at once, 'these are what I need.'

Miss Clarke motioned Barbara to sit and be quiet. As soon as she took her place at the table she wished she had switched on the lamps; clouds were looming over the hills, seeping across the dark clogged sky; the hot dim breathless room reeked of perfume. Perhaps the psychometer would have been distracted by the lamps, for now she had closed her eyes and was holding Angela's dungarees close to her, the cuffs of the trousers standing on her lap. In the dimness, and with her lack of sleep, Barbara thought momentarily that the woman was holding a child.

'Such a beautiful child,' the psychometer said. 'And she is more beautiful within.' No doubt, Barbara thought, that would win over a mother less gullible than herself. Could there be any point to all this except vague reassurances? She kept jerking herself back from belief as though it were sleep.

'Her hair is longer now,' the psychometer said. 'Yes, I can see her, a tall child with long blonde hair.' She could have guessed that from the photograph, or Miss Clarke could have told her. Her vision of Angela seemed suspiciously rapid – or was Barbara afraid to hope too soon? 'There is something on her shoulder,' the psychometer said.

Barbara grew rigid, in danger of trembling. 'What is it?' she demanded.

'I can almost make it out. A badge – yes, a kind of badge. Does she wear a badge on her shoulder?' Before Barbara could decide how to reply, the woman said, 'Wait, I see it plainly now. It's a wound, a wound on her right shoulder.'

'No,' Barbara said dully. 'There's nothing on her right shoulder.'

'Not when you last saw her.' She waved away the discrepancy amid a chattering of bracelets. 'But we mustn't concern ourselves only with her body, my dear. The important thing is her soul.'

If that was the kind of thing she had to offer, as far as Barbara was concerned it was worse than useless. The perfume seemed oppressive as incense; Angela's dungarees were drooping, broken-legged, empty. But the psychometer sat forward, clutching them. 'Oh, my dear, I wish you could see her soul.'

Was she claiming that she could? Apparently, because she said, 'She has so much to give. Already she has great spiritual power. As she grows she will learn how to use it.'

Barbara was about to say that was enough – she had enough nightmares while she was awake about what might be happening to Angela, she didn't need this freak to make things worse – when the psychometer said, 'Has she ever spoken of visions?'

Angela was just a child, a child in danger; how was all this helping her? But it was the first thing the woman had said that seemed more than a lucky guess. 'Some of the things she says are very strange,' Barbara admitted warily.

'She is not strange but wonderful.' It sounded like a rebuke. 'Yet I warn you, not everyone will see her that way. We will find her, you mustn't worry about that, my dear.

But I warn you now,' she said, her eyes opening wide to stare at Barbara, 'that she is in dreadful danger from the people who have stolen her. She must be found before they destroy what she is.'

'Be brave,' Miss Clarke said. 'She'll find Angela, I know she will. All she needs is a map.'

'All right,' Barbara said abruptly, 'I'll get one.' She couldn't bear to sit there any longer, suffocated by the dimness, her inaction, the sickening perfume. Perhaps Keith had left the atlas at home today; if not, she would ask among their neighbours until she found one. At least then she would know if the psychometer had anything other than nonsense to offer.

As soon as she opened the front door she halted, for a large man was trudging from the roundabout, towards the houses. The dimness had smeared everything together, so that she couldn't be sure for a while that it was the police sergeant. For a moment she thought dreamily that he could provide a map.

When he stepped on to her path she seemed to wake: her head was throbbing like a rotten tooth, her nerves were crawling. He closed her gate so carefully before he came to her that she knew he was reluctant to approach.

'Please come inside, Mrs Waugh. I'm afraid I have to ask you a question.'

If he had to ask, he couldn't be sure of whatever it was – yet she was afraid to insist on being told at once. Though her legs were shaky she hurried him into the living-room. He switched on the lamps, and the psychometer stared vacantly, blinking like a bat. 'What are you doing?' Miss Clarke demanded, then saw who he was.

He made Barbara sit down, and squatted beside her. 'Mrs Waugh, you said Angela was wearing a blue and white striped dress with a belt. Was there anything about it you forgot to tell us?'

She couldn't stand this game. 'Such as what?'

'Was there anything about the belt you forgot to mention?'

The throbbing in her head was sharper now; she didn't want to speak. 'She'd lost the belt from that dress, and I borrowed the belt from one of her other dresses. You could hardly tell,' she pleaded. 'It was a shade paler, that's all.'

His face had fallen. 'I'm deeply sorry, Mrs Waugh, but it looks as if they've found her.'

There was something she must remember, something that would nullify the horror he was threatening – 'It doesn't matter about the dress,' she said, close to hysteria. 'If they didn't notice the birthmark on her shoulder then it can't be Angela.'

'A birthmark,' the psychometer cried. 'Of course, that's what I saw.'

He frowned at that, but gazed sadly at Barbara. 'I'm afraid they couldn't identify her like that, Mrs Waugh. Someone had used a shotgun at close range.'

There was nothing but emptiness, inside Barbara and outside her. Somewhere the psychometer was saying, 'When was the child killed?'

'It must have been early this morning.'

The woman rushed to Barbara, tried to clasp her hands. 'Mrs Waugh, you must listen to me. That isn't Angela. She was still alive when I touched her clothes. She's alive at this moment and in danger.'

Barbara jerked to her feet, knocking the woman backwards. She tore the dungarees from her and hugged them to herself, only to feel how empty they were. 'And I suppose,' she said in a voice so full of hatred and betrayal and grief that it was scarcely recognizable as hers, 'that they shot some other little girl to make me think it was Angela.'

The sergeant intervened. 'I think you'd better leave, Miss Clarke, and take your spiritualist friend with you.' It no longer mattered to Barbara; her outburst seemed to have drained the last of her strength, and she could only slump in a chair. He came back soon and talked to her, and after a while Jan and Keith joined him, but she couldn't take in what they were saying or doing. She was aware of nothing but the emptiness of the house.

That was all there was for a very long time. People kept appearing – a doctor examined her, Jan stayed with her as much as she could when Barbara refused to leave the house – but she hardly noticed when they came or when they went away. Sometimes she found that she was facing plates of food which someone had begun to eat a long time ago. She tried to stay downstairs, for the cry of the first three stairs made her wince, but kept falling asleep here and there in the house and forgetting. She seemed not to know who she was or what she had been – at least, whenever she thought of her London job she grew sick with guilt. There were memories of Angela, but she felt she was no longer entitled to them.

After several nights and days had crawled over the hills and through the house, there was a funeral. She seemed unable to grasp that the small closed coffin had anything to do with her. As it was swallowed by the crematorium she imagined the flames of it, streaming away. When she began to shudder Jan moved closer to her, hoping no doubt to comfort her, to pay off a little of her guilt that way. But Barbara had gone even deeper into the emptiness of herself, a dried-up place where there were no tears.

It was later – days later, perhaps – and Jan was saying 'By God, I hope they catch the swine. I know what I'd do to him.' All at once Barbara found her unbearable, for how could that bring back Angela? At last, just as Barbara was about to scream, Jan accepted that she wanted to be left alone. Once she was alone she could admit to herself what she wanted to do.

She plugged in the intercom lead to Angela's room and

waited, hoping, praying incoherently. Static hissed at her, distant metallic voices floated by. The house grew dark, the silence intensified, and at last she realized that she was sitting like a catatonic in the emptiness, hoping blindly for the ghost of her murdered child. That could only lead her deeper into despair. All at once she was disgusted enough with herself to be able to drag herself back.

Early the next day she piled every one of Angela's toys and books and clothes into the car and drove away from Otford. Though she had no idea where she was going, she was soon in Maidstone, where the smell of malt trapped beneath the dull November clouds seemed almost suffocating. When she found a jumble sale in a church hall she left everything of Angela's at the first table, then she fled. Out in the country, among the dark drenched hills, she left the car in a rainstorm and walked in a circle for miles, sobbing and remembering.

She spent days hating herself for needing to go back to work; that need had killed Angela. But if she didn't go back to her job she could only return to the emptiness of herself. Once she was back at her London desk she gave herself so much work that for a while it seemed she would have time to think of nothing else, except that everything nagged at her memories – the things people avoided saying, the way her colleagues and Jan were especially considerate while trying to pretend they were not, the babies and children in half the books she had to read. Those weren't the only reasons why she'd taken the risk at last, had used Arthur's legacy and the cash from the sale of the house to move to London and set up her agency, but the move had helped her to heal, to accept that Angela was gone for ever – except that now, nine years later, a voice on the phone was calling her Mummy.

7

Under the stone dome the night sky was trapped, and light was growing among the stars. At first it was clouds that looked crystalline, intricately patterned whorls of green and blue and crimson that drifted over one another, unfurling. Then there came an enormous scribbling of geometrical shapes, neon mathematics in the sky. Tangles of colours sailed across the stars as though giant kittens were at play, loops of light came swelling down to lasso the audience, geometrical flowers blossomed and closed and blossomed again. There were shapes too rapid to describe, so rapid that Judy forgot she was all of nine years old and squealed with delight.

'That was lovely,' she said when the house lights came up. 'Thank you, Daddy.' She went skipping out of the Planetarium and on to Baker Street while Ted's eyes were still adjusting: he felt as though the patterns of the carpet were about to shift. When he caught up with her, on the fringe of a group of stoned young people, she said, 'Mummy took me to the Museum last week, but I didn't like it nearly as much.'

In the Underground the route map looked like the patterns of the laser show. 'I shouldn't put it to her quite like that,' he said.

'Of course I won't.' The shrewdness of her grin startled him. Glimpses of her growing up often took him by surprise. Of course she was a week older each time he saw her.

On the escalator she clattered down then tried to outrun the steps back to him. Waiting for the train, she held his hand, and seemed at once as ladylike as her ankle-length dress. Did she know how proud he was to be with her? He thought so. As they boarded the train he said, 'Has Uncle Steve taken you both out again?'

'He said he was going to take us on holiday, but he went to South Africa instead. I don't think Mummy liked him very much.'

'That's a pity.' Judy had quite liked him and, from what she'd said, Steve had grown fond of her. Steve had been an accountant, but it seemed he was less dependable than his job. No doubt Helen would distrust men even more now.

They climbed into the daylight at Highbury & Islington. On Upper Street the shops were crammed haphazardly together like boxes left on a shelf to bleach with dust and sun. Flats huddled above the shops, National Front stickers lurked among the badges of credit cards on a restaurant window, a dressing-table leaned outside a discount furniture store, one unhinged wing of the grubby mirror flat on its back. 'Do you like living round here?' he said casually.

'Yes, it's quite good, really. But I liked it best in our old flat.'

He'd thought she would have been too young to remember. He'd hoped so, for he would have expected her memories to be unpleasant: the smallness of the flat, intolerable once there was a baby; the arguments that must have resounded through her bedroom wall, as he and Helen retreated into themselves, found fault with everything the other did. He only hoped she didn't realize that she had been the cause of the arguments.

Workmen were disembowelling white Georgian houses to make room for apartments. Helen lived at the end of the side street, beyond a low archway which might have led to stables but which gave on to a small assortment of flats. She came to the door before Judy could ring, her hands pink as a dummy's with rubber gloves. 'I hope you had a good time,' she said.

'It was beautiful, Mummy, better than *Close Encounters*. And it was ever so funny, the man said that if anyone had brought anything to smoke they had to do it outside. We all laughed, because we knew he didn't mean tobacco.'

When she'd run to her room Helen said, 'I don't think it's at all a good idea to let Judith hear that sort of thing.'

'Good Lord, I only took her to a laser show. Hardly a legalization rally.' He didn't want to argue, for she looked tired and haggard; the band in her hair seemed to draw her face tight, wrinkles tugging at the corners of her eyes. 'She's just trying to seem grown up,' he said.

'Oh, is that what you think?' She clearly felt he had no right to an opinion. Abruptly, with a change of mood that he was meant to notice, she offered him a drink. 'Happy birthday,' she said.

'Here's to finishing my private eye book this year. Here's to promises kept eventually.'

Her smile was so thin it was more a rebuke. However friendly he tried to be, all his visits felt like the aftermath of a row. 'How are things with you?' he said, and hoped that was neutral enough.

'Judith's happy. That's the main thing.'

'But it's not the only thing. What about you? Can I help?'

She stared through him. 'I can't imagine how.'

'Well, for example,' he said, thinking that she looked overworked yet couldn't be earning much at the bookshop, 'would you like me to pay you more now that Judy's growing up?'

'Whatever it may look like to you, I'm managing perfectly well. If I need more I'll apply to the court. Does Judith look badly dressed? Does she look as if she doesn't get enough to eat?'

He could feel the old hatreds rising sourly in his throat. Once she had been so much more intelligent, but motherhood had locked her into itself until she seemed able to think of nothing else. Now she refused to let him reach her at all: she behaved as if the alimony were a punishment he should be ashamed to mention, she called Judy by her full name as though to rebuke him for being too familiar. But here was Judy to save the situation. 'You haven't given him his presents yet, have you?' she said anxiously.

'I was waiting for you.' Helen handed him two packages, a pen with his name inscribed on the band from Judy, a box of handkerchiefs from her – an anonymous present which he suspected was meant to imply how little she could afford. Judy hugged him, Helen offered the side of her face as though turning the other cheek.

'Are you staying for a birthday dinner?' Judy said.

'I'm sorry, darling, I'm already promised.' When he hugged her again she felt limp with disappointment. Helen turned her back on him. Could she have led Judy to believe he might be staying so that he would feel guilty? She still blamed Barbara Waugh for the collapse of their marriage, though she had never been able to prove anything: there hadn't been much to prove.

Out on the street again, when he'd promised to see Judy next week-end, he felt as if he'd left some raw part of himself behind, still trying to resolve the situation. Helen always made it clear that she didn't want him to stay long. She was doling him a series of weekly snapshots of Judy, then snatching them back.

He rather like that image. It might fit into his novel. All at once he felt cheerful; his mind clarified. On the train he was close to glimpsing an episode which the snapshot image suggested to him, until a baby started crying. He could only listen to the yawning pause while it drew breath, the pause during which it seemed that it might have stopped crying.

The pauses were the worst. It recommenced crying at last, louder, more nerve-racking, and the idea he'd almost grasped was gone. Perhaps it might find its way back through the maze of his mind if he didn't nag himself.

By the time he reached his flat it was growing dusk. He showered quickly and changed, then he walked across the Barbican estate to Barbara's. On the balconies, pillars fat as giant barrels looked lagged with rough grey stone. Above the balconies and walkways lamps were coming on, inverted wastebins plugged with light. A tinge of sunset lingered on the tiers of concrete across the rectangular lake.

Soon he reached Barbara's terrace, near half a medieval bastion, a huge stone armchair. A few ducks were waddling across the red-brick plateau which displayed the church of St Giles on the lake. Among the long-stemmed lanterns which rose from the plateau, a willow dangled its mop of doll's hair. As the last of the sunset crept up the church tower it looked as though the grey stone was cooling, turning to ash.

Barbara kissed him Happy Birthday at the door, then she strode ahead of him along the hall. Her dry sweetish perfume drifted back through her long auburn hair, and he glimpsed threats of silver in the auburn. Farewell to our thirties, he said for himself and Barbara.

By the time he reached the main room her long legs had taken her to the couch, under which she stowed a photograph album which presumably she had been studying, then to her desk where she slipped a bookmark into the typescript she was reading, and back down the hall to the kitchen. 'I'll have a sherry,' she called.

Two minutes later she had set the table: salad, chilled hock, avocados. 'How was your birthday so far?'

'Pretty fair.' He'd welcomed the chance to leave the presents at his flat – no point in making her think about

Helen and Judy when he didn't have to – but all at once he felt a need to talk. 'Judy bought me an inscribed pen. She must have been saving for months.'

Perhaps his tone said more than he had meant to. 'Regrets?' she said.

'Well, I like her better now she's growing up. It's hard to believe I couldn't stand her.' He was imagining how much of Judy's development he had missed, and that was why he spoke brutally: he didn't want Barbara to start blaming herself again – something in her poise told him she had problems of her own. 'But you know, I suppose I could have put up with losing sleep for a year, except that was only the start of things. Helen insisted on bringing her to bed with us when she ought to have had her own room, did I tell you that?' Of course he had, here in her flat the night she'd said, 'Don't go unless you want to,' but this was hardly the context in which to remind her of that. 'I blame Helen,' he said, and hoped that wasn't too obvious a reassurance. 'She never stopped Judy from climbing on things. Wherever I hid manuscripts Judy always got to them, and Helen acted as if it didn't matter, I could always ask the author for another copy. Sometimes I think one shouldn't have children at all in this business.'

He was so anxious to reassure her that he made the remark without thinking. What lost faces might she have seen in the photograph album? 'Did you have time to read my chapter?' he asked quickly.

'I made the time, since you were coming.'

'Don't be afraid to tell me it was wasted.' Without warning he felt uncomfortable; you shouldn't ask friends to judge your work, even when their business was judging books. 'I mean, I know how busy you are. Your clients ought to come first.'

'I'm sure you realize that they do. But this could be a strong book if you finish it, Ted. What's blocking you?'

'I don't understand the private eye sufficiently. I can't predict what she'll do.'

'Surely that's a good thing. Try letting the story take over. Write about the situation and see how it reveals the characters. I think you spend too much energy trying to do it the other way round.'

She was at her best when she was enthusiastic; when she was at rest her long oval face looked cool as a sculpture, the long nose and the elegant curves of her cheekbones; now her startlingly blue eyes were even livelier, and he was reminded how passionate her wide mouth could be. Still he had a sense that she was preoccupied, harassed. 'Just recovering from the Paul Gregory auction?' he suggested.

'It isn't really over yet. The big one is still to come, in New York,' she said, and jumped, for the phone was ringing in her bedroom.

Perhaps she had been waiting for a call, perhaps that was why she was on edge. She went quickly up the short staircase and closed the door. Presumably she had left the telephone plugged in there because she didn't want him to overhear, but the flat, which the previous tenant had soundproofed, magnified her voice. He glanced about so that he wouldn't be tempted to listen, at the four-storey hi-fi, the spherical television, the tables nesting as though caught at leapfrog, the leather suite whose chocolate slabs looked to be drooping with the heat, the numerous book-cases. Scattered through the shelves were Melwood-Nuttall books which he had given her. He didn't want to publish his own novel, he wanted someone else to prove to him that it was worth publishing.

Soon she reappeared and carried off the avocados, though she hadn't finished hers. She returned with chicken tikka. 'I don't know if you heard any of that. The girl who was going to Italy with me has decided she can't go.'

Behind her on the wall he saw an Escher lithograph of

61

Southern Italy: the smooth precise planes of the houses and the rocks on which they stood looked carved from a single piebald block of marble; a mysterious entrance was just visible in the distant hills. 'I'd like to see Italy,' he said.

'Come with me by all means if you can be free at the end of next month. I'll see if they'll transfer her reservations to you.' She seemed all at once much happier, and managed to eat most of her chicken before the phone rang.

This time her eyes flickered for a moment before she controlled herself. She looked reluctant, almost trapped. If she was still expecting a call, could she had left the phone in the bedroom because she hoped that would magic the call away?

When the bedroom door closed he crossed to the window. The lanterns on the plateau were lit now; the church was a charcoal sketch, cut out and propped on a red-brick raft buoyed up by swimming lights. Barbara was speaking low, but he thought he heard stray phrases. 'You can't be' – was that what she had just said? A spindly movement by the church distracted him. It must have been the shadow of the willow.

He heard the ring as she replaced the receiver, then there was a long pause. The flattened church hung in the silent dark. All at once she came bustling downstairs. 'Oh, your cake,' she said, wavering between the table and the kitchen. 'You won't mind if I don't have any, will you? I'm afraid I've eaten as much as I can.' He would have asked her what was wrong, except that she clearly wanted to pretend that nothing was. No doubt she would tell him in her own time if she wanted to. But as she cut the cake, having forgotten to let him do so, he saw that her hands were shaking.

8

Though the Underground was stifling, when Barbara reached Notting Hill she found the street was even worse. Beneath the painfully blue sky the air looked pale with dust. Lorries and cars and buses rushed down Holland Park Avenue, staining the grimy trees. The noise was loud as a car factory, and seemed actually to thicken the air. She couldn't think until she found some refuge from the noise.

Eventually she managed to cross to Pembridge Road. It was somewhat quieter, despite the unbroken train of cars. Litter from the dustmen's strike crawled along the gutter. As she hurried past a terrace of shops smoked by the traffic, dogs glared at her with china eyes, one of which was chipped. Further on, scaffolding outlined tall houses, a giant pat of cement glistened on the pavement – but here was the corner of the Portobello Road, and she stopped, to try to think. What was she doing here? Couldn't she accept that she had simply been the victim of a sadistic hoax?

Until last night she'd managed to believe that it was less than that – that the call she'd received at her office had been a wrong number, after all. Though she'd heard the girl clearly enough, that need not have meant that the girl could hear her. Nevertheless she had been on edge for the rest of the week. Sometimes when the phone rang she felt herself grow hollow and fragile, held together by her nerves.

Last night's call during Ted's birthday dinner had come almost as a relief; at least it was something to deal with – at least, that was what she had told herself when she heard the voice, though she felt shaky with heartbeats. This time she wouldn't dump the receiver back in its cradle. 'Mummy, it's me. Please don't go away again.'

Barbara had sat down hastily on the bed, her eyes prickling with tears, even though she'd heard pips and the fall of a coin before the voice. Ghosts didn't feed coins into phones; this wasn't a chance to hear that Angela forgave her, a secret hope which Barbara seldom admitted to herself. 'Don't bother pretending you're my daughter,' she said harshly. 'You can't be. The police found her body in a field in Kent.'

'That wasn't me. They wanted you to think I was dead.'

Whoever it was would have had to say that, yet for an uneasy moment Barbara remembered saying 'I suppose they shot some other little girl to make me think it was Angela.' For a moment that seemed agonizingly possible, but she mustn't let herself be tricked that way; the voice sounded older than it should, trying to pretend it was younger. 'Who wanted me to think so?' she demanded. 'Why?'

'Oh, Mummy, don't ask so many questions. I'll tell you when you come for me.'

'Come where?' Barbara hadn't meant to sound so urgent. 'Where?'

'I'm going to tell you.' Suddenly the voice seemed oddly immature. 'But you have to promise that you won't tell anyone.'

'All right, now tell me.'

'No, you have to say you promise. You mustn't tell anyone about me. You mustn't go to the police.'

'All right, I promise,' Barbara said, though her whole body was struggling to hold back the words. 'Where?'

The pips responded at once, high and inane as giggling, long before she would have expected them. 'Off the Portobello Road. The house with the bricked-up gate,' the voice said in a lull before it was cut off by electronic howling. At least, that was what she'd decided it had

64

gabbled, in the hours when she had lain awake after Ted had left. She had paced the flat when she couldn't sleep, afraid to hope, afraid she would shrink into herself as she had after the kidnapping; she never wanted to feel like that again. By God, she would like to find whoever had made her so nervous and fragile again – and so here she was, at the start of the Portobello Road.

Before she was conscious of deciding, she stepped forward. A corner cut off the uproar of traffic at once. A terrace of two-storey houses, painted green or white or pink, led to a crossroads; some of the paint looked cracked as parched mud. Trees no taller than the houses sprouted from the pavements. A few cars dozed beside the kerbs.

None of the knee-high walls had a bricked-up gate, but of course she wasn't meant to look on the Portobello Road itself. On the sloping crossroad she could see only blinding chalky houses which challenged her not to look away. She might have followed both directions out of sight, except that she'd realized how many side roads there might be, how much time she might have to waste on a hoax. She was wandering when she ought to be at work – but she had treated her work as all-important once before, and she couldn't do so now.

She hurried herself down the Portobello Road, past a terrace of galleries, studios, shops brassy with antiques. Here was Westbourne Grove, but wouldn't the voice have called that by name? Perhaps it might have done so if it hadn't been cut off, or perhaps the hoax was meant to make Barbara wander like this, growing hotter and more irritable. Surely nobody could plan something so pointless.

She tramped up and down Westbourne Grove – white houses glared like lightning – then she trudged back to the Portobello Road, into a clutter of market stalls hemmed in by shops pimply with burglar alarms. The side streets grew more numerous, and she had to cross back and forth to examine all of them. Suppose the voice hadn't said 'a bricked-up gate' but something else entirely?

Suddenly she halted, between bollards like metal candles that closed off Lonsdale Road. All the side streets had names; why hadn't the voice named the street before describing the house? Could there have been any reason other than to prolong the joke? Suppose the caller had read about Barbara in the Sunday supplement and had resented her success? Suppose the caller were unbalanced enough to want to make her suffer?

All at once Barbara was furious, determined to find the house if it existed, for surely the owner of the voice would be waiting there to see if she'd taken the bait. She struggled onwards, though the crowd made the street even hotter, guzzled the air. Stallholders were shouting and arguing, blocks of shoppers obstructed the narrow pavements in front of the stalls. A tall, heavily-built man, thickly bearded and dressed even in that weather in Cossack boots and fur hat, squeezed past her. She was conscious of every one of her sticky movements.

Here was another side street, more white houses cracked as senile faces. Cheap sunbleached curtains of all colours made the pairs of windows look unmatched and cataracted. Those houses which could afford paths had gates, however staggery, or at least spaces between the gateposts. She turned away, and came face to face with a woman who was watching her.

She was dressed in black: black stockings, fat black trousers, black sweater sprinkled with white, perhaps from her dyed hair. Her round teenager's face was made up to disguise how much older she was, and bore a vague meaningless smile – exactly the look one might expect of the person who had made the call. For a moment she seemed about to speak, but was that surprising, given the way Barbara was staring at her? Barbara dodged past her, feeling

66

idiotic, angry, ashamed of herself. When she glanced back from the corner, the woman was still watching her.

At least the end of the market was in sight, beneath a flyover loaded with traffic, above which the air was grey and wavering. Now the crowd seemed to be full of teenage girls – of course it was the school holidays – and all of them stared at her. No doubt that was hardly surprising, if she looked as she felt. Shops sprang open like Jacks-in-the-box; the presence and uproar of people and animals, dogs kicked away from the stalls, was oppressive as a traffic jam. She tried to hurry and almost knocked down a wire mesh bin of shoes.

When she reached the flyover it offered no relief. The roar of traffic overhead was dull and overwhelming. People clustered beneath the flyover like derelicts under a bridge, fingering clothes that staggered along racks of hangers. Everything looked grey and shabby, the faces as much as the clothes. She thought it was less the shade than the noise which was befogging her vision, choking her thoughts.

Beyond the flyover it was worse, an absolutely constant roar of white noise from the heavy traffic, so intense that it was physically sickening. She had to halt beside a line of grubby parked cars and shove her hands against her ears, and even then most of the noise seeped through. Her mind seemed to have been wiped like tape. Everything looked flat as the blue plastic sky which was dovetailed into all the spaces between the chimneys of the terrace which paralleled the flyover. She could only stand and stare while she tried to grow used to the noise.

The three-and four-storey houses were so nondescript that she seemed hardly to be seeing them at all. Flaking pillars supported their porches, several windows were broken, greyish curtains hung beyond some of the holes. Other windows were bricked up, as was one of the gates.

9

It looked like very little: an abandoned house, the feeble ending of a cruel joke. None of the windows appeared to be curtained except by dust. Even so, could she be certain that it was empty, even if both adjacent houses clearly were, without going to look? Either a tipsy shadow of the porch was leaning against the edge of the front door, or the door was ajar.

Eventually she crossed the road to the adjacent garden, before she could drown in heat and noise. A fractured armchair, apparently dropped from an upper window, had broken the fence between the gardens. As she clambered over she glanced towards the market, both from guilt and in the hope of glimpsing whoever had enticed her to the house. One or two people were watching, but as far as she could tell at that distance, they looked sympathetic. Perhaps they took her for a squatter.

Jumping down from the armchair, she made her way quickly to the porch. Litter clung to spikes of bleached grass – yellowing newspapers, torn pages from a book, a sherry bottle – or lay on the ragged greenish drive. Fragments of the porch crunched underfoot as she climbed the steps. Yes, the door was ajar, and she pushed it wider. The floor of the hall was covered with dust, but there was no sign of footprints.

So that was that, as she had been almost sure it would be. She gazed out of the porch, more relieved than angry with herself. Perhaps she had been gullible, but it was over now. She was still gazing – the market beneath the flyover looked quaint now, even the noise was almost bearable – when something looked out at her from one of the windows beside the porch.

She turned so violently that she almost fell from the steps. She grabbed a pillar for support and felt it crumbling beneath her fingers. But the shape at the window had only been cobwebs, lumpy with dust. She saw an edge of the grey mass slithering down the pane a moment before it sank out of sight.

She glanced towards the crowd beneath the flyover for reassurance, and thought she saw a face she recognized. Yes, a white-haired woman dressed in black was watching her from the shadow of the concrete. As Barbara made for the gap in the fence, the woman fled into the crowd.

That was enough. Now that she remembered the woman's vague smile it seemed knowing. If Barbara caught her she wouldn't have much to smile about, she would really have something to resent Barbara for – but Barbara had wasted enough time. When she reached the pavement she turned away towards Ladbroke Grove.

In the quiet of the Underground her head felt hollow, a rusty bell without a clapper, still echoing metallically. On the train she brushed dust from her clothes. It was rather dismaying that her success could make someone she'd never met hate her so much, try to hurt her so cruelly, but at least it was over. Certainly the woman would never dare try anything else when she knew that Barbara had seen her face.

By the time she reached Dover Street she felt surprisingly light-hearted. Taxis black as beetles crawled up from Bond Street and Piccadilly, and she could outstrip them easily. She was glad to be back at her office. Here she was in control, here the game had rules.

Louise consulted her pad of messages. 'Fiona says she's sorry but they won't hold her reservations for Italy.'

'Aren't they bastards. They love their little rules, don't

they.' Perhaps she and Ted could work out an alternative. 'What else?'

'Paul Gregory doesn't think the publishers should get a percentage of the film rights. End of messages. The mail's on your desk, mainly some rejections and a manuscript. Oh – '

Barbara was impatient to get going, after the false start to the day. 'Well, go on.'

'I was wondering if I could bring Hannah in sometimes during the holidays, when I'm taking her on somewhere.'

'Of course you can. Why on earth not?' Presumably, now that she'd read about Angela, Louise hesitated to bring the child to the office, but of course there was no need. Yet for a moment Barbara wondered if she herself was too eager to dismiss the events of the morning, to put Angela out of her mind. She mustn't start brooding: Angela had died nine years ago, and she had come to terms with that; to allow her guilt to interfere with her work now would be a mockery of concern, and unfair to her memory of Angela.

Arthur was watching over the mail on her desk. She pushed him closer to the phone to give herself more space. American letters enthusing over *A Torrent of Lives,* an author complaining that a small publisher had plagiarized him just before it went bankrupt in order to recommence business under another name, an agent who was trying to sell the American rights which she had already sold on one of her books. The sooner she opened an American office the better. Here was a manuscript returned by one of the larger publishers, its disordered pages stamped with coffee-rings. Here were three exercise books from a vicar in Cornwall: *The Salt Has Lost Its Savour, Hip-Hip-Hip-Hooray.* His letter was in the same impeccable handwriting: 'I read the article about you in the Sunday journal, and I wondered if you might have the time to place a little book which is by no means fashionable, but, I hope you will agree, the better for it . . .' Since the publication of the article she had been besieged by letters of sympathy about Angela and by manuscripts, most of them typed with grey, almost invisible ribbons: *Rapunzel the Medusa, Ferry Bus to Erebus, The Old Man Covered With Oil*. All were unpublishable. It unnerved her to imagine how much frustrated creativity there might be in the world.

Well, it was an average working day. First she wanted to sort things out with Paul. Eventually his phone stopped ringing. 'Who's that?' a child's voice said.

'Could I speak to Paul Gregory, please? This is Barbara Waugh.'

'It's Barbara somebody,' the child shouted. After some time a woman's voice arrived. 'Actually, I wanted to speak to Paul,' Barbara said. 'This is his agent, Barbara Waugh.'

'He isn't here at the moment.' Paul's wife sounded guarded. 'Do you want him to ring you?'

'Yes please. Tell him the Americans are panting for his trilogy. They'll be lining up when I go to New York.'

'You'll have to talk to him about that,' Mrs Gregory said, and rang off at once. Was she the one who had changed Paul's mind about the film rights? Now that her husband was making real money, did she feel that Barbara was giving too much of it away? Barbara was impatient to clear up the misunderstanding, but here was Louise with the afternoon mail – a new manuscript from Cherry Newton-Brown.

Barbara read the opening pages and felt heartened at once; if the whole book was as engrossing then they had a winner. She could take a few chapters over to the park to read. She was still reading as she reached for the phone, to ask Louise to get her a sandwich – the novel was better than engrossing, it was compulsive – and for a few moments she didn't realize why her hand was hovering aimlessly above the phone. Then she heard someone in the outer office with Louise. They were arguing.

Barbara picked up the phone as soon as it rang. 'I have a Ms Margery Turner in reception,' Louise said. 'She hasn't an appointment, but she insists on seeing you.'

'What does she want?'

'She says she has to tell you that herself.'

'Oh, one of those.' One unpublishable author had tried that trick in an attempt to browbeat her into handling his work. 'Do you think she has anything to offer?'

'Decidedly not, I'd say.'

'Tell her to write us a letter. Oh, and when you've got rid of her, could you go down and get me a sandwich? Anything with salad.'

She tried to read on, but she couldn't concentrate, for Ms Margery Turner was still arguing, a slow blurred petulant sound. She found herself reading the same words over and over: he couldn't help himself, he couldn't help himself. The argument stopped abruptly, and Louise came in. 'She won't go away,' she hissed.

'Oh yes she will. I've taken enough bullshit for one day.' Barbara strode into the outer office; she could already feel how cold and brisk her voice would be – but she halted between the rooms, staring at the woman's dyed white hair, her round teenager's face and vague smile.

10

One thing was clear at once to Barbara: if this woman had had anything to do with the two phone calls, she would never have come here, especially not when Louise as well as Barbara could see her. But that re-opened far too many questions which Barbara had thought safely closed. She didn't know what to say, she could only stare at Margery Turner and feel herself growing nervously fragile until the woman said, 'Can I speak to you in private?'

Barbara regained some control; after all, this was her office. 'That depends on what you want.'

'The same thing you do. The same thing you're looking for.'

'Which is?'

'You know. Why you went to that house.'

'Perhaps I don't know.' The conversation was growing maddeningly insubstantial. 'Perhaps you can tell me.'

The woman peered suspiciously at her. 'I will if you want me to, but can't I tell you by yourself?'

The main thing was to find out what she wanted, what she knew; Barbara felt as though she herself knew nothing at all. 'I have to go out,' she said abruptly. 'You can walk down with me if you like.'

As she fetched her handbag Arthur's eyes glared like a warning, but that must be a stray reflection of sunlight on the glass. 'I'll be about an hour,' she told Louise and hurried out, to give herself no chance to wonder what she was inviting.

On the stairs Margery Turner said, 'I didn't want to say much in front of her. I don't like people who treat you as

73

though you're a criminal. When I said I was looking for the same thing as you, I meant the people at that house stole my daughter as well as yours.'

Barbara managed not to react. She mustn't give anything away until she knew what the woman's game was. Perhaps there was a way to make the woman talk more freely. 'Why don't we discuss it over lunch?' she said.

She hurried Margery Turner into Mayfair, down Hay Hill and through Lansdowne Row, where the gutter that split the pavement looked like a crack which the heat had opened. Walking down Curzon Street, between the two-tone buildings of red brick and cream, felt like entering a kiln; she could smell the walls baking. Beside the great stone-pillared half-shell of the Christian Scientist church, a men's hairdresser's breathed out after-shave. A mound in the window was planted with dozens of shaving brushes, stranded desiccated anenomes.

Barbara couldn't chat all the way to the wine bar, and it seemed bad strategy to stay forbiddingly quiet. 'What do you know about the people at that house?' she said, which seemed vague enough not to betray her ignorance. 'Where are they now?'

'I'll show you the letter when we're sitting down.' Margery Turner's voice was as slow as her large body. 'I expect you're wondering how I knew to get in touch with you.'

'Well, yes,' Barbara said, though her other unspoken questions had given her no chance to wonder.

'I'm afraid I followed you to your office. I don't like people who do that sort of thing, but I felt I had to. You see, I recognized you from your photograph when you came into my street – I'd read about you in the library. So when I saw you going to that house I knew what you were after.'

That didn't make sense. 'What did you think I was looking for?'

'Your little girl, of course.' Though the vague smile hadn't faltered for a moment, her eyes looked wary, suspicious. 'I forget her name,' she said.

'Her name is Angela, but why should you think I was looking for her when she was killed nine years ago?'

'What do you mean?' The woman sounded outraged. 'Who says she was?'

'One person who says so,' Barbara said with a kind of bitter triumph, 'is the writer of the article you read.'

For a moment she was sure again that Margery Turner had made the phone calls, until she saw how bewildered the woman was. 'I didn't read that part, I only read about Angela. I hadn't any reason to be interested in you then, had I?' she said petulantly. 'Some of the library staff treat you as if you're there to steal the books. I don't wonder I missed that part.'

It was too clumsy to be a lie. 'Anyway,' she said, 'you can't believe she's dead, or you wouldn't have gone to that house.'

'I don't want to talk about that just now,' Barbara said for lack of a better response, and led her through the arch, hardly larger than a front doorway, that gave into Shepherd Market. At the centre of the small paved court a prostitute wearing an abbreviated fur coat stood beside a clump of telephone kiosks, their red no brighter than her lipstick.

'I thought we might help each other,' Margery Turner said.

That sounded ominous. 'Surely the police can do more than I can.'

'Police?' Her smile turned sour. 'They won't do anything, because Susan's over seventeen. They say they don't think she's in danger, but they just want to keep her away from me. You know how a mother by herself gets treated. Now I don't know who to turn to.'

'Well, at least you can tell me about it,' Barbara said carefully, and led the way down to the wine bar.

Boxing photographs yellow as old skin patched the wall above the steep stairs. After the sunshine the dim orange light could hardly be perceived as light at all. As Barbara made her way to a tiny table she felt as though she were groping through marmalade.

A waiter came to the table at once. Margery glared at him, daring him to throw her out. 'Whatever you're having,' she said when Barbara asked what she would like.

Soon the wine arrived. Margery had seemed reluctant to speak; she'd kept glancing at the nearby diners, their sloughed jackets on the backs of their chairs. Now she half-emptied her glass and sat forward. 'I want to be straight with you,' she said. 'They didn't steal Susan in the way they stole your little girl. Susan ran away from home.'

Barbara could only nod, but that seemed to be enough. 'She couldn't stand the people where we lived,' Margery said. 'They were no older than you or me, but you'd have thought they were Victorians. If you made a mistake and then couldn't get married they treated you like a leper. Susan used to say they didn't dare to think there was anything worthwhile outside themselves.'

She pushed her plate of Swiss sausage out of the way and drained her glass, which Barbara refilled. 'Susan was artistic, you see. She was brilliant, and yet she never did anything with herself. I kept on and on at her to go to art school – oh, I must have kept at her solidly for a year or more. You see, I was never much good at school, I didn't want her to end up like me. When she ran away I thought perhaps she'd gone to art school, until I got her letter. Then I knew she'd gone because of the neighbours, even though she didn't say so. Artistic types can't stand people who are false.'

'You were going to show me the letter,' Barbara said.

'Oh, not that one. That was just to let me know she was all right – at least, she said she was, but if there was nothing she wanted to hide she wouldn't have left out her address, would she? I showed it to the police, but they wouldn't do anything. We're supposed to be equal now, but they treat us like halfwits unless we're the Queen or the Prime Minister,' she said, a feeble joke that dared Barbara not to laugh.

She was peering in her frayed black handbag. 'This is the letter I meant. She addressed it to the wrong house, she'd forgotten where I lived. It was delivered just at the other end of the street and yet they didn't bring it to me, they crossed out their address and posted it again. That's the kind of thing I had to suffer. If they'd brought it to me I might have found Susan while she was still at that house.'

It was only the last page of the letter, with something drawn on the back. At least the large rather childish handwriting was easy to read in the marmalade light. Margery loomed close, ready to retrieve the letter as soon as Barbara finished.

but now i can take drugs or leave them alone just like men or women or life for that matter – so i was ready to move on when i met the people im with now – you wouldnt like or understand what were doing but we dont fully understand it ourselves – we wont know what it is until weve done it but i dont care – at least well see what no ones ever seen before – im not supposed to tell anyone about it but i thought id see if i could tell you so youd know i wasnt dead – im not supposed to use my name either but i will in case youve forgotten it – thats all from
susan the bastard

Barbara felt acutely uncomfortable. The letter was embarrassing, but what did it prove? She turned it over to glance at the drawing, and recognized everything at once: the market beneath the flyover, the house with the bricked-up gate, a few lines of adjacent houses that faded into nothingness. A face was staring out of an upper window of the house. Its eyes were minute empty circles, absolutely blank.

Margery hid the letter quickly in her bag and glared

suspiciously at a waiter who happened to be passing. 'Don't let the way she talks fool you. It sounds as if she's just trying to shock, doesn't it? But just think about what she says. That letter is a cry for help. She's not supposed to write to anyone or even to use her own name, she can't get away from those people even if she wants to – you realized that, didn't you? She mustn't be supposed to say where she is, and I think she drew the house because drawing wasn't really saying. Their minds aren't like ours once they start taking drugs.'

Barbara could imagine her poring over the letter, finding more with every reading. 'Aren't you assuming rather a lot? I mean – '

'You don't have to take my word for it. Someone agrees with me. Perhaps you should meet her.'

'Perhaps I should. Who is she?'

'Her name is Gerry Martin. You know who she is, don't you? You ought to know her. She's a writer.' For a moment she looked suspicious again. 'Well, perhaps she isn't your kind of writer – she writes for newspapers. She wrote a lot about these cults who steal young people from their families, and I got in touch with her. She thinks the people who've got Susan moved because she told me where they were. Now Miss Martin is trying to find them.'

'Well then, someone *is* helping you.'

'But I couldn't just leave it all to her and do nothing myself. Could you?' she said, and Barbara remembered the empty nerve-racking weeks she had waited in the house at Otford. 'When I found that house from the postmark and it was empty I just wandered about like a madwoman, like one of those old women you see walking the streets with nowhere to go. Then I saw a vacancy in that street where you saw me and do you know, I really felt as if God had put it there. I go to the house by the flyover each day and stay there as long as I can, just in case. Susan knows that's the only place I know to look for her.'

For the moment Barbara felt nothing but sympathy. 'Did you ever look inside the house?'

'I didn't dare to, in case someone had me arrested. People are like that, you'd be surprised. We could go in together, though, couldn't we? They'd have to believe you.'

She'd landed herself in that one, Barbara thought wryly. Still, it was easy enough to refuse, to plead pressures of work, and she was about to do so when a stray thought made her pause. Suppose the people Margery was searching for were the people who had kidnapped and killed Angela? Suppose the purpose of the two phone calls had been to alert Barbara to their existence, however obliquely? Suppose the caller hadn't dared to be more explicit? At least she might have a chance, however small and belated, to make amends for her neglect of Angela.

'All right,' she said, not at all sure of herself or of how she was becoming involved, 'I don't suppose it will do any harm. I'm busy today and tomorrow, but tomorrow evening is clear. I'll pick you up at your flat about sevenish.'

'It's number eight, flat three. My name isn't on the bell. It doesn't do to let people know too much about yourself.' She blackened her eyes with mascara as Barbara called for the bill. 'Oh, let me pay half,' she said, so mechanically as to leave no doubt that she hoped Barbara would refuse.

She made for the staircase as Barbara paid for them both. There she stumbled, almost pulling someone's coat from the back of his chair. She hurried upstairs, smiling apologetically. It seemed she had spoken freely because she was drunk, but Barbara wondered if she had left anything unsaid.

'If we don't find anything at the house,' Margery said when Barbara caught up with her outside, 'we could help Gerry Martin, couldn't we? Then there would be more of us to search. The only thing is, I couldn't pay for much travelling.'

'We'll see what happens,' Barbara said, for she felt she was being drawn deeper too quickly. She watched Margery vanish into the minor maze of side streets, then she made for Curzon Street. She must think of a plausible story to tell Louise, something that would save her from having to explain, for now that she thought about it she had little idea what she was doing, or why.

11

Margery sat on her bed and gazed from her window. Above the peeling bleached houses, the blue drained from the sky; somewhere nearby a man and a woman were shouting. Margery was reading a large novel about a brilliant young actress who used her talents to rob and seduce and blackmail her way into international society. It was a book for people who liked to imagine themselves in the role of criminal but who needed to believe that nothing of the kind could happen to them or perhaps to anyone else, and it was dedicated to the author's agent, Barbara Waugh.

Where was Barbara? To judge by the sky, she must be late by now. Margery leaned out of the window. The white houses hung like holey sheets above the grey pavements; the man had stopped shouting, the woman was screaming; two men strolled by, ignoring the screams. Margery liked people to mind their own business, but sometimes she felt that round here they did so too well.

She slipped the book under the bed with the others. She'd had enough of it, had enough of lies. Susan gazed down from the narrow shelf above the bed. The sun never reached her there, and she looked to be gazing out through fog rather than glass, up among the shadows or stains of damp which clung beneath the ceiling. If Margery switched on the light beneath its dusty fez the dark patches were still there, and Susan was wiped out by a slash of light on the glass.

Susan was holding a book of Picasso, which she'd chosen as a prize at school. Margery hadn't liked most of the paintings, which looked like things that vandals drew on walls, but then she'd never claimed to be artistic; if they helped Susan with her art, that was all that mattered.

If only she had kept along that path! Margery had tried to encourage her to do better, but Susan had scarcely worn the presents her mother brought home. Before she had left school she had begun to turn against everything that Margery wanted her to be. Too late Margery had seen that people were turning Susan against her, reminding Susan of her mother's mistakes. That was confirmed by the way so many people – the neighbours, the police – had been delighted when Susan left her.

And perhaps Barbara Waugh was among them. She'd seemed generous when she had drunk less than Margery, but perhaps the wine had been meant to make Margery overlook questions she ought to have asked. How could the agent have known so little about the people who had lived in the abandoned house, when she had known enough to trace her daughter Angela there? What had she meant by saying that Angela had been killed? Perhaps she had only been pretending to be sympathetic, so that Margery would let these things go unexplained.

Today she had gone to the library to look up the article about Barbara Waugh, to see if it really said that Angela had been killed, but when she'd said she didn't know the date of publication the staff had treated her as if she couldn't read. They hadn't kept it, they told her without even checking. She was glad she'd stolen their copy of the book she had noticed in Barbara's office – they would never have let her borrow it – but it had given her no insight into Barbara Waugh. How could she be sure of the woman? Was she even coming?

The *Charlie's Angels* theme was blaring in the flat next door. In the days when she was allowed to rent a television, she had used to watch the Angels with faint contempt – they were so impeccable and fearless and unreal – yet part of her had wished she could deal with problems as capably as they did. Of course they didn't deal with real life, that was too messy and disappointing. They were reminding her how disappointing it was, for their theme meant that it was eight o'clock, that Barbara Waugh wasn't coming.

So the evening was wasted. If there was anything that needed to be found in the house by the flyover, it would stay hidden while they took Susan even further away. Everyone had been right after all: Margery was an apology for a mother, she could do nothing to save her child.

All at once she rallied. They'd nearly had her there, but she was the one person they couldn't turn against Margery Turner. They'd almost cowed her into becoming the person they all wanted her to think she was, but she wasn't so easily beaten, not while Susan was in danger. The market was closed now, there might be nobody to wonder what she was doing at the empty house. Let them have her arrested, she had Susan's second letter to show why she was there. She'd give as good an account of herself as Barbara Waugh could have.

And by God, Barbara Waugh would have to help if necessary. She could vouch for Margery; after all, she'd trespassed at the house herself, if that was trespassing. Maybe she'd thought she had got rid of Margery by lying to her, but her behaviour in front of her receptionist had shown she had something to hide; Margery could play on that if she had to. Smiling at herself in the mirror above the sink, where a jagged patch of wall pierced by a rusty screw left a piece out of the top of her head, she made up her eyes and went out.

Apart from the stampede of traffic on the flyover, the streets were quieter than during the day. Now that the light was subdued everything had the chance to be itself, and she was able to look directly at the white houses. She could see each line of mortar in the sharp-edged frieze of chimneys.

As she walked past open windows, Charlie's Angels ran from house to house.

The Portobello Road seemed much wider now that the market had been put away. Window displays were quiet as museum cases, if more dusty. She halted beneath the flyover, amid litter which was dozing fitfully, and stared at the house beyond the bricked-up gate. She mustn't lose her nerve. Perhaps there was nothing to find in the house, but she would still have proved that she could face it by herself, she needn't rely on other people when they were all so unreliable. She stopped her mind at that and made herself emerge.

The noise blotted out her thoughts at once. She'd walked some way before it became actually painful, otherwise she would have had to retreat. She felt as if the noise was in her head and bursting outward. She scrambled over the armchair that had broken the fence between the gardens and stumbled to the porch, to take refuge from the noise. She no longer cared if anyone was watching.

She hesitated when she saw that the front door was closed; surely Barbara Waugh had left it wide open. But it opened readily, revealing a hall which led past a staircase to a kitchen. Through the kitchen doorway she could see a window, beyond which rubbish was smouldering. A door stood open on either side of the hall. The floor, the carpet that was too narrow and too short for the stairs, the stairs themselves, all were pale with dust.

When she stepped forward the noise accompanied her. Though she felt dust gritting underfoot, it seemed to make no sound. Glancing down, she saw her footprints following her. There were no marks in the dust ahead. Gratified that she was able to think despite the uproar, she closed the front door and hurried down the hall.

The kitchen was a mass of closed doors: wall cupboards, a battered refrigerator, a chipped stove wrenched away from the wall, its umbilicus dangling. The stove was empty, but there was an unidentifiably rotten object at the back of the refrigerator. When she managed to open the cupboards, their sliding doors grinding in dust, she found several jars that looked sticky with grey fur.

She went back to the hall. The noise was dull but omnipresent, a medium in which the house was drowning. She'd glanced into the rooms beside the hall on her way to the kitchen – rooms the length of the house, bare except for dust – which was why she faltered now, heart jumping painfully. But the grey lumpy mass just inside the right-hand doorway was a tangle of cobwebs and dust or stuffing from a chair, not an animal at all. She dodged past it, into the room.

There was nowhere to search. Apart from a fireplace which had once been painted white, the room was absolutely featureless. Oily black ash came flaking towards her as she stooped quickly to the grate. She strode back into the hall, ignoring the flurry of the mass of cobwebs.

The room across the hall was empty. The sash of the back window lay broken on the floor. If the entire house was as bare as this, what point was there in searching? But she wouldn't know unless she looked. Why should she be afraid to go upstairs? It didn't matter that she would be further from the front door, not when the house was so obviously disused.

Nevertheless, as she climbed the stairs she felt that someone was standing absolutely still and watching her, she couldn't tell from where. It was the sort of thing anyone might feel in a deserted house. The smell of dust gathered in her nostrils, the air looked grey and dimmed and restless. Above the stairs a dangling socket swollen with brownish dust swayed almost imperceptibly.

All the doors on the first landing were open. The bathroom contained a dried-up toilet from which a spider was crawling; a coffin-shaped patch on the floor showed where the bath had used to be. Both of the larger rooms were completely bare. Tattered cobwebs hung from the ceilings, groped feebly over the walls.

She was glad not to have to linger in the rooms; she had been nervous when she couldn't see the stairs. But the only footprints climbing towards her were her own, and there were no prints on the staircase above her. She was beginning to feel irritable: could Barbara Waugh have tricked her into coming here alone to teach Margery not to pester her? She was only trying to dissuade herself from going up to the top floor; it was nervousness that was making her irritable. She glowered at nothing, as if that would scare away her nervousness, and hurried up the stairs.

They were darker than the rest of the house. The heat and the dust seemed to have massed up here, a dark oppressive presence beneath the roof. She took short quick breaths as she climbed, but her nostrils still felt clogged. Suddenly she recalled what she'd seen from outside the house: the left-hand window on the top floor was bricked up. No wonder it was dark. She hoped she wouldn't have to go into that room.

But of course she had to, even though she could see through the doorway that it was darker in there than it ought to be. The front window was bricked up, but why was there no light from the back? She glanced uneasily at the dim staircase – nothing but her footprints – then she made herself go into the room.

Beyond the doorway was a passage no wider than a telephone kiosk. At first she thought that was the cause of the dark, then she managed to distinguish the room itself beyond an open door at the end of the short passage. The room was even darker. She ventured forward, and realized why. Not only the front window but the back had been filled in.

She was reaching into the darkness in search of a light-switch – if the Waugh bitch hadn't let her down she wouldn't be so fearful now – when the smell came drifting out at her. Though it was too faint for her to define, it was utterly horrible. For a moment she thought she was trapped, that the door to the landing would close, locking her in with the dark and the smell. Nobody would hear her screams. Then she had stumbled out on to the landing, and slammed the door so hard that the slam resounded through the omnipresent noise, down through the house.

Susan had lived in this house. Margery's dismay at that was so intense, if unspecific, that she was afraid she might be sick. It was her dismay that made her go into the last bare room, though she could see there was nothing to find. On impulse she glanced from the back window. Behind the house a bath was almost buried under a smouldering pile of rubbish that looked as though it came from all the houses. If there had been anything to find, perhaps it was in that pile.

She was hurrying back to the landing – she'd realized that if the door to the bricked-up room should open she would never hear it, though she wasn't sure why that should make her nervous – when a floorboard moved beneath her feet. Was the dilapidated floor giving way? She almost fell, and that was how she glimpsed the piece of paper beneath the dislodged board.

Her excitement faded when she saw what it was: a crumpled page torn out of a book, just like the pages she'd seen littering the garden below the porch. Nevertheless she fumbled the page from under the board and smoothed it out on the floor. It came from a book called *The Bedroom Philosophers*, and it described the torture of a mother. Through the thin paper she could dimly see an illustration on the next page, but if it was as disgusting as the text, Margery didn't want to look – and yet wasn't it part of the life that Susan was leading? Reluctantly she turned over the page.

87

The drawing didn't illustrate the text. It was one of Susan's portraits. She read what Susan had scribbled beneath it, then she gazed at the sketched face. This was more than she could have hoped for. Barbara Waugh couldn't refuse to help her now.

Suddenly she was afraid. For no reason she was sure that she wasn't meant to take the drawing out of the house, that she had endangered herself by finding it at all. Every vague fear she had suffered since entering the house was lying in wait for her on the landing. She rushed herself out there, before she was too afraid to do so.

The door of the bricked-up room was still closed. She ran downstairs, frightened of her own clattering; she couldn't hear for the noise of the flyover, but suppose she could be heard? More than the heat and the dust seemed to loom about her now.

At the next landing she balked, staring. Her footprints in the dust led down, pretending that it would be easy for her to retrace them – but they looked blurred, as though something had trailed over them. Perhaps a draught had blurred them or perhaps, she thought desperately, they had looked like that before. Time enough to wonder once she was out of the house.

She stumbled down to the half-landing, clutching the banister – a splinter stabbed deep into her palm – but there she had to stop. Her lungs were heaving; the dust seemed to have left no room in them for air. Only one more flight of stairs, and she could see the front door below her. But she could also see through the doorway where the mass of cobwebs had gathered or been left, and the mass of cobwebs was not there.

She didn't know what made her turn, crumpling the torn-out page in her hand: certainly not a noise. Of course a draught might have shifted the grey mass from the doorway, and perhaps a draught was making it, or something like it, come flopping down the stairs towards her. In the ground-floor room she had been reminded of an animal, but this looked hardly formed, a foetus covered with cobwebs and dust or composed of them. It was so quick that it had swarmed up her body and was almost at her face before she began to scream.

12

Barbara's car stalled before it had even left the car park
under the Barbican. She used it so seldom in London that it
had had several weeks to go wrong. She wouldn't have used
it today, except that otherwise she would be late for her
meeting with Margery. Now she couldn't even leave it, for
it was blocking the ramp.

By the time she found someone to help her move it – a
tweedy bespectacled man who had been looking at the
remains of the medieval bastion and who seemed reluctant
to go down the stairs with her – she had wasted ten minutes.
When at last they'd manoeuvred the car to a space in the
herd of parked cars she was clammy and panting. She wiped
her blackened hands on her jeans. At least she was dressed
for exploring the dusty house.

She ran through the Barbican to the station. She'd said
sevenish to Margery, but it was twenty-five to eight by now.
If only Margery were on the phone she could cancel the
meeting; the day was already enough of a mess without this
pointless expedition – but she had to see Margery in order to
ask the question she should have thought to ask yesterday.

In the dark beyond the platform, trains were chasing
their tails around the Circle line. They would take her to
Notting Hill, but not to Ladbroke Grove; ought she to catch
one and run the rest of the way? She was sure it would be
ultimately quicker to take the Metropolitan, even though
that meant she would have to wait on the empty platform
and brood over the news about Paul Gregory.

At a quarter to eight a train carried her away. Stations
idled by. Halfway there two Americans in deerstalkers got

90

off at Baker Street, and there were still five stations to go. The Newton-Brown book at least was even better than she'd hoped, and she had submitted it at once. *The Salt Has Lost Its Savour* read like the first sign of madness, the vicar muttering to himself.

At ten past eight she was running up the escalator at Ladbroke Grove, though part of her was sure that running was absurd: what on earth was the point of searching the empty house? She had enough complications for one day – she had the news from an editor friend that Paul Gregory had been seen at lunch with a rival agent, Howard Eastwood. So that was why Paul was quibbling over contracts, why he was never available when she phoned.

Still, the immediate problem was Margery. Barbara hurried through the whitish streets. Chalky dust blew in her face, houses played like radio sets, wavebands leaking from one window to the next. She reached Margery's house – number eight, flat three – and rang the bell.

When there was no answer she felt momentarily relieved, but why? She had to meet Margery, to find out how to get in touch with Gerry Martin. Louise had called the *Daily Telegraph* Information Service, but they had no listing for a journalist of that name on any newspaper. Perhaps the reporter had traced the people from the house by now – the people who might have killed Angela.

After several tries at the bell she made for the flyover. It was just possible that Margery was waiting for her by the empty house. But when she reached the flyover there was no sign of Margery. Could she be inside the house? In any case, now that Barbara was here she might as well go in, get it over with.

She was bracing herself for the onslaught of noise when a police car appeared from the direction of Ladbroke Grove. She turned quickly and pretended to stroll away beneath the flyover until the police car had gone. So long as they didn't see her entering the house, why should she be nervous of them? Her furtiveness irritated her. She strode across to the broken armchair.

Apart from the rush of traffic on the flyover she could see no movement anywhere. She made her way through the parched drooping grass, the scattered pages from a book or books, and climbed the steps to the porch. She pushed open the door and was almost in the house before she saw what was inside.

Margery lay halfway down the first flight of stairs. For a grotesque moment Barbara thought she was standing on her head; certainly her head was bent back at too sharp an angle on the stair below the one that held her shoulders. Her skirt had ridden up, revealing a glimpse of pasty thigh above the black stockings. Her right hand was trapped beneath her body. She wasn't smiling now, even though she looked as if she was; her lips were wrenched back from her teeth.

Barbara tried to think as she ran to the fence: would any of the callboxes be working, or ought she to ask to use someone's phone? When she saw the police car she began to wave frantically as she tried to climb one-handed over the shaky armchair. The car was drawing up before she wondered how much she would have to explain.

The policeman was young. Like most of them, he wore a moustache to make himself look older. He vaulted over the bricked-up gate, then almost lost his footing. At once his face was a mask that warned her to take him seriously.

'There's a lady in this house,' she shouted into his ear. 'I think she's dead. I think her back's broken.'

He waited for her to accompany him into the house. His breast pocket was crackling and muttering. As soon as he saw Margery he took out the radio and called an ambulance. Barbara turned away from the stairs; the dust that hovered about Margery's open mouth reminded her of flies.

The policeman surveyed the ground floor, then went out

to glance at the adjoining houses. 'Were you and this lady together?' he said close to Barbara's ear.

'We were supposed to meet here.' He was so close that she could smell his uniform. 'I was late, and I found her like that.'

'When the ambulance arrives I would like you to answer some questions at the station.' He turned his back on her as though she had no choice, and went to collect the scattered contents of Margery's bag, which lay at the foot of the stairs. He brought the bag out with him and stood near her on the porch. His silence was a threat of questions. How much would she have to tell the police? How unconvincing would the whole thing sound?

When the ambulance came he gestured the men into the house and gripped the handbag as though it was a suspect he was holding by the scruff of the neck. Barbara lingered – perhaps Margery wasn't dead, she'd heard of people who had lived despite a broken back – while the men loaded Margery on to the stretcher. One of them glanced down at Barbara and shook his head, and she was about to go with the young constable when the piece of paper came sailing downstairs.

It was a torn page, which had been trapped beneath Margery's body. Had Margery been holding it when she fell? As Barbara hurried to the stairs the page settled almost at her feet. Though it was crumpled and fluttering slightly, she could make out what was drawn on it. It was a sketch of herself.

At once she recognized the work of Margery's daughter, but why had she made Barbara look so young? Then it stopped fluttering for a moment, and she realized that it wasn't her face at all but a face that resembled hers. It was a sketch of a teenage girl who looked like her. Perhaps she cried out – nobody would have noticed, especially not her – when she realized who it was.

She was stooping so quickly that her vision blackened – something was scribbled beneath the drawing but she hadn't time to decipher it now, not until she got hold of it – when the page sailed away from her, into one of the empty rooms. She felt as if a shutter were closing over her eyes, but she ran wildly after the paper, fast enough to see it flying through a gap where the sash of a window had been. She reached the window just in time to see the page fall on a bonfire of rubbish. The page blazed up at once. In a few moments it was black ash, tattering in a breeze.

When she turned, feeling shaky and hollow and utterly bewildered, the constable was waiting for her. 'Are you ready now?' he said in a tone which suggested he thought that she'd tried to escape. But she made him wait, even if it made her situation worse, while she examined every one of the pages in the grass beside the porch.

13

'I'm afraid you've been the victim of a hoax,' the inspector said.

The walls of his office were the colour of tripe, unnaturally bright beneath the chained fluorescent tubes. Blotches of light clung to his desk, to the leather padding of the chairs, to the bell of the spindly desk-lamp; a blotch floated like turned milk on the surface of Barbara's untouched cup of tea. Everything looked flat as a page, on which she could see the drawing of Angela's face.

She had to stay calm, however brittle she felt, or she might say too much. 'No, I don't think so. I'm sure this cult exists.' She was growing confused: had Margery said it was a cult? She'd had to pretend that Margery had said Angela was involved with the cult, and even that seemed to betray the promise of secrecy she had made to the voice on the phone. She was anxious to keep that promise now, but how much did she believe? 'I don't understand why you think it's a hoax,' she said.

'Well, for example, if she was so worried that her daughter had joined this cult, why didn't she come to us?'

'I assumed she had.' Hadn't Margery said that they wouldn't help because Susan was over seventeen? 'In fact, I believe she said so.'

'I think you must have misunderstood her, Mrs Waugh. Perhaps she meant that she approached us when Susan originally left home.' He was being gentle with her – his round placid face with its pipe-stained moustache made her think of someone's favourite uncle – but she sensed that he was building up to something. 'Let me return to your point about the hoax. You say that Turner got in touch with you and convinced you that your daughter was involved with a cult of some kind. I don't see how she could know that, but we'll let it pass for the moment,' he said, to Barbara's relief. 'Tonight you were supposed to meet her at her flat, but when she wasn't there you went to the house she described. Didn't it strike you as odd that she lived so near that house?'

'No, not really. She'd moved there in the hope of finding her daughter.'

'That's the reason she gave you.'

All at once he was so gentle that she grew more nervous. 'Yes,' she said, 'and she didn't like the people where she used to live. She was glad to move away.'

'I'm sure that's true, but did she tell you why?'

'She didn't tell me in so many words, but I gathered she didn't trust them.'

'I'm afraid it was the other way round. She was glad to move somewhere the people didn't know her. You see, she was a convicted criminal.'

It didn't matter what Margery had been, that couldn't alter the truth of the drawing of Angela. Nevertheless the lurid room was flattening, losing perspective. 'What had she done?' she demanded.

'She was a thief. She underwent treatment for it at one time, but that didn't seem to do her any good. I suspect that when she reported that her daughter had left home we weren't very anxious to reunite them, under the circumstances. It must have been all to the good that the daughter made a life for herself, don't you think so? Excuse me,' he said as someone knocked at the door.

While he and another policeman murmured outside his office a scene was replaying itself relentlessly: Margery stumbled on the stairs of the wine bar, grabbed at someone's jacket, hurried away. What did her left hand do after it grabbed? Seize the banister to help her upstairs, or dart to her handbag? But there was something more important that Barbara must remember.

Before she could, the inspector returned to his desk. 'Did Turner ever ask you for money?' he said.

'No, certainly not,' she said, and then she remembered Margery's last words: 'I couldn't pay for much travelling.' What else was going to turn on her in retrospect? 'At least,' she said glumly, 'not in so many words.'

'Well, you see what I'm getting at. In fact she was convicted of obtaining money under false pretences. The Lord only knows what else she may have got up to. We're just now sorting through the contents of her flat.'

At once Barbara knew what she was trying to remember. 'And her handbag too?'

'Yes, obviously. Why do you ask?'

'You think she invented this cult to extort money from me, but I can show you that's wrong. Among her things you'll find a letter from her daughter which proves it exists.'

He seemed to think better of objecting. 'All her things are here. You may as well show me.'

He took her down to a basement room. There were no windows; fluorescent light had congealed on all the walls. A young policewoman, her face scrubbed and rigid, was sorting through the items on a table. 'If you'll keep them in order,' she said to Barbara.

There were library books, a wad of money that looked as though it had come from a wallet, a selection of clothes which seemed never to have been worn, several pieces of jewellery. The sight of all this, exposed beneath the pitiless light, made Barbara uneasy: was there anything that belonged to Margery, any trace of her at all? Yes, there was a photograph of a schoolgirl holding a book, and there were homework books with 'Susan Turner' written on the covers in a hand which became surer with the years, until at last it was exactly like the handwriting of the letter that Barbara had seen.

But there was no letter. She shook the clothes and the library books, while the policewoman grew disapproving and the light seemed to intensify jerkily. 'It must be in the house by the flyover,' she said.

'But you've searched there, Mrs Waugh. The constable said you checked all the litter in the garden. I take it that was what you were looking for.'

Could she tell him about the sketch? It seemed too close to breaking her promise. She yearned to tell someone, anyone who might know what to do, and she might have given in to the temptation if he hadn't said, 'I think you must face facts, Mrs Waugh. Turner read about you in the newspaper and decided to see how much she could take you for.'

It took her moment to see that she had been tricked, but not by Margery. 'You knew all the time who I was. You think my daughter died nine years ago, and so nothing I've told you can possible be true.'

'I'm sure nobody could forget what happened to your daughter, Mrs Waugh. Rest assured that the case isn't closed. One day we may bring the culprits to justice. But you must see,' he said, ushering her away from the policewoman who was sorting disdainfully through Margery's clothes, 'that's the only hope we have now. You mustn't let people like Turner raise your hopes. Her sort feasts on the misfortunes of others.'

'No, she wasn't like that. That wasn't why she came to me. I accept she was a thief, but she was genuinely concerned about her daughter.' Now she was determined to defend her, since Margery couldn't do so for herself. 'Look, if it was all a hoax, why did she go into that house? That wouldn't have persuaded me of anything. She must have been looking for something.'

He closed his office door behind her. 'Mrs Waugh, you'll be telling me next that this cult pushed her downstairs to shut her up.'

Though she hadn't thought anything of the kind, the suggestion made her uneasy. 'No, I'm sure she just lost her footing and fell downstairs. But that could have been because she was excited over something she'd found.' A shudder went through her as she remembered vividly what that was.

All at once he was less gentle: he was a policeman, and policemen don't like to be wrong; he seemed to resent her attempts to play detective. 'All the evidence suggests that Turner invented this so-called cult and wrote the letter as well. If the letter had been as convincing as you want me to believe, she would have brought it to us.'

He took her silence for agreement, and became kindly. 'You haven't drunk your tea. Would you like a fresh cup?'

'If you've no further questions, I'd like to go home.' She wanted time to think uninterrupted, but at once the idea dismayed her: she would be alone with the meaning of the sketch of Angela.

'By all means.' As he held open the door for her he said, 'I know it must be difficult to believe that anyone would play such a cruel trick, but there's really no alternative to believing that, is there? You know that your daughter is dead, you had the courage to face that. Many people wouldn't have been able to rebuild their lives as well as you have.'

Outside, the roar of traffic was waiting for her. A dingy sports car sputtered past, belching fumes the colour of the sky. In the dimness the white houses of Ladbroke Grove shifted and smouldered like ash. There were so many shadows where a watcher could hide, so many gardens obscured by bulging hedges. She hurried towards Holland Park Avenue, the carpet of light outside the shops, the Underground.

The tiled corridors were deserted. Escalators unfolded their steps and sent them down to crawl up the underside, back to the top. As they carried her down, faces with their eyes poked out sailed by, scrawled with gibberish. There was nobody on the platform, nobody was watching her except David Hemmings flattened like a pinned moth on the wall, and it didn't matter if anyone was; she had kept her promise.

In the Barbican the walkways were shadowy and ominous as unknown empty streets; each pillar could hide an entire group of watchers. Inverted lamps trailed in the lake, beneath the hovering church. Her thoughts had chattered louder than the train, and they were still chattering: if Angela were still alive – and there seemed to be no other way to interpret the drawing – where was she now, and with whom? Were they the people whom the reporter Gerry Martin was trying to trace?

Even when Barbara locked herself into her flat she felt watched. She was growing hollow, her nerves felt exposed, and there was only one reason why she didn't feel completely helpless: she had to find Gerry Martin. But when she did so, wouldn't she have to break her promise? All at once her raw nerves felt worse. Even if the scepticism of the police had let her keep her secret in effect, if anyone had seen her going from the empty house to the police station – anyone who had Angela at his mercy – then she might as well have broken her promise.

14

The neck of the receiver was solid in her fist, the distant
phone rang against her ear, but as soon as she glanced at
Arthur's photograph she was back on the escalator. Dimness clung to everything like grime; she could feel it
clinging to her. Perhaps it had seeped into the works,
perhaps that was why the stairs kept jerking and faltering,
and she felt she would never reach the top of the sloping
tunnel. Was that it, the blotch of darkness high above her,
or was that just more of the dimness, intensified by
distance? The eyes of framed posters gleamed at her from
the walls. Whenever she tried to climb, the stairs began to
slip backwards.

Arthur went by on the downward escalator, and she had
the impression that he wanted to tell her something. He
couldn't, for he was only a photograph of himself, unable to
speak or move. She watched him dwindle into the dimness
where the trains were slithering. When she looked up she
was nearly at the top, and there was Angela.

Behind her was nothing but darkness, a darkness that
seemed to be moving, but she was almost within reach. It
was only when Barbara tried to run to her that she began to
recede. The stairs were toppling downwards too fast for
Barbara to outrun, and something was happening to
Angela's face. It wasn't Angela but a sketch of her, Barbara
had told herself as the stairs rushed her down into the dark
in which she woke, crying out and alone. Now she had
forgotten in what way Angela's face had looked so dismaying, but the sense of it was still with her, so that when a

voice said 'Hello' it took her a moment to recall what she was doing.

'Hello, library?' Now she remembered, and it was urgent. 'Can you tell me which newspapers you buy?'

She scribbled down the names as the voice listed them: *Times, Telegraph, Guardian* . . . She had to be sure. 'I'm correct in thinking that a Margery Turner used to read your newspapers?'

'Yes, you are.' The voice, a pale tenor that sounded fussy, had hardened. 'And that isn't all she did. May I ask to whom I'm speaking?'

Barbara felt trapped. 'Just a friend,' she said, and rang off.

The other phone rang at once. Her mouth grew sour and dry, her heart felt as though it was hiccuping. There was only one voice she wanted to hear – but it was Louise. 'Paul Gregory is here,' she said.

'I'll see him in a few minutes. Can you find out for me if a journalist called Gerry Martin works for any of these newspapers?' When she'd listed them she felt slightly less helpless. 'All right, send him in,' she said.

Paul was wearing a deep blue silk shirt with a matching cravat and expensively faded jeans. 'Well, Paul,' she said.

'Well,' he said, coming to the point with a directness that was new, 'I was wondering how you'd feel if someone else were to handle my American rights.'

'Someone such as Howard Eastwood.'

'Oh, you know he approached me?' Though she must have take him off guard, he didn't let it show. Success had filled him with confidence.

'Publishers and agents are part of the same community, Paul. News travels. Of course it's entirely up to you who represents you.' For the first time today she felt sure of herself, able to forget her worries and deal with the moment. 'I'm building up a good deal of American interest in *Torrent*. Do you want me to withdraw the books so that Eastwood can resubmit them?'

'Can you do that? I mean, might it weaken the American interest?'

'Well, yes, I'm afraid it might.'

'Oh, then you mustn't do it.' His confidence was stumbling. 'But couldn't you, ah, sort of – '

'Hand over the negotiating to Eastwood? No, Paul, I won't do that. Apart from the fact that it was wholly unethical of him to invite you for lunch, I've no respect for him. He's notorious for selling rights which he isn't entitled to sell. Frankly, if you decide to let him handle your work in America, I shall feel uneasy about handling it here.'

'Oh, I hadn't committed myself to anything.' His face was trying to stay calm, but he was rubbing his shiny forehead. 'As far as I'm concerned it was just a free lunch.'

'You weren't to know.' As she settled back, Arthur's glazed eyes flashed at her. 'But believe me, an agent who tries to poach someone else's clients isn't to be trusted.'

He was obviously relieved that she had let him off so lightly. 'Anyway,' he said, 'I wanted to tell you the idea I had for my next novel.' It sounded promising – a man donates his sperm for artificial insemination only to learn a terrible secret years later about his heredity, and has to trace his children and decide what to do – but she felt depressed, perhaps the after-effect of winning him back, and on edge to hear from Louise.

Soon Louise appeared, with coffee and bad news. 'I can't trace Gerry Martin,' she said.

'Gerry Martin? Now where have I heard that name?' Paul frowned and sipped his coffee slowly, as though that might stimulate the memory. At last he said, 'Maybe I'm thinking of someone else.'

Barbara suspected that he'd never heard of Gerry Martin, that he had simply wanted to seem willing to help, so as to wipe out his lapse with Eastwood. 'Could you find out if she's written any books,' she told Louise, and managed not to sound as edgy as she felt.

She got rid of Paul as soon as she could, and occupied herself with amending contracts for some of her authors. Arthur watched her, his unblinking eyes a question which she couldn't answer, until she turned the photograph away. She had to phone contractual amendments through to editors at Cape and Gollancz and New English Library, and she kept thinking how that engaged one line. Still, the other phone was free; Angela could reach her. Why did she need the reassurance of a call? There was no reason to suppose that anyone would have been watching the empty house by the flyover, that anyone had seen Barbara and the policeman there. Perhaps there was even less cause for her to worry, perhaps Margery had made the calls and forged the letter and gone into the house to plant the drawing there; Barbara had only her word for it that she couldn't draw. The worst thing was that she could be sure of nothing.

Louise came in to remind her that she was due for lunch with an editor from Secker and Warburg. 'I'm sorry,' she said, 'Gerry Martin doesn't seem to have written any books. What do you know about her? Maybe there's another way to find her.'

'I don't know anything, Louise. Never mind, it doesn't matter.' But of course it did, and she realized how much when she reached Piccadilly. Children clung to balloons and to their parents' hands; a little girl's face perched above her father's. Their voices were borne away by the crowd, and Barbara could only tell herself that Margery might have invented Gerry Martin too.

She wished she had arranged to meet her editor somewhere other than that same wine bar in Shepherd Market. She had to ask the waiter if any money had been stolen here on Monday, and he seemed to regard her as little better than an accomplice of Margery's, even when she told him where to contact the police. The man from Secker's tried to put her at her ease, and made offers for two promising first novels she was handling, but her mind chattered uncontrollably throughout lunch: where else could she search for Gerry Martin? Whom could she ask? She could think of nobody, but by the time she left the editor one thing was clear to her: she must tell someone what was happening to her.

As soon as she reached her office she called Ted. 'Can I visit you today? Just a friendly call, or perhaps I ought to say a cry for help.'

'Glad to see you any time. Come over now.' He sounded as if he might want to swap problems. 'Tonight I have to lecture at our local library about publishing.'

'I'll be over in an hour or so. Set up the drinks.'

She hurried through her correspondence, among which she found confirmation of her New York hotel suite. How could she risk going to New York, or to Italy with Ted, when the drawing of Angela might not have been a fake? But she had at least to go to New York, to conduct the auction. She had almost finished drafting the replies when Louise called. 'Paul Gregory is on the line.'

She's had enough of him for one day. 'You deal with him, Louise. Say I'm not here.'

She scribbled the last of the replies and took them through to Louise for typing. 'I have to go over to Melwood-Nuttall for a couple of hours. Call me if you need to.'

She was at the door when Louise said, 'Oh, Paul Gregory –'

'What about him?' Barbara hadn't meant to speak so sharply, but her burst of work had twisted her nerves tighter. 'Can't it wait?' she said more gently.

'I suppose so. It was only that he'd remembered about Gerry Martin.'

After Barbara turned the room seemed to continue turning. 'Remembered what?' she demanded.

'Where he'd come across her name. Apparently she writes for an underground newspaper, the *Other News*.'

'Good God.' Of course the library wouldn't buy that; it would be donated. 'Tell him that I had to rush out again but I'm very grateful,' she said.

She was so elated by her release from helplessness that she was nearly at Melwood-Nuttall – Piccadilly, Shaftesbury Avenue, Charing Cross Road were a single jumble of sun and faces – before she thought of looking for the *Other News*. She found several issues in Words & Music; apparently it was doing its best to be monthly. A title on one red and white cover led her to four pages at the centre: *The God Trap,* by Gerry Martin.

She leaned against the pole beside the pedestrian crossing – above her head a green man kept flickering, marching on the spot, but his red twin failed to show up – and glanced through the article, which exposed several religious groups which demanded complete faith and all their money from members. She could see from the opening paragraphs how thoroughly researched the report was.

Though she felt guilty, she knew what she ought to do now. She would only be wasting time if she tried to explain everything to Ted when Gerry Martin, whoever she was, already knew about the cult – perhaps knew things which Barbara should know. She hurried back to her office.

Louise looked surprised. 'I called Paul Gregory for you. He wants you to have dinner with him and his wife.'

'Thanks, Louise.' Directory Enquiries gave her the phone number of the *Other News*, but there was no reply. She rang Ted to apologize. 'You don't mind, do you?'

'So long as you're all right,' he said, and again she felt

guilty; if his problems related to his ex-wife she felt bound to help if she could, to comfort him at least. 'I wasn't going to tell you anything that can't wait,' he said.

She rang Paul to accept his invitation for the end of next week, then she kept calling the *Other News* intermittently throughout the afternoon, without success. She managed to work, but her elation faded a little each time she put down the phone. Gerry Martin existed; did that mean that everything else was true? Was Angela somewhere, thirteen years old and in someone's power? Her feelings were splintered, unable to fit together. If Angela were still alive, she thought bitterly, then her captors had taken better care of her than Barbara had done.

On her way home she stopped at the garage where she knew the proprietor and asked him to repair her car. He left her in the car park under the Barbican and towed the car away. The low ceiling pressed down like a stormcloud, the fluorescent tube above her was shaky as lightning. As she made for her flat, to recommence trying to call the *Other News*, she wondered dully if anyone had cleaned the car park lately; one of the dark corners looked thick with cobwebs.

15

Gerry Martin was less impressive than her article. She'd sounded offhand almost to the point of impatience, and younger than Barbara had expected. Of course, Barbara reminded herself, journalists were often disappointing when you met them, just like writers. 'I have to be at the paper tomorrow night,' the journalist had said grudgingly. 'I suppose I could see you then.'

Tomorrow was now, and Barbara was back in Hornsey, having toiled up from the station. The streets climbed to a main road which fell away at once towards Crouch End. By the time she reached the road she was short of breath, her head felt soft and throbbing as her heart. She crossed the road and descended the far slope, where terraced houses stepped down steeply as organ-pipes.

The office of the *Other News* was a terraced house just like its neighbours, opposite the empty cage of a schoolyard. A privet hedge lolled into the street, leaned over the path, obscured most of the minute garden. When she squeezed past she felt the thumping of the press in the basement, the tell-tale heart of the house.

She rang the doorbell and waited. Twilight came welling over the hills, which looked ragged with green baize; a radio mast was a pin in a cushion. A hairy young man who wore an orange singlet, his hands tattooed with print, opened the door. 'Gerry Martin is expecting me,' she said.

'She isn't here. Do you want to see the editor?' He turned his back on her at once and went into the house.

She followed, though she'd already had one brush with the editor. The ground floor had been made into a single room. Several young people were collating the latest issue of the newspaper on two long trestle tables, beneath an assortment of lamps. Four armchairs, none of them matching the others, sagged in what space was left. A boy of about twelve ran up from the basement, bringing pages and a hot smell of oil and ink. Barbara sat in one of the armchairs and tried to avoid the springs.

Eventually the editor came downstairs. His denim waistcoat and trousers might have been the ones he'd worn last week. He was stout and thirtyish, with a drawl that was almost Oxford, a faint supercilious smile. Last week, when she'd despaired of getting through by phone, he had interrogated her with maddening thoroughness, though she had told him little except that Margery had put her in touch.

Now he stared at her. 'Ah yes,' he said at last. 'Gerry is out on a job. Wait if you want to, but I wouldn't be too hopeful.'

Once he'd gone, his buttocks slouching from side to side in their denim bag, she shifted to a marginally more comfortable armchair and earned herself a sympathetic grin from one of the collators, a young man with an earring. When he made coffee he brought her some in a chipped Donald Duck mug. The coffee was atrocious, and speckled with milk, but she made herself sip it while she wandered about, reading the pamphlets that were tacked to the walls: a report on private security forces, the Race Relations Act, what to do if you're arrested. She read as slowly as she could, for she was determined not to leave until she met Gerry Martin. She had already been waiting for almost an hour.

When the front door banged open she turned quickly, but it was a spotty young girl wearing jeans and a faded shapeless sweater with holes in the elbows. The girl hurried upstairs, her sandals flapping, her lank hair wagging from two rubber bands. 'The pigs are harassing the travellers all right,' Barbara heard her saying. 'And someone dumped broken glass all over one of the caravan sites. I got some of the travellers to talk.'

The editor said something muffled. 'Is she still here?' the girl said, and came strolling down to Barbara. 'Barbara Waugh. I didn't notice you.'

She was older than she'd seemed at first glimpse – in her early twenties, Barbara judged – and her eyes were quick and sharp. Nevertheless Barbara must have looked dissatisfied. 'Don't let my scruff bother you,' the journalist said. 'I had to look unobtrusive today. What did you want to tell me?'

'I rather hoped you might be able to tell me something.'

'Well, first I need to know what your interest is. Are you looking for the people who killed your daughter?'

For a moment Barbara felt shaky, until she realized that the journalist – like everyone Barbara met, it seemed – had read the article about her. 'I mean,' Gerry Martin said, 'nine years is a long time unless you've got some kind of a lead.'

'I'm not sure that she's dead.' Barbara grew uncomfortably aware of the people at the tables. 'Is there somewhere private we can talk?' she said, and heard herself echoing Margery.

Gerry Martin led her upstairs to a small room opposite the editor's, who frowned at them as they passed. The room contained a rusty filing-cabinet, three scratched office chairs and two desks; there wasn't much space for anything else. On one desk a scummy mug of coffee acted as a paperweight beside an ashtray snaggletoothed with butts. Gerry Martin struggled to the other desk and gestured Barbara to sit on the third chair. 'Why do you think your daughter's still alive?'

Barbara told her everything. It didn't matter that the journalist was nondescript – no doubt that was a positive quality in investigative journalism – for Barbara was so relieved to share her tale that it felt almost like giving birth. Despite her promise, she told the journalist everything.

'Yes, I thought it was strange when I heard about Margery Turner,' the journalist mused. 'Mind you, she didn't move too well, did she? The kind of person you could imagine falling downstairs. So you never got to search the house.'

'No, not yet, anyway. Have you?'

'I meant to, but I've been busy with assignments. Too late now. It must have burned down shortly after you left.'

Barbara stared at her. 'I didn't know. There was a fire behind the house. I suppose that could have spread, but doesn't it seem odd that the house was destroyed as soon as someone tried to search it?'

'Maybe.' Gerry Martin shrugged. 'But listen, there's something you need to explain. If it really was your daughter on the phone, why would she send you to a house that had been empty for weeks?'

Barbara had wondered that herself; it was a reassurance she'd kept at the back of her mind, a reason to believe that it couldn't have been Angela on the phone. 'Well, maybe there is an explanation,' the journalist said. 'If she's been in the power of the cult for nine years, maybe she can only think of the places it has lived. If she was scared to meet you near wherever it is now, she might have thought of the place before that.'

The vibrations of the press reverberated faintly through the house; Barbara couldn't tell if she were shuddering too, and had to close her eyes. 'I'm sorry, Miss Martin. I'll be all right in a moment.'

'Call me Gerry.' Now she seemed concerned. 'I don't want to upset you, Barbara, but are you assuming that the murder of your little girl was deliberately faked?'

'Maybe.' Barbara's voice was shuddering now.

'I agree it's possible. Say one of their women wanted your daughter because she couldn't have a child of her own – it's exactly that sort of fucked-up mind that gets taken over by fringe religions. It isn't usual to steal a child as old as yours was, but it happens. It really sounds more like that than a ransom kidnapping. If they were after money, why did they never get in touch with you?' She was thinking aloud, and seemed hardly aware of Barbara. 'All right, let's see. Maybe they felt they would draw less attention to themselves by keeping your daughter than whatever else they might have done. So they have to call off the police. They dress up this other little girl and kill her. The question is, where did she come from? Why wasn't she reported missing? It's a nasty idea, but maybe she was one of theirs.'

Barbara felt sick. 'You can't believe that, surely.'

'There's a whole lot I wouldn't have believed until I researched *The God Trap*.' She looked belatedly reassuring. 'But everything I said is hypothetical, obviously. The important thing is that you think your daughter's still alive, and I'm inclined to agree with you because of the drawing you saw. I mean, Margery Turner wasn't my idea of an artistic personality.'

By now her agreement was less reassuring than dismaying. 'But what is this cult? Do you know where it is?'

'No, I don't know that. I've got a lead I haven't followed up – someone who may have been one of them. And I did piece together a few things about them.'

'What things?' Barbara demanded, afraid to know.

'Principally how secretive they are.' She unlocked her desk and found a notebook. 'While I was researching fringe groups I kept coming across rumours of people who had no names. The earliest rumour I can trace was current in London in the late forties. Then the rumours go to Dartmoor, Manchester, Inverness, Liverpool, London again, Newcastle, Birmingham, Sheffield and back here to

London. You see, there's no geographical pattern and, as far as I can trace, the times never overlap. There are gaps I can't account for, which I take to mean they hid themselves successfully. It looks as though they have to keep moving so that nobody finds out about them.'

'Why can't it be just one rumour that's travelling? It doesn't prove that they exist.'

'There were more than rumours in some places. In London about 1970 and in Manchester in the mid-forties, kids were lured away by other kids who said they had no names, to see their parents who didn't have names either. Luckily the kids were scared and didn't go. And in some of the other towns the Salvation Army got wind of the group. They never traced them, and couldn't find out much about them, but their general impression was that they were really bad.'

She was closing her notebook. 'Is that all?' Barbara said incredulously.

'And what Margery Turner said. Her daughter's letter started me fitting together some of the things I'd heard, and I did some more research. Actually, there was one thing I remembered that had already started me thinking along those lines. You remember the Manson trial, obviously. One of his women said something to the effect that maybe people thought the Family was bad, but there was a group that made them look like Disneyland. They were people with no names who were into things even Manson wouldn't touch.'

When she saw Barbara's eyes she said hastily, 'I don't mean they're the same group, of course. People are freakier in California. That kind of thing doesn't travel. But all the same, the group you're looking for needs finding. You saw the letter Margery Turner had, so you know what I mean. They don't issue literature, which is suspicious in itself for a fringe group that's survived so long, and they don't even seem to need money. Anything that secret has to be pretty bad. You can find out about the freemasons if you know how, but just you try to find out about the CIA.'

Barbara thought some of the links in her reasoning were tenuous, but she hadn't time to quibble. 'You said you'd traced a member of the cult,' she said.

'That's right.' Gerry unlocked a drawer of the filing-cabinet and produced a clipping. Girl With No Name Comes Home To Her Parents, the headline said. According to the report she had escaped from an obscure religious sect. 'We keep calling her Iris in the hope that she'll remember,' her weeping mother said.

'I checked with my press contact there,' Gerry said. 'It sounds very much like the group you're looking for.'

One thing was clear to Barbara: the girl Iris could confirm whether or not Angela was in the hands of the cult, whether she was alive at all. 'Have you been to see her yet? Shall I come with you? She might be more forthcoming if I tell her about Angela.'

Gerry looked doubtful, but had no chance to reply before the editor came in. 'The stuff on the travellers is good,' he said, standing in front of Barbara as if she wasn't there. 'Now I want you to see what you can find out about those Rhodesian loans. I smell something big and shitty there. It'll need a lot of research.'

'Are you giving that to me now? I wanted to follow up that group I mentioned, the people who give up their names.'

'That's Sunday tabloid material, establishment newspaper stuff. Too minor for us. Too vague.'

'I have a lead that looks very promising.'

'Not for us. Anyway, I shouldn't think you'll have time while you're investigating these loans.' When she demurred he said, 'It's up to you if you want to go over to establishment journalism. Just let me know soon if you're through here.'

'Well, I tried,' Gerry said when he'd gone. 'It's the same

whatever the newspaper. You have to do what the proprietor says, however arseholed it is. I'm sorry I can't be more help. To be honest, I more or less gave up the story when I heard Margery Turner had died.'

Barbara stood up impulsively and closed the door. 'Suppose I could sell your report to a mass circulation newspaper? If you wrote something as strong as the article I read we'd sell it with no trouble. Maybe it could be a series. I wouldn't charge you a commission,' she added, and wished she hadn't, for it showed how desperate she was.

Gerry stared for a while at her notebook. At last she looked up. 'All right, I'll go with you to see this girl in Hemel Hempstead. I can probably get more out of her than you could. After that, we'll see. When do you want to go?'

'As soon as possible. Tomorrow.'

'Well, first I have to arrange the interview. We can't just go down there, not in a case like that. I'll call you as soon as I've made contact, all right? That's a promise.'

When Barbara reached the street the pavement seemed to be quaking. As she walked down to the station, through the whitish mould of light beneath the street lamps, she had to steady herself against garden walls, yet why should she be so unsteady? The journalist thought Margery couldn't have forged the drawing, but that was hardly conclusive. A breeze dragged shadows of foliage over houses, which went toppling downhill like dominoes. She was remembering the last words Angela had ever said to her in Otford: 'Will you bring me some more books I can read?' And then, more vivid and even more painful, she saw Angela looking up from her book and wanting to be admired, saying, 'Shall I read to you?' 'Some other time, love,' Barbara had said, busy with a manuscript, but there had been no other time. She felt trapped in a limbo between her memories and her trudging body; all of them were out of reach. Perhaps there was rain in the air, or perhaps she was weeping.

16

On the Edgware Road Gerry began to talk about her editor. 'He overheard me calling Hemel Hempstead and he wasn't very pleased. I'd have called back later, but I was having enough trouble persuading her to let us see her daughter.' She raced a red light and veered around a turning bus. 'And then he still tried to pretend he wouldn't use the story because the people with no names don't seem to rip anyone off. That isn't the reason at all.'

Barbara could only suck in her breath and wish she were driving – the Edgware Road was mined with crossings, by no means all of which were controlled by traffic lights – but her car was still at the garage. 'What is the reason?' she said, for Gerry was glancing at her.

'Why, that it might alienate the readers. Quite a few of them must be into the occult, mysticism, that whole trip. To criticize anything like that would be like saying that smoking dope gives you a hangover, though of course it does.'

She brought the car screeching to a halt as a little girl stepped on to a crossing. 'Anyway, he obviously felt he'd persuaded me not to write the story, so I had to tell him you were selling it for me. You will be able to, won't you?'

'Of course I will. A couple of papers are already interested.' She'd had two days to talk them into it, and a great deal of determination. 'Depending on how substantial a piece you eventually write,' she said, 'it might be worth thinking of a book.'

Gerry drove straight on to the twin roundabouts which led to the motorway. In the August heat the oncoming traffic quivered like jelly; pangs of sunlight sprang from windscreens. A tanker and a lorry boxed in Gerry's Fiat, a juggernaut lumbered overhead; Barbara felt she was about to be crushed in the thin metal shell. On the motorway Gerry's driving grew wilder still. Transporters big as bungalows raced each other at speeds that Barbara found terrifying, yet Gerry dodged among them, from lane to lane. 'He got quite pissed off about it,' Gerry said. 'He said I sounded as if I wanted to join the system we were committed to attacking, and I told him I was trying to grow out of my prejudices,' but Barbara had managed to detach herself – someone else was belted into the passenger seat, not her – and had to make an effort to recall what Gerry meant.

Hemel Hempstead wasn't much of a relief. 'She said above the canal,' Gerry remembered, and sped through the town, slowing only when she reached the shops. A multistorey car park spun a striped ball on the tip of its concrete nose. Beyond the shops was a two-way roundabout, and Barbara closed her eyes. When she opened them she was by the canal: barges passed quietly as clouds, swans slept beneath their wings. She must be near her goal, and at once she felt apprehensive.

Soon Gerry took a road which led above the canal. On the door of a dressmaker's called Sarah-Boo, a Snoopy poster declared Peace on earth, goodwill toward everyone. Gerry turned left into a street which climbed through a mound of semi-detached houses, clustering like barnacles. Rock gardens blazed purple and yellow. 'It's somewhere here,' she said.

Higher up they reached a maze of anonymous streets and closes, crammed with small boxy houses. A garage door occupied a quarter of each frontage. Before each house an unfenced patch of grass twice the area of a car's floor lay stranded between concrete paths. Gerry had to slow down, scrutinizing the street names, for every time she turned a corner the street appeared to have cloned itself.

'Here we are,' she said before Barbara was ready. She slipped out from behind the wheel and smoothed her dark skirt; she had obviously dressed for the interview. Barbara felt hemmed in by the deserted streets; through a gap she could see the buttercup-yellow Hertfordshire hills beyond the Kodak building like two dozen strips of unexposed film, but otherwise there were only the houses, singing their morning song of vacuum cleaners. The cars had been let out for the day, the housewives were locked in.

When Gerry rang the nearest doorbell a stocky man opened the door at once. His shirt was buttoned over his wrists; perhaps his face and hands were angrily pink from the sun, not from truculence. 'What do you want?' he demanded.

'I'm Gerry Martin, and this is Barbara Waugh.'

'I know who you are right enough. What do you want?'

'Well, I explained that on the phone.'

'Not to me, you didn't.' He looked ready to close the door. Barbara started forward, opening the photograph album she had brought – surely the photograph of Angela aged four would move him, she was less and less able to look at it herself – as a small square woman, hardly five feet tall, appeared behind him, wiping soapsuds from her hands with a souvenir of Brighton. 'Don't argue on the doorstep, George,' she said with an accent similar to his, on the border of north and south. 'At least we can let them in.'

She led them into the front room, where the wallpaper was patterned discreetly as a civil servant's suit. Doilies were spread on a sideboard, a ballerina of lustre pottery gleamed purple on the windowsill. 'You're the lady who is looking for her daughter,' the woman said to Barbara.

'This is a photograph of her.'

The woman glanced sharply at Gerry. 'You said she was older than this.'

'That's the most recent photograph I have.' For a nervous

moment Barbara thought that the couple were going to reveal that they had read the article about her. 'I haven't seen her since,' she said, her eyes blurring.

Perhaps the woman was remembering her own grief. 'Oh, George, I don't think it'll do any harm if we show this to Iris.'

'Don't you be so sure, Maisie. We told the doctor we'd give her peace and quiet. That's what she needs.'

'We came down from London on the understanding that we could see her,' Gerry said.

'And I've had to take the day off from Kodak because of it.' He turned to Barbara. 'Look, I'd help you if I could. I just don't see what good it will do for you to bother Iris. She couldn't tell us where the buggers were who did that to her. She must have wandered away from them one day and come back here somehow. They won't still be where they were then, will they? Call me unfeeling if you like, but I think you're wasting your time.'

'I don't expect to be led to them. I just want to be sure if they have my daughter.'

'A bit late to worry about her, isn't it?' At once he was shamefaced. 'Look, that's how I feel about myself and Iris. I don't know anything about you and your daughter. I should never have let Iris leave home, she'd follow anyone and not see where they were leading.' Reluctantly he glanced at the photograph. 'Show her if you must,' he grumbled. 'Otherwise you'll go off thinking we ought to have helped you. But you'll leave when I tell you to.'

His wife led them upstairs, past a flight of plaster swans. 'Don't speak suddenly,' she said low. 'She doesn't like noise.'

'Aye, and she won't like so many strangers, either. You stay outside,' he said abruptly to Gerry. 'I'll leave the door open. You'll be able to hear if there's anything to hear.'

Barbara's first impression was that Maisie had opened the

119

wrong door: was the woman at the bedroom window a companion or a nurse? She looked over forty, twice as old as Iris; her striped summer dress, and the pink bow in her greying hair, were too young for her. But Maisie went straight to her. 'Iris, there's a lady here to see you.'

Iris turned painfully slowly. Barbara thought of a mechanical figure whose machinery was running down; the eyes and the face seemed a single unbroken surface, smooth and artificial as plastic. It might have been a life-size doll which Maisie had dressed in her daughter's frock, faded by months of sitting at the window. 'The lady is looking for her little girl,' Maisie said to the doll. 'She wants you to tell her if you've ever seen her.'

Barbara stepped forward, holding open the album. By the time Iris lowered her head to look – her head moved as though her eyes were fixed – Barbara's hands were shaking with the effort to hold the album still. Was there a glimmer of recognition in the girl's eyes? Perhaps it was only an indifferent reflection of the album, for it had faded when Iris looked up. She gazed towards Barbara as if nobody were there.

'The little girl is older than that. Thirteen years old,' Maisie said when Barbara mouthed it. 'She would have been twelve last year, Iris. Did you see her last year before you came home to us?'

Barbara shifted her grip on the album; her fingers came away from the celluloid page with a sound like the smacking of lips. 'She may be very thin,' she said, remembering the drawing. 'Her eyes are very blue, at least they were,' and found she was weeping.

'I'm sorry,' Maisie said after a static pause. 'Some days she just doesn't want to talk. I'm afraid this may be one of those days.'

Suddenly Barbara realized how Maisie saw her daughter: she'd fallen into bad company and gone through a bad phase, but she was home now; all she needed was peace and her family, she would right herself in time. Barbara turned away defeated by Iris's blank stare, and dabbed at her eyes.

'If you leave me a photograph I'll keep showing her,' Maisie said. 'I can let you know if she says anything.'

'Thank you,' Barbara said dully, and handed her the album; she didn't feel capable of selecting one herself. She gazed about the room, at a model lighthouse which must light up with a battery, a school magazine for 1969, a mandala which was composed of tiny people and which focused on an unreadable eye, an exercise book open at a poem in an adolescent hand ('O let me go down in the warm wet dark'), a doll with the pupils scraped out of its eyes, which reminded her unpleasantly of the face which had stared from the sketch of the house. Presumably all this was meant to recall Iris to herself, but it seemed to have failed; what chance did Barbara have?

When Maisie gave her back the album she headed for the landing. George turned gruffly towards the stairs, Gerry gave her a smile and a shrug that she must have meant to be encouraging. Maisie left the photograph in the room, and had almost reached the door when Iris said, 'They made me get someone from New Street.'

At first Barbara wasn't sure that she was hearing the voice, it was so scrawny and blurred. But when she hurried into the room, Maisie stepping back reluctantly to let her in, she saw that Iris's lips were moving, though for the moment without sound. Eventually her voice caught up with them. 'I had to wake him up. He went back with me, and . . . After that we went to Sheffield, and . . .' Her voice kept fading like a worn-out radio. 'I left them one day and came home,' she said.

'Was there a little girl with you while you were away?' Barbara tried not to speak too abruptly, but she had to

121

make contact while she could. 'A little girl about twelve who looked like this?'

Perhaps Iris would have examined the photograph, except that a bird began singing outside the window. She turned to the window as if she dreaded to do so; her shoulders hunched, her head sank down like a tortoise's. Her voice seemed to come from somewhere the sunlight couldn't reach. 'When I was little I found a bird in the garden. I thought it was asleep. When I turned it over it started moving, but it was things crawling inside.'

Her mother clasped her hand, but she continued tonelessly, staring. 'Where I had to live with them, things kept coming alive. The bad got into things and made them move.'

'Don't go upsetting yourself, Iris. You know it's only your imagination. You're home now.'

'It got into us. It made us do things.' She dragged her hand out of her mother's grasp. In a voice half choked by self-disgust she said, 'I like remembering them.'

That was her last word. Her gaze had sunken inwards, she was hugging herself as though to keep everything out. 'She's never said anything like that before,' Maisie said, plainly blaming Barbara.

'You can't believe some of the things she says,' George reassured her. 'That's what they did to her. Don't you remember, she wrote to us that she was leaving the country. They must have made her say that so we wouldn't look for her.' As he hurried Barbara and Gerry down the stairs he said, 'Now you see why I didn't want you bothering her. You'd better hope you get your daughter back before she's the same.'

He sounded bitter, yet in one way he was reassuring: if it had really been Angela who had made the two phone calls, she was certainly far more stable than Iris. But was Iris an example of the company she was keeping? When Barbara emerged the sunlight pierced her eyes, as if the jagged clutter of her thoughts were not painful enough.

Gerry saw how she felt. As soon as they reached the car she said, 'I don't know if your daughter's alive, but I'll do what I can. I think I can track these people down.'

It was too sudden. Barbara could only stare at her as the car sped downhill. 'I've got another lead,' Gerry said, 'but I wasn't sure what to do about it until just now. Exposing Rhodesian loans isn't going to help anyone, but these people need stopping. And you're sure you can sell the reports when I write them.'

The canal flashed by, the two-way roundabout carried the car along between lorries and sent it speeding onwards. 'I'm going to try and infiltrate the group. You may not hear from me for a few weeks, but I'll let you know if I find Angela, when I can.'

Barbara tried to sound casual. 'Where are you going to look for them?'

'I'd rather keep that to myself for now, Barbara, if you don't mind. If you search for them as well you may drive them into hiding before I can join them. Try not to worry if you don't hear from me for a while.' The car shot on to the motorway; in the distance the traffic and the landscape were melting and changing. 'You know,' the journalist said, 'I have the feeling that this may be a turning point in my life.'

17

As Barbara drove past Regent's Park the evening sky was the colour of steam. Beyond the railings the darkened leaves looked moist and tropical. A jungle smell drifted through the open window of the car, harsh odours of animals, an overpowering scent of blossoms. Monkeys screamed beyond the trees, a lion roared. Barbara's hands were glued to the wheel by the heat, her clothes felt steeped in humidity. She was uncomfortable enough without having to dine with Paul Gregory and his wife.

In Camden Town all the pub doors were propped open; couples stood on the pavements, drinking beer. Opposite the dusty marquee of the station, people queued for a Max Ophuls film. As Barbara steered into the side road where the Gregorys lived, in a flat overlooking a bank, a man hurried out of an Indian restaurant, fanning his mouth.

She parked the car in front of the house and rang the bell. The pillared porch was a trap for breezes, cooler than the car. A dozen racing cyclists sped by, multicoloured as a musical routine. Perhaps the evening wouldn't be too difficult, especially if Paul gave her as much alcohol as he drank himself. At least she wasn't at home or at work, waiting nervously for the phone to ring.

A tall woman in a long black dress opened the door. Presumably the dress was meant to be ankle-length, but it showed that her ankles were as bony as her arms and her pointed face. 'Barbara Waugh,' she said, and shook Barbara's hand once. 'Sybil Gregory.'

On the ground floor someone was practising scales on a flute, on the first floor a police car was howling. The

Gregorys lived on the top floor, under the sloping roof. In the main room, where the ceiling stooped to the wall, the first thing Barbara saw was a telephone. She couldn't help worrying, though Gerry Martin had had only a couple of days to find the cult. It was unlikely that she would be calling Barbara so soon.

'Paul, your agent's here,' Sybil said briskly. 'When you've given her a drink, will you put Bevis to bed? Katrina, you should be dressed by now. Come and talk to me in the kitchen, Barbara, when you've got a drink.'

When he'd poured Barbara a Stolichnaya vodka, Paul hurried apologetically into the bathroom, his small son under his arm. She made for the kitchen, past a tiny room with a double-decker bunk, where a little girl was buttoning her Brownie uniform.

Sybil was grilling steaks. A lion roared in the park, as if it smelled the meat. 'There's Imogen and her father now,' she said to the little girl when the doorbell rang. 'You go and make me proud of you. She's nearly a Guide,' she told Barbara. 'Were you ever in the Guides?'

Barbara had almost thought of something, but it was retreating beyond her grasp. 'No, I never was,' she said.

'I was for years. I made Katrina join the Brownies, and Bevis will be a Cub as soon as he's old enough. There's nothing like it for licking them into shape.' Perhaps she was just what Paul needed, a grown-up Girl Guide who could run the household and make do with whatever they had – but Barbara was still trying to grasp the thought she'd almost had. Somehow she felt that if she managed to define it she would wish she hadn't done so.

'Watching them grow up helped me through our bad time,' Sybil was saying. 'Nothing can replace the family, whatever some people would like us to believe.' Barbara nodded vaguely, for she had just realized where Paul must have written *A Torrent of Lives*, at a desk in the corner furthest from the stove: bad time indeed. 'Oh, I beg your pardon,' Sybil said, 'that was tactless of me. Paul told me how you lost your husband and then your little girl.'

She made it sound like negligence, but how could she know she was right? Barbara couldn't tell if she was being paranoid, she could only drain her glass. 'You've finished your drink,' Sybil said in surprise or reproof. 'Do pour yourself another if Paul is still busy.'

Barbara sat on a double bed disguised as a couch and lingered over pouring the vodka while she tried to sort out her feelings. Jackets of Paul's early novels curled on the walls, suitcases like Chinese boxes gathered dust on top of a wardrobe. She had to be content that Gerry was searching. There was nothing she could do now except get on with her job.

Back in the kitchen Sybil said, 'What do you think of Paul as a writer?'

'I think he has the potential to write something even better than he has.'

'I think he's the finest writer I've ever read.' She wasn't the first writer's spouse that Barbara had heard say something of the kind. 'Name a better living writer,' Sybil said.

'He's extremely good.' Barbara ignored the challenge, whatever it was meant to achieve. 'He was telling me the plot of his next novel. Has he started work on it?'

'Not until we move.' She turned wary. 'We're thinking of moving to Ireland once we see some money from the sale you made. They know how to treat artists over there.'

'Yes, several of my clients would agree with you.' Writers paid no tax in Ireland. Barbara managed to direct the conversation to the ways in which different societies treated writers, a subject where Sybil's traps were easier to avoid. Nevertheless, halfway through dinner Sybil said, 'I gather you objected when Paul met another agent.'

'Paul is free to change his agent whenever he chooses.'

Paul was blushing like a small boy who had to keep quiet while adults discussed him. 'But I believe it would do him no good.'

'Well, of course you do. I hope you'll forgive my bluntness, but I want to be sure that his books earn every penny they can. I want to make absolutely certain that our children never go through another bad time. Of course I'm sure they won't, Paul, but still,' she said to Barbara, 'how can you do as well for him in America as an American agent would?'

'Because I can be there in less than a day whenever I need to go. I shall be in New York next month to conduct the auction. Since I'm handling all the English language rights I can negotiate a better deal overall than if I had to wrangle with another agent over who gets which territories. I'll negotiate terms Harold Eastwood wouldn't dare consider.'

'Forgive me,' Sybil said, 'but we can't really prove or disprove what you're saying.'

'Eastwood is a fucking awful agent.' Barbara realized she'd had a good deal to drink, but it seemed not to matter. 'He advertises in half a dozen magazines. No good agent needs to advertise.' Why attack Eastwood when she could be promoting herself? 'It goes without saying that we'll make better money in the States than here,' she said, 'but I can promise you it will be even better than you hope.'

It was only later, as she drove cautiously home along the Euston Road, that she wondered if she had fallen into the biggest trap of the evening. She'd assumed tonight's dinner to have been a peace offering, but had it been meant to take her off guard? In one way that was unimportant – she was sure she would do as well in New York as she had promised – but it meant that she was committed to going there next month, whatever else was happening. She had to believe that she'd done all she could, that it was up to Gerry Martin now.

She was glad to leave the car park under the Barbican. More of the fluorescent tubes were failing; above the dim humps of cars the light made the low roof judder. A shadow caused her to glance towards the corner where she'd seen the mass of cobwebs. Someone must have cleaned up in here, for the corner was bare. She wished he would do something about the lights, about the dark jerky movements behind the cars.

A small inverted head peered through curtains deep in the lake. The church of St Giles looked stilted by the reflections of its lamps. When she was ready for bed Barbara had to turn off all her lights, which she hadn't been conscious of switching on. Eventually she fell asleep, still trying to recall the thought she had had before dinner. She was sure it related to Angela.

She seemed hardly to have slept when her morning call woke her, but sunlight was thinning the curtains. She groped for the phone, feeling resentful because half-awake. Nothing could wake her in the mornings but speaking to someone. She fumbled the receiver on to the pillow. 'Hello,' she croaked.

Was this the worst line she'd ever had? She couldn't make out the voice at all. 'Hello,' she said more distinctly, and after a pause the voice rose slightly. 'It's me, Mummy,' it said.

Barbara clutched at the receiver, only to send it crashing to the floor. It must sound as if she had thrown it away. This time she was sure the voice was Angela's, not a hoax at all, and all at once she realized how eager she had been to explain the calls away, to believe that Angela was safely dead and buried. She scrambled desperately on to the carpet, pain bursting in her head, and grabbed the receiver. 'Where are you?' she cried.

The murmur of response was less clear than the meandering of static. 'I can't hear you,' Barbara said, close to breaking down. 'Speak louder.'

'I can't speak much louder. I'm calling you now while everyone's asleep.' But not everyone was, for just then Barbara heard a man's voice over the phone. Though she couldn't make out the words there was no mistaking the tone, which was cruel and mocking. At once the line went dead.

Barbara managed to dial the operator, though her fingers felt crippled. When at last the operator responded she told Barbara haughtily that it was too late to trace the call. Barbara hung on to the receiver for ten minutes while the phone rang at the *Other News*, and grew appalled with herself, with her failure to respond. At last a woman's voice snarled sleepily at her and gave her Gerry Martin's address and phone number to make her go away.

There was no reply at Gerry's number. Barbara rushed to Gerry's flat, in a Brixton house which looked sooty and crumbling. She didn't know what she wanted: she was afraid the cult would now be on the lookout for a spy; she was more afraid to delay Gerry, in case they knew that Angela had betrayed them to her mother. But the girls who lived across the landing said that Gerry had paid her rent two months in advance and left no forwarding address. Wherever she was, she was beyond recalling.

18

Halfway across Regent's Park the sky grew puffy and black. Gerry was too far from the zoo to shelter there. She dodged beneath an oak, her torn canvas bag bouncing on her hip bone, as the first large drops began to fall. When she leaned against the tree trunk her eyes closed at once; a cloud of sleep gathered around her, muffling the roughness of bark and the ache of her feet, absorbing sounds. She dozed and waited for the shower to pass.

But it was a downpour. When she woke for the second or third time, she thought she was standing on an island in the middle of a stormy lake, for it sounded that way. The air was a mass of taut grey fibres that drenched her whichever side of the oak she stood. Rain cascaded down the layers of foliage above her, finding every gap. All around her, grass was struggling as it drowned.

It could be worse, she thought wryly: she could still be working for a local newspaper, still be trying to scale the molehills of news – weddings, traffic offences, lectures in the church hall – on the way to genuine journalism. Or she could be writing for the *Other News*, which had been another dead end: however strong *The God Trap* had been, the issue hadn't sold many copies. The smaller the paper, the less chance you had to make a name for yourself. Well, here she was, a freelance investigative journalist at last, and it felt like the wettest and grubbiest job this side of North Sea Oil. She was living the role for which she needed to be mistaken, and she could only hope that made her more convincing.

At last the rain pattered away. The circular blade of the sun tore a gap in the clouds. Gerry dug her second pair of shoes out of her bag, then she squelched through mud and drooling grass towards the Euston Road. All the buildings looked washed and put out to dry; the roofs of cars steamed like blocks of ice. She hurried to the station, which was beginning to feel like home.

The high spacious anonymous hall of Euston was crowded with queues that trailed out from the ticket barriers. Here were a dozen teenagers loaded with rucksacks, here were Scotsmen whose knees looked boiled, here was a blind man following his dog through the maze of suitcases and trolleys. Escalating commuters sailed up from the Underground, past a series of posters dominated by a credit card, like frames in a trick film.

Gerry locked herself in a cubicle in the Ladies', then she stripped naked and rubbed herself dry with the towel from her bag. She'd brought a change of underwear, but there had been no room for other clothes. While her T-shirt and jeans dripped on the back of the door she sat on the toilet lid, nodding off in search of a week's lost sleep. She had been a vagrant for a week now, and nothing had come of it. Could she be on the wrong trail?

All her inferences had seemed to fit together perfectly. There was a rumour of nameless people in London, which confirmed what she'd deduced: if Angela was dominated by the cult she wouldn't dare to venture far from them to meet her mother – since she'd promised to meet her by the Portobello Road that meant they were in town somewhere. The young woman Iris had said that she'd had to wake a man on New Street, which could only mean the station in Birmingham, the group's home immediately before Sheffield. The Salvation Army in Manchester had heard that vagrants were approached by people who refused to name their organization or themselves. That must be how they recruited members, and so Gerry had become a vagrant in the hope that they would recruit her.

She swayed against the water pipe and recoiled, shivering. It was one thing to congratulate herself on piecing together the hints, quite another to live out the consequences. The last week had seemed endless – pretending to sleep at Euston and sometimes not pretending, napping on park benches in the daytime – but why should she have expected to make contact so soon? She had no idea how large the group was, how infrequently it sought recruits. If she had only been able to question Iris she might have been more prepared now.

She mustn't weaken. She must prevent the little girl in Barbara's photograph from growing like Iris, if she could. Despite what she had said so as not to raise Barbara's hopes, she thought it very likely that Angela was alive. Besides, this investigation was going to make Gerry's name. Suddenly apprehensive, she grabbed her notebook out of her bag, but the plastic carrier within the bag had prevented the rain from reaching the book; she was learning the tricks of poverty. Her notes looked sparse for a week's work, but they should jog her memory when she came to write the articles.

When she lolled against the pipe again she made herself get dressed. Her clothes were still damp, the knees of her jeans were soaked, but a walk in the sun should dry them. She stumbled into the Euston hall, past a pale young man like a starved monk whose tonsure was longer on one side, and for a moment it was too much for her; the crowd was too rapid and chaotic, the noise was huge, incomprehensible, terrifying. If only she could sneak home for a day or so and catch up on her sleep! But that might be the very day the group was looking for recruits. She had to stay available.

However irrational it was, she was beginning to feel as homeless and friendless as she looked. She was tempted to call Barbara Waugh, but she had nothing to tell her. No, there was something better she could do to make herself feel less vulnerable.

Outside the station, she fed her Barclaybank card into the slot in the wall and typed her code. When she'd stuffed twenty pounds into her pocket she felt a good deal more secure, until she realized that if a member of the group had seen her she had ruined her disguise. She glanced about, but the people who were staring at her clearly wondered if she had stolen the card. That was encouraging.

In five minutes she was in the Tottenham Court Road, and sneezing at the sunlight. Mexican food ought to help fight her cold, if she had one coming. But they wouldn't let her into Viva Tacos. 'Tables all reserved,' the waiter said expressionlessly. She was living her disguise.

Eventually she found a snack bar where they would serve her sandwiches through a window. She sat on a bench opposite a television store, where a man's face in various colours and sizes was mouthing. Her eyes kept closing as she ate. A Scientologist approached to offer her a personality profile, but she waved him away. She hoped the group that she meant to expose had less power than the Scientologists, who had sued the Olympia Press out of existence for criticizing them.

She restrained herself from going back to Euston at once, and struggled along Oxford Street for a while, through the swarm of tourists. Now and then she took refuge in a store, some of which were cooler, but the store detectives followed her until she left. Though she was glad to be so convincing, she could hardly afford to be arrested.

At Marble Arch she turned along Park Lane. Silver limousines glided by, uniformed doormen glowered at her in case she thought of approaching their hotels. She managed an hour's sleep in Hyde Park, but woke shivering, despite the sunshine. In a chemist's she bought Beecham's

Powders – she ought to have done so earlier – and persuaded the shop-girl to give her a glass of hot water in which to dissolve the lemony medicine.

She wandered along Piccadilly to Leicester Square. Above the roofs, cranes groped about the sky. She felt as though her mind was up there with them, trying to catch hold of something, perhaps her body. When she'd sat for a while in Leicester Square she went to see a film called *Eraserhead*. At least the cinema should be less humid, and the film might wake her up; the film buffs at the *Other News* had said it was hilarious.

But she was asleep before it began, and when a snore jerked her awake a man was disembowelling a deformed baby with a pair of scissors. She closed her eyes hastily, until the cries of the baby woke her halfway through the identical scene. A lump of darkness with eyes the colour of snails was glaring at her over its shoulder. She stumbled out of the cinema before she could be asked to leave, only to find that the day had vanished. She'd entered the cinema in broad daylight, yet now it was dark except for headlights sloshing over the wet road. She'd slept through two performances of the film.

She hurried down the Charing Cross Road, over pavements stained with neon. The Tottenham Court Road felt like a film of the start of her afternoon walk, a film running jerkily in reverse. Her haste stoked her body, which was prickling. Before she reached the Euston Road she had to cling to a lamp post in case she was about to be sick.

When she arrived in the Euston hall she slowed, panting. Her sounds were thin and unreal, too tiny even to echo. A hovering voice boomed, announcing trains. A few people stood about, dwarfed by the hall and the voice. She went in search of a seat, her legs trembling.

The few seats – narrow ledges obviously meant to deter sleepers – were all occupied. Were there seats on the platforms? If she bought a platform ticket, would the collector let her past the barrier? If he did she would be out of sight of anyone who came looking for vagrants. She was faltering near the barriers when she saw a journalist she knew, striding towards her up the slope from the Edinburgh train.

She had almost acknowledged him before she realized what she would be doing. Instead she dodged into the Ladies', and felt absurdly furtive. No doubt she might feel more absurd before her search was over.

The matron in charge of the Ladies' gave her a glass of hot water in which to take another Beecham's. 'Are you all right, dear?' the woman said anxiously, and Gerry had to say that it was just a mild cold. In the mirror she saw what the woman was seeing: her spots were worse, accentuated by her unhealthy pallor; her bunches of hair looked like muddy rope. Even more than sleep, when all this was over she looked forward to lying in a hot bath for hours.

Now she had to go out into the station hall. She'd grown almost used to sleeping upright – that way she was less likely to be moved on – but tonight she was afraid she didn't have the strength. Everything would wake her, the bundles of newspapers thumping the floor like falling drunks, the amplified voices calling for the staff, the winos breathing in her face, the policemen who were there when she opened her eyes as though they were waiting to arrest her. The only people she wanted to wake her had no names.

Eventually she found a pillar to lean against, in the middle of the hall. She made sure that the von Daniken book protruded from the bag between her feet, to advertise her as gullible and in search of some vague mystical secret, then she closed her eyes. Perhaps she was delirious, for she seemed to sink at once into a cocoon; the pillar at her back turned soft and horizontal. The warm subdued light behind her eyelids drew her down into itself.

'I said, would you like to come to us for the night?' It was a Salvation Army officer, who looked patient when she peered blearily at him, even when she mumbled ungratefully. She couldn't be sure that he wasn't a dream, derived irrationally from her Salvation Army research. Everything seemed unconvincing as the clock which said she had dozed for an hour.

The awakening had left her unable to sleep, and her cold was worse. The pillar was tilting, the floor was a deck in a storm, the captain was a giant who stooped towards her, shouting about trains. Of course she was in a station, Euston Station, and people were wandering about listening to radios, or were those the voices of the people? It was impossible to tell, they were so small and blurred. One thing seemed clear: if she were given the chance now to infiltrate the group, she would be very little use.

She had no choice. She must go home for the night and try to sleep off the cold, and hope she hadn't missed her chance. Surely one night wouldn't matter. When she came back to Euston she'd make sure she was better prepared for the climate.

She swayed against the pillar and blinked at the clock, which had somehow gained half an hour. How was she to get home now that the trains had stopped for the night? She'd been ignored sometimes by cabbies when she had looked more presentable than this. If she queued in the rank below Euston surely a cabby would take her when she showed him her money. She forced her eyes open, and thought she was misreading the clock: how could it be ten minutes later than a couple of thoughts ago? Yet it was, and a shabby young woman with hair like combed tar was gazing at her. 'Do you want a bed?'

Gerry was about to refuse when she felt how ill she was: the long-faced young woman, the station, her own body

136

were distant and ungraspable as ice. She couldn't face an argument with a cabby. 'Where are you from?' she said.

'The London Refuge. We've got a van outside. It doesn't matter if you haven't any money.'

No doubt that meant the bed would be the worse for wear, but the offer seemed irresistible. If other people were dossing at the London Refuge, perhaps they might be able to tell Gerry something about the people with no names; dossers were one group she hadn't questioned, yet they might be the ones who knew. She followed the young woman into the drizzling night.

When they reached a nondescript van in a side street a young man, tonsured like an untidy monk, came up behind her. She hadn't realized he was following. 'You'll have to ride in the back,' he said, unlocking the doors.

Gerry thought there was room on the front seat for three, but she didn't feel like arguing, even when she saw the clutter in the back, boxes and rusty tools and bricks, so grimy they almost looked merged. She clambered over them into the available space, and the doors were locked behind her at once.

She'd hardly settled herself when the van jerked forward. The partition behind the driver was windowless, and she couldn't see much out of the back windows except for street lamps, fleeing into the night. She managed to prop herself against the side of the van, and attempted to decide whether she had seen the young man and woman before. Hadn't she glimpsed them several times at Euston? On the way to the van she had noticed white hairs showing through the woman's dye.

Whenever the van slowed Gerry craned towards the windows, and so when it reached its destination she saw where she was: Earls Court, just off the Cromwell Road. She could almost have recognized it from the noise.

When the young man unlocked the doors she found she

was in a driveway beneath a tangle of trees, in front of a three-storey house. All around the porch the ground looked scurfy with paint. Perhaps the trees helped trap the noise, for it seemed even louder here. Certainly the swaying foliage sounded like the lorries which went roaring nose to tail towards the motorway. She felt clogged with noise and catarrh.

When she looked up at the house, Barbara Waugh was gazing at her from an upper window.

For a moment she thought she had grown more delirious, then she realized that it was a thin young girl who looked like Barbara. It could only be Angela, and she gasped – but she had stumbled against a corner of the van, and her escorts must think that was why she'd made the sound. 'You're tired,' the young woman said indifferently as they led her to the house.

Gerry glanced up without moving her head before they reached the porch. Angela was withdrawing into the dim room, and seemed to be surrounded by several figures; were they urging or forcing her away from the window? The woman from Euston unlocked the scabby front door as Gerry climbed the cracked steps. Beyond the door the hallway and the unshaded light bulb were a dingy shade of brown. Quickly, in case they wondered why she was hesitating, she stepped forward into the house.

19

When the front door closed behind her she was afraid that she wouldn't be able to act normally, that she was too tired or too ill to keep up the pretence. But she had only to behave as if she was tired, and that was no task. In fact she almost dropped her bag, having forgotten that it was in her hand, as the woman led her upstairs.

Within the house the noise of traffic was muffled, a dull blurred static mass of sound. It seemed to merge with the dingy light into a single medium that choked her senses. Perhaps the wallpaper was brown, perhaps the patches of carpet on the stairs had a pattern and a colour. Were voices muttering beyond the door of the room where she had seen Angela? She couldn't be sure.

There were three doors on the first landing, and three at the top, where the woman led Gerry. Beside the greyish light bulb a skylight was boarded up. The woman opened a door and clicked a switch, but the room beyond stayed dark. 'Not working,' she said flatly. 'You have the bed nearest the door.'

When Gerry ventured forward she could just make out two ranks of mattresses against the walls, three beds in each rank. The light from the open door barely reached the one she had been given; dim shapes were huddled on the others. The woman waited as Gerry stripped to her panties and pulled the single blanket over her, then she closed the door.

For a moment Gerry was afraid of being locked in, but the women went downstairs at once; the creaks of the stairs just pierced the sound of traffic. Gerry lay hemmed in by the other beds, by darkness that smelled musty, even through her cold. She had managed to infiltrate the group. It was as easy as this.

She had no doubt they would try to draw her in, perhaps as soon as she woke in the morning; fringe religions, much like any other kind, must seize you when and where you were most vulnerable. She was less apprehensive now, and felt all at once less delirious. They could try their best to brainwash her, she wouldn't end up like Iris. That sort of thing could only work on personalities less susceptible than hers.

She needed to sleep so as to be ready for them, but would she be able to do so? Sleeping in a room with people she had never seen made her obscurely nervous, and besides, there was the noise. Presumably the group chose to live in houses such as this because the noise brought down the rent, assuming that they didn't move in as squatters, as it seemed they had near the Portobello Road. She was wondering if she would be able to doze when she fell asleep.

When she woke it was still dark, yet she felt refreshed and not at all delirious. Only her throat felt so ragged she was glad not to have to speak. She lay and waited for her eyes to adjust. The window was uncurtained, but the trees were as good as shutters; glimmers of rain trickled over the leaves. The traffic noise had acquired a whining note. Apart from that she could hear only her clogged breathing. She could hear no breathing from the other beds.

Of course the rumble of traffic could swallow most noises, yet all at once she was nervous. She levered herself upright on the bed and leaned towards her neighbour. The huddled figure seemed to be making no sound at all. Gerry held on to the edge of her mattress and leaned further, but her grip was weaker than she thought, for she lost her balance. Her free hand poked the shape on the next bed: poked deep into the shape.

She managed not to cry out, for she'd realized that there

had never been a figure, only a pillow entangled with blankets. Shouldn't the sound of her fall have woken the people in the other beds? She made herself go quickly to each, though she was nervous in case one of them loomed up towards her in the dark. All of the figures were unmade beds.

She stood beside the window, where there was marginally more light. Her bed looked as if a figure lay there now. She had no reason to be uneasy that she could see – presumably the people who slept in this room were elsewhere – and yet she was seeking one. Suddenly she realized what was wrong: though she was nearer the traffic, the whining was further away. It had nothing to do with the traffic. It was the cry of a child in the house.

Well, she knew the group had children, and presumably they cried sometimes. After a while she went back to her mattress, but instead of lying down she squatted there, straining to make out the child's cry. Outside the window branches dripped and shifted, disturbing the dim figures on the mattresses. What was wrong with the crying? Why did it sound so muffled?

At last, reluctantly, she stood up and eased the door open. However slowly she turned the doorknob, it squeaked. She tiptoed on to the deserted landing, between two closed ominous doors. The wailing was somewhere below her, and she could hear what was wrong. It sounded not only muffled but gagged.

She ought to ignore it. If she betrayed herself now the group might flee before they could be stopped – but how could she ignore the crying? Suppose it was Barbara's daughter? It didn't matter who it was, Gerry had to find out what was being done to the child. She dressed hurriedly, then she picked up her bag in case someone might find her notebook and crept to the stairs.

By walking down close to the edges of the stairs she

managed to avoid their creaks, but the banister was wobbly. Halfway down she swayed and had to grab it, only to find that it gave with a loud creak. For a moment she thought it would fall away, throwing her into the stairwell. She clung to it for minutes while she tried to catch her breath and wondered if anyone had heard the creak.

Eventually she reached the lower landing. In the brownish light the three doors looked unreal, sketched and painted on an unbroken wall. Beyond the middle door, in the room at whose window she'd glimpsed Angela, she was certain that voices were muttering. The traffic noise must have prevented whoever was there from hearing the banister. Did that mean that if anyone came behind her she wouldn't hear them for the noise?

The cry was still below her. It seemed distant as ever. She tiptoed past the doors and down the stairs. The hallway looked steeped in soupy light as it floated up towards her. All at once the cry stopped, and so did she, halfway down the last flight of stairs. She could see the front door, and now she realized it was mortice-locked. Whatever she found, she wouldn't be able to leave that way.

But she had to stay here until she found out everything about the group. Surely she wasn't putting herself at risk, surely they would understand that anyone would have come down to help the child – anyone, not just a spy. Perhaps the child was all right now, but she had to be sure.

When she reached the hall she glanced uneasily up the deserted stairs, then she made herself turn her back on the locked front door. There were four doors to the hall, including one beneath the stairs; presumably that led to a cellar. Metal outlines gleamed in the kitchen at the end of the hall. That left two rooms. She went to the first, between the stairs and the front door.

When she pushed the door a garment fell within. She heard its fall, and felt the soft obstruction as she continued pushing. She was afraid that the garment would make the door judder, make her more audible, but there was no sound beyond a faint slithering. Before long the door was open wide enough for her to look in.

This room was less dim than the one on the top floor had been; more light seeped between the tree trunks than through the foliage. A few moments passed before she was able to see. She stared towards the uncurtained window and ignored the illusion of movement beside her. As her eyes grew sharper, she made out that the room was completely bare. There was nothing at all behind the door, not even a hook where a garment could have hung.

At once she was so frightened that she wasn't sure she could move. She leaned there, half into the room, her hands clutching the door frame one above the other, unable to let go. Most of all she was afraid to look up. She didn't have to, she could see that the child wasn't in the room, she could let go, she could shove herself away from the door frame, out of the room. She fell back into the hall and barely managed not to slam the door as she closed it tight.

There was one more closed room, towards the cellar and the kitchen. She had to go on, she couldn't get out of the house. Nevertheless she went first to the kitchen, whose open door made it less threatening. In the gloom she distinguished the outlines of a sink unit, a cooker, a table attended by a few chairs. There was nothing else to see.

She couldn't delay any longer. Whatever was to be found was in the last deserted room. She crept towards its door, supporting herself with one hand on the damp coat of the wall. The door knob felt cold, almost slimy. Her shadow, a furry blotch whose shape seemed quite unlike hers, cowered back.

When she edged the door open she found the room was dark. She had to grope along the unseen wall in search of a light switch. Here was something round, a socket into which her finger scrabbled. It was the switch, its lever broken off. She pressed down the stub.

There was no child in the room. Beneath the shadeless bulb was a straight chair and a lame desk, a filing-cabinet, a bookcase piled haphazardly with books. A dark curtain thick as a blanket was nailed over the window. She stepped forward at once, and eased the door shut behind her. Perhaps this room would give her some idea of the aims of the group.

However untidy the books were, their themes were all too orderly. *Encyclopedia of Murder*, *A History of Torture*, *Cannibalism and Human Sacrifice*, *The Scourge of the Swastika* – the obsession with sadism was almost suffocating. Here was an illustrated edition of de Sade, next to a lithographed book called *The Manson Mandala*. One shelf was full of books in unmarked jackets, which she preferred for the moment not to open: the group's preoccupations were already clear enough.

It wasn't her cold that made her feel ill now. She was recalling Iris's tone of appalled disgust as she said, 'It made us do things. I like remembering them.' She thought of Angela, of the child's cry. Why had it stopped? She must be trying to delay her search by going to the filing-cabinet, for she was sure the drawers would be locked.

When she pulled the top drawer it rattled out at once, so loud amid the muffled thunder of the traffic that she was near to choking. It contained tapes and cassettes and reels of film in boxes identified only by numbers, and she felt dismayingly relieved not to be able to tell what was recorded on their contents. But the second drawer was unlocked too, and it was full of photographs.

She grabbed the first handful and took them to the desk beneath the glaring lamp. She had to hold up a photograph to rid it of the glare, but as soon as she made out what it showed she almost threw it away. Instead she forced herself to peer closer, in the desperate hope that her scrutiny would prove it to be faked.

The picture had been taken in a forest. She identified the giant trees at once: sequoias, in California. Spiked to one trunk was a naked body. Though it was abominably clear, she could tell neither its sex nor its age. Far too much of it had been removed.

She sorted through the handful of photographs, while her body twitched, desperate to turn away. The rest of the photographs were even worse. Several had been taken in California. She remembered the group that one of Manson's women had described as worse than the Family: perhaps there was a connection, after all.

Most of the photographs had been taken in houses much like the one in which Gerry was locked now. The rooms were evidently English; might some of them be in this very house? Her hands were beyond her control, unable to stop turning over the photographs. By now she knew that the pictures weren't faked; they were too undramatically framed, flat as police photographs, appalling in their indifference to what they were showing. Perhaps she had been wrong to assume that the group chose houses in noisy areas because they were cheap; perhaps the noise was meant to drown sounds from within the houses.

She was unconsciously crumpling the photographs as she realized how much more was in the filing cabinet – what must the tapes and films have recorded? – when the crying recommenced. She hadn't yet looked in the cellar. For a moment she was swaying on the chair and afraid she was going to faint, then she was running to the door, forgetting Barbara Waugh, her disguise, her mission. She knew only that she had to save the child.

She ran on tiptoe to the kitchen and found a carving-knife in a drawer beneath the sink. She winced as the blade slit the skin of her thumb, but the sharpness was reassuring.

She strode to the cellar door, though her legs felt wobbly, and shoved it open, holding the knife low.

A cramped passage slanted downwards, enclosing a flight of steps, to a second door. The stagnant light from the hall gathered dimly in the passage and gleamed on a switch at the bottom. The crying had stopped while she was in the kitchen, but it must have come from down there. As she descended she felt as if the slant of the ceiling were forcing her downwards. When she kicked open the door and found darkness beyond, she jerked the light switch down at once.

The cellar was large, with walls of unplastered brick, and it appeared to be quite empty. The single bare bulb left the corners in shadow, but certainly none of them hid a child. Bewildered, she stepped down into the open. Something the size of a child ran out above her at once, across the ceiling.

Her start was so violent that she dropped the knife, which clattered on the concrete floor. But there was nothing above her except herself: the ceiling was covered with mirror tiles. She stared nervously up at herself, hanging there inverted, dwarfed and helpless. She had just begun to wonder if the mirror tiles were there so that victims of the group could watch what was being done to them when she heard footsteps coming down into the cellar.

She snatched up the knife and backed away, only to wish that she'd hidden just inside the door. It would have done her little good; there were four men on the steps. They came into the cellar and stared at her, their faces blank with purpose. They closed in quickly, keeping between her and the door.

They hadn't reached her when someone else ran lightly down the steps. It was a girl about six years old, in pink pyjamas covered with blue rabbits. Grinning at Gerry between the men, she put two fingers in her mouth and wailed monotonously. It was the gagged cry that Gerry had heard.

146

Gerry had been lured down here like an animal to the slaughter, and she realized what she ought to have deduced sooner; the group didn't seek recruits among the vagrants at all, it sought victims. The little girl was giggling, and sounded innocently pleased with herself. Gerry raised the knife and clung to the handle, which was slippery with sweat. 'Keep back,' she said to the men.

They came forward, watching her eyes. They were spreading out now; the knife could never deal with all of them. 'Don't try anything with me,' she said, her voice rasping her throat. 'I'm a reporter. I was sent here to investigate you.'

The left-hand man smiled cruelly, revealing a few decayed brownish teeth behind his thick moist lips. 'Of course you are,' he said.

'I am. Look at this if you don't believe me.' She managed to wrestle her notebook out of the canvas bag beneath her left arm, and flung the notebook at him. 'My paper knows I'm here,' she lied.

He caught the notebook and tore it in half without a glance. The little girl squealed with delight. The men were unstoppable as robots, and they had almost reached Gerry; overhead she hung by her feet as the men closed in. She was nearly at the wall. 'Barbara Waugh knows I'm here,' she said, and realized they knew she was lying; she hadn't known where she would be brought. 'Angela's mother,' she said desperately.

'Names don't matter here,' said the left-hand man, as the one on the right darted forward to twist her arm until she dropped the knife. The man with the thick lips picked it up. The little girl watched fascinated as the other men held Gerry while he cut the tendons in her arms and legs.

20

East Anglia was a green table-top which ended jaggedly in cliffs. Gulls swooped along the beaches, searching the frills of the waves. The North Sea sounded like an enormous stormy forest; waves exploded against the rocks of the cove above which Ted was standing. 'Mummy said it would be nice if we could all go out for a drive sometime,' Judy said.

The wind on the cliff-top made his beard itch and tried to throw his voice over his shoulder. 'Now, is that really what she said?'

'Yes, because she said if we could afford a car we could go to new places on our holidays.'

That sounded like Helen, and no doubt she'd hoped Judy would tell him. 'I'll speak to her,' he said.

On the drive home, the horizons of the flat land had the unreal closeness of backdrops; clouds that were propped on their straight-edged bases supported models of churches. The car was nowhere in particular when Judy said, 'Are you definitely going away next week?'

'Yes, I have to, love.' He had the option of an Italian trip that would more or less coincide with Barbara's. Now Barbara was saying that she didn't think she would be able to go, but he could tell that she needed a holiday. 'Since you're into things Arthurian I'll take you to Glastonbury as soon as I get back.'

'We thought if you weren't going you might want to come with us.'

He was sure Helen had thought nothing of the kind, whatever she might have said to Judy. 'I'm afraid I'm already booked,' he said.

'Are you going away with Barbara?'

'What?' The accusing note in her voice was an unpleasant shock, though he knew who had put it there. 'What do you know about Barbara?' He had never even mentioned her name.

'She was the lady you used to visit when we were in the old flat.'

She couldn't have known that at the time, she had been too young. 'Yes, Judy, I'm going away with her. Just as you and your mother were going away with your Uncle Steve.'

It didn't please him to score the point. The whole purpose of the divorce had been to protect Judy from similar hostilities. He was about to ask if there was anyone new – it seemed childish to call them uncles, but what else could he call them? – when Judy said, 'Mummy says you prefer Barbara to us.'

'Not to you, Judy.' He restrained himself from saying more, though the monotonous landscape gave him little to do except grow angrier. Nevertheless, by the time he'd taken Judy home and she was washing noisily in the bathroom, he was calm; it would achieve nothing to lose his temper. 'Helen, I don't think there's much point in talking to her about Barbara Waugh.'

'Why should that bother you?' Helen was cutting one of her old dresses into dusters, no doubt to show how she had to economize. 'Does it make you feel guilty?' she said without looking up.

'Yes, of course it does. Everything you say to Judy about me is calculated to do so. I mean, telling her that we could go away together – would you really have wanted that?'

'It's obvious that you wouldn't. You begrudge her one day a week.'

'Where in Christ's name do you get that idea?'

She stared at him. 'Don't try to be funny. You haven't changed that much, don't pretend you have. Has your

149

Barbara Waugh seen you in one of your moods? I expect you're more careful with her. She doesn't depend on you as we used to. She can always leave you when she's had enough.'

He knew what was coming – innuendoes, accusing silences, stares that meant he ought to know what she was thinking, that if he didn't that put him further in the wrong – and yet he couldn't stop at this point; he had never been able to. 'What moods are those?' he demanded.

'Why, the one you're in now is a mild example. Don't tell me you've forgotten your years as man of the house. For all I know you're just the same now when you take Judith out. She says you aren't, but I only hope for your sake that's true.' She glared at him as her scissors chewed through the last section of cloth. 'Do you know that each night before you're going to take her out she has nightmares?'

'I'm not surprised.'

'If that's meant to mean something, it certainly means nothing to me.'

That was always guaranteed to make him lose his temper. 'It means that you've got her into such a state she doesn't know what she feels. I'd like to know what kind of shit you feed her about me.'

'You're as filthy as some of the books you publish. That's something else you can teach her, except I won't give you the chance. You just remember I've got custody. I can soon make sure you don't see her if you give me cause.'

'Maybe you wouldn't have custody if I contested it now.' He was trapped in an argument that he didn't even want to win. 'You'll have to show the court more than this kind of hysteria to keep me away from Judy.'

'Do you think they'd believe you care about her? Not if I tell them how much you care for a woman who couldn't even look after her own child. No wonder you used to take it out on Judith. Nobody made you feel guilty except yourself.'

She was almost right, by mistake: when he'd come home

after sleeping with Barbara he had been nervous in case he seemed too happy, which in turn made him anxious not to appear secretive – but Helen had already suspected him for months of having an affair with Barbara, and living up to her suspicions had relieved him of the illusion of guilt, made him feel freer than ever before in his life. Perhaps Barbara had helped to end the marriage, but hardly in the way Helen meant.

'I'm sorry, Helen, I won't argue about Barbara.' He knocked on the bathroom door as she watched him coldly. 'I'm going now, Judy. I'll take you to Glastonbury next time.'

On Upper Street a carpet like a roll of sacking leaned against a shop window. A ragged man who had been leaning next to it staggered towards Ted, but the empty wine bottle missed the car. No wonder Helen was depressed, Ted thought as he drove past bleary shops. The argument had been too familiar on the whole to hurt, and he was sure that Helen didn't seriously intend to keep him and Judy apart. Did she really think so little of the books he published? No doubt she sold *Signed Adolf Hitler* in the shop quite happily. He'd rejected that book nine years ago, but the gold swastika in the sunburst was in every bookshop now. He wished he'd asked her which books she was accusing him of, except that she wouldn't have told him; she was too devious for that. She was as devious as his private eye would be.

By God, of course she would. He punched the wheel, which shouted at an empty street. Of course, that was how the private eye would approach her job, not like Philip Marlowe in drag at all. He drove home fast, rewriting chapters in his head.

As soon as he reached his flat he began writing, crossing out whole pages, scribbling between lines. All at once everything that was wrong with the chapters he'd written

151

seemed clear and manageable. He reworked three chapters in two hours, and the energy he'd generated drove him to begin a new chapter. There he found himself stranded halfway down the page. The private eye was herself now, she had none of Philip Marlowe's adolescent bitterness that the world was less romantically perfect than he wanted it to be, but the story demanded a betrayal next, a test for her compassion. What could it be?

Barbara might help. When he glanced across the lake he saw that her window was lit; behind her roof a raw sunset was blackening. She answered the phone before he could hear it ring. 'Yes?' she said urgently.

'Hi, Barbara, it's Ted.' He felt he should have said, 'It's only me.'

'Hello, Ted.' She was doing her best not to sound disappointed. 'What's up?'

'I've done some work on my novel but now I've reached a block. Do you fancy a drink?'

'Yes, come over and I'll give you several if you like. Just let me have a few minutes.'

He'd meant they could go out to a pub. Still, at least he would be able to talk to her; they hadn't spoken at any length for weeks. She sounded too exhausted and on edge to bother with his novel. He'd concentrate on persuading her to go on holiday, with or without him. Certainly she needed the break.

He played a Charlie Parker record to give her a few minutes, and searched for a buttock to insert in the half-arsed *Playboy* jigsaw, then he strolled across to Barbara's, beside the pinkish lake. Beneath the church of St Giles, strings of white light squirmed like grubs. A thin pallid youth, tonsured like an untidy monk, stood by the willow on the red-brick plateau and watched Ted as he rang the bell.

Ted managed to clench his fists in his pockets rather than

show his dismay when Barbara answered the door. She looked worse than overworked: her face was haggard, almost colourless beneath the make-up; her eyes seemed unable to take any more. Something had happened since he'd called her.

'Come and sit down.' She was doing her best to sound in control of the situation, but he could see how much of a strain that was. 'There's something I have to tell you,' she said.

21

'Just let me have a few minutes,' Barbara said, and sat with her hand over her face. She felt so dizzy she was certain that if the prop of her elbow moved she would slump across her desk. Whether she was here or at the office, she was at the mercy of the phone.

Did she wish that Gerry would phone or that she had never sent her in search of Angela? She'd wished both, desperately and irresolubly, ever since she had heard the cruel mocking voice of one of Angela's captors. She could only hope that he hadn't seen that Angela was phoning, hope that Gerry had infiltrated the group by now, but it seemed so much to hope. Even if she dared break her promise further she couldn't call the police, in case they drove the group into hiding before Gerry could infiltrate. In any case, they wouldn't believe her. It had taken her too long to believe in Angela herself.

She'd made herself work harder at the office and at home, to be sure her clients didn't suffer. Some days she suspected herself of making call after call in order not to sit brooding over the phone. Frequently she thought she was being watched, especially on the balconies and walkways of the Barbican. Alone in bed, too exhausted to sleep, she felt like a figure of rusty wire. She felt worse than she had after the police had told her Angela was dead. At least that had seemed final.

She let go of the receiver at last and trudged to the bathroom, where she revived herself with splashes of cold water. She lingered a few minutes over making up her face, though that couldn't make her eyes less uneasy. She seemed to spend most of her nights climbing the escalator, which crept steadily backwards. Sometimes Angela was waiting at the top, sometimes she looked like Iris, grey and haunted. Last night Arthur's face had stared up, no larger than a pinhead. Angela was waiting against a restless darkness that looked impatient to take shape, but when Barbara glanced back at the top of the escalator a snake with a swollen head, pink and moist as a foetus, was waiting.

She hurried out of the bathroom, for the mirror gave her nothing but the apprehension in her eyes. What could she do while she waited for Ted? A manuscript lay in two piles on her desk, but she doubted she had time to read another chapter. She was surrounded by books, by stories. She felt walled in by unreality. There was nothing she could grasp.

Ted's window was still lit. She was on her way to her desk, to tell him to come over as soon as he liked, when the phone rang. Surely he wasn't calling to cancel his visit. 'Yes?' she said anxiously.

'It's me,' Angela said.

Barbara grew drunk with relief, and sat down hurriedly. Her captors mustn't have seen her phoning, after all. Nevertheless Barbara demanded, 'Are you all right?'

'Yes, of course I am.'

She sounded cross as any child who thought her mother was being too protective. Barbara felt obscurely cheated: how could she sound like that when she was in danger? Before she could think as well as feel she said, 'Why are you calling?'

'Because I need you.'

Barbara managed to hold back her tears, in case her weeping made her unable to hear. Angela must have reinterpreted the question, for she said, 'Because we're going away.'

'Where to?' Barbara's ear was aching, she was pressing the receiver so hard against herself. Angela must be in her captors' house, for she was speaking low. 'Scotland,' she said. 'I can't tell you where.'

Were they moving because they knew Gerry was looking for them, or had she passed herself off successfully? There was no way Barbara could have asked, even if Angela hadn't said, 'I can't talk any more now. I've got to go.'

For a while after the phone went dead, Barbara felt almost heartened. Angela was unharmed. She'd sounded impatient when Barbara had asked about her welfare simply because she didn't realize that she was in danger. But the more Barbara thought about that, the more dismaying it seemed. What might they be doing to Angela without her realizing? If Gerry hadn't found them by now, Barbara was the only one who had any idea where they were going. How could she bear to do nothing with that knowledge?

She was pacing the cage of her flat, glimpsing Ted's extinguished window and a monkish youth who must be admiring the church, when the doorbell rang. She couldn't keep her plight to herself any longer. 'Come and sit down,' she said. 'There's something I have to tell you.'

She told Ted everything, over drinks which neither of them touched. He gazed steadily at her, one hand hiding his mouth and his feelings. When she'd finished she wished she had told him sooner; though he wasn't as informed as Gerry, he might be more supportive. But he said, 'I don't understand how this cult is supposed to have faked Angela's death.'

'Gerry Martin thought they might have killed one of their own children.'

'Gerry Martin sounds rather a sensationalist. Does it really seem likely that the parents would let their child be killed just because someone else wanted Angela?'

Her forehead was tightening; she wanted comfort, not confusion. 'Can you think of a better explanation?'

'If it weren't for the evidence that this cult or whatever it is exists, I'd suspect you were being set up for extortion.'

156

'I don't see that at all.'

'Well, to begin with, it seems awfully convenient that Angela should start calling just after the article about you was published, don't you think? That could mean someone read the article and thought you must be making enough money to be worth trying. All these phone calls could be to soften you up so that when someone comes offering to bring back Angela you'll agree to anything. I'm not saying you would, only that they might think so. After all, the fact that the cult exists doesn't mean that Angela does.' He sat forward and took her hand, which she let slump in his. 'As far as I can see,' he said, 'the only reason to believe she's alive is that Margery Turner gave the impression she couldn't draw. Suppose that was part of her plan?'

'No, Ted. The reason to believe that Angela's alive is that she has called me several times – twice since Margery's death.'

'If that was Angela. If it wasn't Margery's accomplice, who has decided to carry on even though Margery is dead.'

She managed not to snatch her hand away from him. Arthur would never have tried to argue her out of the truth, he would have stood by her until Angela was found. 'Ted, I know you want to help, but you can't help by trying to tell me I'm wrong. I know it's Angela who calls.'

'Are you sure? Has she ever said anything only you and she could know? Have you ever asked her to? Barbara, you don't dare to consider that she might be a fake. You're wrecking yourself, and it may be for no reason.'

She felt trapped by his concern for her, by the confusion he was creating. His large untidy face crowded her, and she felt like a child overborne by an insensitive adult, except that she wasn't a child.

'I know you blame yourself to some extent for what happened to Angela – '

'Oh, for God's sake, Ted. I don't blame myself to some

157

extent, I blame myself totally. I have to be sure that this time I do everything I can.'

'Well, just as you like. The last thing I want is to upset you further. It's only that looking at the situation objectively I find it hard to believe that anyone would have gone to the trouble of faking her death so that they could keep her.'

'That's because you never wanted your own child. She was so much of a burden that you couldn't even live with her. Yet I wanted Angela more than anything else in the world, and I let her be stolen. It isn't fair.'

She stopped, appalled. She wouldn't have blamed him if he had left without another word, but he said, 'So you'll be going up to Scotland next week.'

'Yes, I have to. I've got to try and find her.'

'You can't drive all over Scotland by yourself. It's a good job you didn't manage to get me those reservations for Italy.'

She didn't trust herself to speak in case she broke down. He must have realized that, for he held her without speaking for a while. Eventually they went into the bedroom. Though she wanted to make love, she fell asleep in his arms at once. Except for his promise of help she had already forgotten everything he'd said.

22

Outside Lancaster grey rock began to rise, tearing the fields and woods. On the Lakeland horizons mounds of haze were just distinguishable from the sky. Sometimes the mounds came closer, looming hundreds of feet above the motorway. Streams and rivers glittered softly in crumbled valleys, sheep or boulders stood in the grass of the fells.

Beyond Carlisle the map was veinous with rivers, but there was nothing to mark the Scottish border except a roadside sign and the sudden twist of apprehension deep in Barbara's innards. Soon the horizon looked layered with storm clouds, except that the closer layers were tinged green by grass. Above the road the slopes were pinstriped with bare earth or spiky with ranks of firs. Where the road grew straight she drove faster, anxious to reach the towns, dark enigmatic blotches on the map.

Dumfries was almost deserted when they reached it, a riverside town where nobody could direct them to a restaurant for dinner. At Kilmarnock factories stained the sky, featureless council estates boxed in a valley and relics of Robert Burns. She searched both towns desultorily; she couldn't imagine anyone trying to hide in either of them.

Glasgow seemed more promising. It was even larger than the blotch on the map had led her to believe, and appeared to be growing. Its edges ripped fields apart and strewed them with rocks and litter, scattered grey fragments on the map. Further in, the buildings crowded out the green; pylons and tower blocks and factory chimneys stood over what was left. She had been in Glasgow two days now, and had scarcely explored the city centre. She was beginning to realize how futile her search was.

She stepped off Sauchiehall Street and into the hotel, through blades of light trapped by the revolving doors. The chandelier above the foyer looked foggy; one of the nymphs supporting the balcony had a broken nose. In the lounge, residents were watching Ronald Colman as the Prisoner of Zenda on a chipped black and white television; one old lady was rapping the floor with her stick and crying 'Donald' for a porter. She went upstairs.

Ted wasn't in his room. She had a shower in her bathroom, then she sat at her window. Office buildings Gothic as Chicago stepped down towards the River Clyde, cars jounced down the steep ramps of the streets; a few spires stood like faceless totem-poles among the tower blocks on the far bank. A man whose face was red as biddy sat on the pavement opposite her window and managed eventually to remove his shoe so as to examine his bare foot. Along the street towards the Ocean's Eleven pub, from a passage where a feeble neon sign said BILLIARDS, she heard the click of balls through a lull in the traffic. Shoppers and tourists thronged past her window, and she couldn't help searching their faces, even the distant faces which shifted in the heat and were never what they'd seemed. A Scottish publisher had once remarked to her that if you stood on Sauchiehall Street for long enough you would see the world go by. There was only one face in the world that she wanted to see, and the tradition seemed a cruel joke now.

The more she searched, the more difficult it grew. The simplest tasks were tortuous. The police and the Salvation Army were no help, but she couldn't tell if they had withheld information because she was so evasive. She mustn't tell them anything that might give them a reason to search; she didn't know if it had been Gerry Martin's search that had driven the group out of London. She could only hope that Gerry was with them now, finding out about them.

Why should they be in Glasgow? Barbara knew it was Scotland, and Gerry's list of places had implied that it would be a large town or a city, but Scotland had a dozen of those. She could only search doggedly and hope that her search was redundant. In the Mitchell Library, where girls let books out on parole from behind the counter, a librarian who obviously regarded her as a pestering eccentric directed her to the University, in case a researcher in local history could help. Nobody could, and she was reduced to wandering the streets, peering at buildings and faces. Half the time she felt she was being watched. No wonder Ted was worried about her.

Of course that was why he had come with her, not because he believed her. At least she'd persuaded him to go off by himself today. He'd noticed a bar beside the Inner Ring Road, and no doubt he was making the most of the liberal licensing hours, but she'd sent him off so that he would have a chance to write to Judy. After what she'd said to him about Judy, that was the least she could do. She mustn't destroy whatever was left of his family life.

But now that he'd left her alone she could only brood. Though she'd brought material to read, she couldn't work just now. The interminable parade of faces went by in the street, the head of the shower snaked out of the dark of the bathroom mirror. When she began to stare at the phone she made herself go downstairs. She kept phoning Louise to ask if there were any personal calls and to leave her latest number, but if Angela or Gerry had phoned at all they might well have rung off as soon as they heard she wasn't there.

She lingered in the foyer while she tried to rid herself of the thought of Angela phoning the flat, at who knew what risk to herself, and getting no reply. In the lounge residents were knitting or doing crosswords, Ronald Colman was dashing about heroically. The residents looked faded as the armchairs; there was a faint musty smell of lavender-water, a sense of growing old and trying not to notice. The street would be more bearable, despite the heat and the crowds. She could watch the faces and pretend she was looking out for Ted.

Better, she could buy the evening papers. That felt a little like hope. Perhaps a headline would give her a lead, or a paragraph somewhere in the paper would, or even an advertisement; there was always hope. She pushed through the revolving doors toward the faint unconvincing luminous crowd that became real once she was out of the glass, into the sunlight and dust and the roar of traffic.

The nearest kiosk was recessed in the corner of an office building. A woman with a pink cardigan draped over her shoulders sat behind the small counter, knitting a baby jacket. When Barbara had tried her hand at knitting for Angela, her attempt at a jacket had begun to unravel as soon as it came off the needles, and all she could do was laugh at herself. Now she bit her lip so that the pain drove out the memory. She grabbed the evening papers and looked for something else to read.

The *Cosmopolitan* was last month's, which she'd read, and nothing else seemed worth reading. She found herself staring at *Fate* magazine, which both reminded her of the occult fringe and seemed to suggest that she resign herself. She picked it up unwillingly. She ought to look in there too, she couldn't afford to ignore any possibility of a lead. 'I hope you find comfort there,' the woman behind the counter said.

'Pardon?'

The woman withdrew quickly into herself. 'Just the way you looked. No offence.'

162

'I wasn't offended.' Barbara fumbled in her purse. 'I didn't understand what you said.'

'So long as you don't think I'm prying.' The woman gazed at her over the chattering needles. 'Whoever you've lost, don't despair.'

'I try not to,' Barbara said, staring at her money to keep control of her emotions.

'Maybe you'll hear from them if that's what you want. Have you been to the Spiritualists?'

Barbara thought of hearing Angela's voice out of the air or from a medium's lips. 'God forbid.'

'Just asking.' The woman had withdrawn again, it seemed this time for good. She pinched her needles together in one hand, took Barbara's money with the other. 'So how are you liking our city?'

'I'm sure I'd like it,' Barbara said, feeling that she'd somehow been unreasonable, 'if I had less on my mind.'

'You poor thing.' As the woman passed her the change she squeezed Barbara's hand. 'Maybe there's someone better than the Spiritualists to help you.'

Barbara managed to look interested and grateful. 'Who's that?'

'Someone who buys these magazines you read told me about it. She's only been once but she says it changed her. They meet down on Broomielaw, under the bridge. I think she said Thursday nights.'

That was tonight. Perhaps it was a lead, perhaps there might be people in the group who could help Barbara, people who might know of other, more secretive groups. 'Is that all you know? What do they call themselves?'

'That's all she said, but I'm telling you she was a different woman. I thought you might be interested, that's all.' She recommended knitting, with an air of having done all she could. 'I don't know what they're called.'

'Thanks anyway. Really, you've been very kind.' Barbara

made herself smile before she turned away. The woman called after her, and then Barbara was hurrying to find Ted, to tell him they must go to the meeting tonight. Her eagerness felt close to panic, for the woman had called after her 'Maybe they haven't got a name.'

23

Broomielaw was a four-lane dual carriageway that ran by the Clyde. When they arrived it was growing dusk; traces of light flickered like dying neon in the river. It had taken them twenty minutes to walk from the hotel, and Ted had insisted they eat first. 'Of course we must go,' he'd said, 'but we may need the energy.'

Like most dock roads at night, Broomielaw was almost deserted. Neon names of whiskies towered above the pavements; presumably there were drinkers in the bars underneath the signs. A few men drank from bottles on benches by the river, but they weren't watching her. However watched she felt, why would anyone have followed her from the hotel?

She saw the bridges at once, a railway flanked by roads which spanned both the river and Broomielaw. Beneath the bridges, on the wall furthest from the river, two orange lights were glaring, so stark they were almost white. Between the lights the roadway was bare and so, apart from carpets of shadow behind the pillars, was the pavement. There was nobody at all.

Perhaps the woman in the kiosk had mistaken the day, or perhaps they were simply too late; they hadn't known what time to arrive. Reflections of lamp-standards fished in the river, patches of pollution oozed by; on the water naves of arches dripped loudly. Her elongated shadow dangled its head in the water. She mustn't blame Ted for having delayed her, yet she did.

But it was Ted who saw the door. It stood ajar in the wall between the orange floodlights. Because it was covered with posters she had assumed that it was peeling away from the wall. She hurried across, screwing up her eyes against the dazzle.

Just within the doorway stood a two-faced board which said UNDYING LIGHT in large bold letters. Presumably it had stood outside on the pavement to advertise the meeting. Whoever they were, she reminded herself, they might be able to help. When Ted managed to shift the door, which reluctantly gave a foot or so before becoming wedged, they went in.

The passage was dim, with dog-eared wallpaper, and all the dimmer for the brightness of the room beyond. Someone in the room was talking fast and lively as a salesman. When Barbara reached the end of the passage she thought for a dislocated moment that she'd found a pop group by mistake: four scrubbed figures in white robes were chanting on a podium, expertly picking up one another's cues, for an audience seated on wooden folding chairs. But a small man in his sixties, wearing a robe too big for him, came whispering to her and Ted at once and tried to hustle them into the nearest available seats. He was enough to show that this was meant to be a religious meeting.

Barbara resisted his urging and found seats as near the front as possible, so that she would be ready to question the people on stage as soon as they'd finished. Milky blurs coated the whitewashed walls; behind the stage, pockmarks outlined the circle where a dartboard had hung. As she sat down her chair creaked sharply, but the usher had time only to glower at her before he flapped away to seat another latecomer.

The quartet on the podium was selling reincarnation. Their accents varied between Scottish and mid-Atlantic; it was impossible to tell where they came from. 'All of us are destined to have better lives than this,' the younger woman said, but the more Barbara gazed at them the less alive they seemed: they looked manufactured by whatever factory produced families for television series, a fresh-faced young man and woman between an older couple, all their instant identical smiles gleaming. Only the grubby elbow of the older woman's robe, which must have brushed against something on her way to the stage, seemed other than calculated.

The audience was grey. Everywhere she looked she saw clothes or hair the colour of the stale smoke that half the audience was sucking from ragged cigarettes. They looked like people who worked in dingy offices or in shops in half-derelict streets if they worked at all, people who grew old looking after their parents and who would die unmarried and almost alone in their parents' senile houses. They were here tonight because they were starved for faith, for anything that would explain their lives.

And the quartet was telling them exactly what they wanted to hear, telling them so slickly that nobody had time to think between their claims. 'We are all good, but some of us have forgotten,' the young man said, and his young wife or sister responded at once: 'It's easy to forget. That's the difficulty that God puts in our way so that we have to have faith. But with faith every one of us can remember. We can remember all the good we did in our other lives.'

She sensed that Ted was restless, and she was growing impatient too: how could this glib quartet tell her anything about the occult except their own routine? But she mustn't leave without making sure. She felt more than ever that she was being watched. No doubt that was because she was on edge.

The maternal woman was speaking. 'Whatever our present lives may be, we have had better lives and will have again. Once you remember those good lives your present sufferings will seem less than a dream.' She wavered forward a step, and Barbara realized she was crippled; that must have made her blacken her sleeve. 'We can give you the key to those lives,' she said.

Now came the sales pitch, Barbara thought, but the older man said, 'yet there is one thing you must remember. You have done bad as well as good in those lives. Every one of your most secret evil thoughts is something you have already done in another life. It isn't wrong to think these thoughts, because they are done and already forgiven. To realize that will help you rise above them.'

A train bowled overhead, emerging from Central Station or dawdling in, and gave Barbara the chance to look over her shoulder without seeming paranoid. Nobody was watching her, but someone had been, a large-nosed woman on the back row who had come in after her. Or perhaps the woman had only been gazing at the stage and had glanced away nervously when Barbara turned; most of the audience looked timid, hoping not to be noticed. At any rate, the woman had turned her face aside.

The older man was still speaking gently but firmly, a father who had to communicate unpleasant facts of life. 'You can't put those thoughts aside. They will only burrow deeper in you and grow there. That is how corruption begins, when you pretend to yourself that evil has nothing to do with you. That's how you begin to lose control of yourself and what you can do.'

This didn't seem quite what the audience wanted or expected – Barbara could tell that some of the listeners were ill at ease, a few of them were muttering – but nor did it help her find Angela. It was beginning to remind her of Miss Clarke's psychometer friend, for it was just as unhelpful. When Barbara used the muttering as an excuse to glance back, there was no doubt that the woman with the strawberry nose was watching her, perhaps because Barbara looked out of place. The woman's face turned aside at once, hair trailing over one eye.

'But we all have it in us to do good,' the young woman said, to the relief of the audience. 'Good cannot be killed. It will always be reborn. None of us is ever beyond redemption unless we give up everything that makes us human. To be human is to be potentially good.'

It must be the gaze of the large-nosed woman that made Barbara feel on edge, yet she felt there was something else, something she had just failed to remember. The effort to identify it rasped her nerves. 'But the good that is in us can be corrupted,' the young man shouted. 'We must guard against those who would destroy it. There are always those who have turned their backs on their humanity, on everything they could achieve for good.'

All at once Barbara remembered what she had almost forgotten or perhaps couldn't bear to recall. 'Even their names?' she said uncontrollably.

'Names?' The young man's reassuring smile wavered; he hadn't been interrupted at rehearsal. 'Turned their backs on their names, you mean? Yes, some of them even give up their names, maybe.' He was faltering, and the maternal woman took over quickly. 'Few of us will meet anything that could corrupt us absolutely,' she told the audience, but Barbara could hear only what Miss Clarke's friend had said.

Ted was clasping her hand as if he knew what was wrong, but all her senses seemed overpowered by the psychometer's voice: 'Already she has great spiritual power. She must be found before they destroy what she is.' The babble on stage had reminded her of this, but it could certainly not reassure her. The psychometer had been right to claim that Angela was still alive, she must have been right about everything. Barbara turned away, unaware that she was pulling her hand out of Ted's, and saw at last that the woman with the strawberry nose had a lopsided face.

A train rumbled overhead like stage thunder on cue, but Barbara was on the train where the lopsided woman had sat next to Angela. This couldn't be the same woman, she looked much more than nine years older, yet as Barbara grabbed Ted's arm, dragging him to his feet as she rose, she could see that the woman was afraid of her. She remembered the fear and loathing in the woman's eyes as she had gazed at Angela, she remembered how Angela had shrunk into herself as if with a premonition, and the nightmare seemed close to fitting together. She stepped into the aisle, and the woman fled into the passage at once.

'That woman,' she gasped to Ted. 'She's one of them.' Perhaps he wondered how she knew, but he followed without speaking. Folding seats clattered behind them, the man in the too-large robe tried to detain them until his robe tripped him and dumped him back in his chair. In the passage the board rocked, fell against the wall. She ran past, knocking it aside.

The deserted street looked flayed by orange light. Beyond it the river and the sky were dark; night gathered like smoke under the bridges. Barbara was just in time to see movement dodging behind one of the left-hand pillars. 'Head her off,' she cried as she ran across the roadway.

When she reached the pillar there was nothing but a grey bird which flapped away amid a migration of echoes. She ranged desperately about the cage of pillars, peered behind each one, darted back to the main road, along which Ted had halted, at a loss. Her shadow, a stylized hand on an elastic arm, made grabs at the dark.

Eventually she went back to the riverside. Arches dripped sharply, segments of inverted pillars squirmed. Flies that had swarmed from a drifting object tickled her face, but she was too intent to brush them off. To her right, against the low arch of the road bridge, an irregular patch might be the woman's bluish dress.

Barbara crept forward. A train ticked over the railway bridge; rats' tails of light dangled in the water. She could

170

hold on to the woman until Ted came to help, no matter how the woman fought – but perhaps the bluish patch wasn't the woman at all, perhaps it was a stain or a clump of weeds. She had almost reached it before it darted away beneath the arch.

'Over here, Ted!' If Barbara hadn't ducked as she ran, the edge of the low arch would have split her scalp. The riverside walk was darker than the road, but that meant she could see the woman, outlined against distant lights and drowned streaks of light. The walk felt rough as rubble underfoot, and she stumbled more than once. Round-headed dwarfs lined up in her way – bollards which she barely managed to avoid. Nevertheless she was gaining, however hoarse her breathing was.

Suddenly the woman dodged on to the road. Barbara panted after her, skidding on a scrap of lawn that smelt of mowing. The woman raced across into an empty side street which was shiny with orange light. Ted came pounding along Broomielaw and reached the side turning just as Barbara did.

She hadn't time or breath to speak. They ran along the deserted street beneath windows blackened by the light. She could hear the strain in his breathing; he must be as out of condition as she was – but the woman they were chasing had looked much unhealthier, and they were closer to her by the time she dodged to the left.

When Barbara reached the corner she saw the station ahead, its great arched windows bright as a cathedral's. The woman was running under the wide bridge which led the railway lines towards Broomielaw, running through the rugs of light outside a dozen shops. As she ran past a bus queue, faces peered out from behind one another like a high hand at poker, and Barbara thought of crying out to them to stop her. But she no longer had the breath to spare, even supposing she would have been able to convince them to help.

As Barbara passed the queue, her open mouth dragging at her breaths, the woman turned left into Union Street. She glanced back at Barbara, then she seemed to make a final effort. When Barbara arrived, panting jaggedly, at the corner, she thought the woman had managed to lose her. Then, beyond a few scattered window-shoppers, she glimpsed the woman dodging into a doorway between shops.

Ted saw this too, and ran to the opposite pavement, surprisingly fast for his large frame, in order to head her off. He was ahead of the doorway, and running back across the road, as Barbara came up to it. He already looked defeated, and when she reached the doorway she saw why. It wasn't a shop doorway at all. It was a passage that led into the railway station.

As she toiled up the steps into the station she heard a train leaving. At the top of the steps a drunk tried to detain her, but she threw him aside. The station hall was crowded with people, staring up at announcements that hands were removing or placing in windows; it sounded like a theatre during an interval. Hands were withdrawing a placard for the Edinburgh train, and she ran to that barrier. 'Did a woman,' she gulped at the ticket collector, 'just come through here?'

'A woman? Aye, a whole lot of them.'

'Just now.' He was turning away, and she had to restrain herself from clawing at him. 'A woman in a blue dress.'

'Aye, blue and green and yellow and rainbow with pink spots. They'd better all have tickets, I can tell you.'

It was useless. She could hear trains leaving for other towns, and she couldn't check them all. She slumped and might have fallen if Ted hadn't supported her. There was one last faint chance. 'We've got to go back,' she said.

But the door under the bridges on Broomielaw was closed and padlocked; the Undying Light had gone. She trudged wordlessly back to the hotel, up the giant sloping steps of the streets. A light rain tingled her face and bare arms, but she was beyond being refreshed. She dared not call the

172

police, she could do nothing except hope that Gerry had found the cult, hope for another phone call eventually. No doubt the cult would move again as soon as the woman reported that Barbara had spotted her.

'Never mind,' Ted murmured, taking Barbara's arm. 'We'll try and find them in the morning.' He was guiding her towards the stairs, and she knew that he meant to help – but now she would have to explain to him why she had chased the woman, which meant that at last she would have to admit to herself all she feared.

24

When he was sure that Barbara was asleep Ted went next door to his room and phoned down to make sure she wouldn't be disturbed. He stood at his window and tried to think. Rain was performing a spiky dance in the street; lit windows piled above the Clyde, floated along the dark river towards the sea. The anonymous cheerfulness of his room seemed to hinder his thinking. He went downstairs.

The bored young woman at the desk didn't seem much enlivened when she found that he only wanted her to let him know if Barbara called his room. Eventually a porter took his order for coffee. In the lounge the extinguished television was showing a swollen reflection of armchairs; a faint smell of pipe-smoke and talcum powder hovered among the glazed half-empty bookcases, the tables scattered with disintegrating magazines. He sat in an armchair that smelled of tobacco, and thought about Barbara.

It looked bad. He could see she realized that herself. Apparently she had felt watched for weeks, and tonight's encounter with the woman under the bridges had convinced her she was right. That might not be entirely paranoid – the lopsided woman must have had reason to flee – but it was trivial, not to say reasonable, compared with the things she imagined about Angela.

They seemed to go all the way back to the kidnapping, to the claims a so-called psychic had made, which surely proved how bad her state of mind was: could this really be the Barbara Waugh who used to refer to occult books as idiot traps? That Barbara would never have gone anywhere near an outfit like the Undying Light, but now she believed

174

that Angela had psychic powers which the kidnappers were trying to destroy: she had seen her father and talked to him after his death, she had an aura of peace which calmed everyone who came near her. Everyone except the killers, apparently: they were the people with no names, who must believe she was some kind of threat; the lopsided woman was one of them, who had sensed her powers one day as she'd sat next to her on the Victoria line. That was why they had gone to such lengths to steal Angela. The Undying Light had made it clear why the nameless people couldn't simply kill her: the threat to them would only be reborn.

He couldn't tell how much of this Barbara believed, and perhaps she wasn't sure herself. Perhaps she meant only that the cult believed Angela was beyond killing, not that she was. Nevertheless he'd tried to disentangle her thoughts – hearing her husband soon after his death, and believing that Angela had seen him, could be wishful thinking; surely Angela could have pacified people and still have been quite a normal child – until he'd seen that he was making her more tense. He'd had to persuade her to take two of the sleeping-pills he sometimes had to use, and then he had needed to reassure her that whatever he'd said, he would help. Of course he would, but how?

When the porter had gone he drank sweet scalding coffee and hoped that would sharpen his mind. He still felt that her search would lead nowhere – one reason he'd come with her was to support her if she gave in to despair – but perhaps he wasn't as objective as he liked to think. Did he secretly hope that she wouldn't find Angela, that Angela had died nine years ago? Wasn't her childlessness part of her appeal for him? Perhaps, but he was being unfair to himself; he cared about her more deeply than that. If the nameless people really had Angela, if Barbara managed to reclaim her, what would the child be like after nine years? He suspected that Barbara didn't dare wonder.

His logic was growing tangled. There was no need to think along those lines. He was still convinced that Angela was dead and that Barbara was being set up for extortion; certainly that was the simplest explanation. The lopsided woman must have been following her to see if the false trails had softened her up. He only wished he could get his hands on her, on any of the bastards who were doing all this to Barbara.

And by God, perhaps he could – perhaps there was a way to help, at any rate. He set down his cup with a thud on the tray. Now they knew what one of her persecutors looked like, they had to tell the police. He would have to persuade Barbara that Angela could come to no harm: either she was dead or, if the nameless people had really stolen her for the reasons Barbara had suggested, they didn't dare kill her. Of course he would put it to her more gently, but she must accept that this was their first real lead.

All at once he felt a great deal more useful. He finished his coffee quickly, then he went to stand for a while beneath the hotel awning. Smells of Greek and Indian food drifted through the rain, window dummies stirred beyond tendrils of rain on their windows, reflections swam by under cars. He was standing there when a porter came to him. 'Mrs Waugh,' the porter said.

'Is she awake?' He'd hoped she would sleep until morning. 'All right, I'll go up.'

'No, it's someone wants to speak to her. You said she wasn't to be disturbed.'

It was after midnight. Could this be the girl who was pretending to be Angela? If he could only meet her face to face – But when he answered the phone in the foyer alcove, the girl's voice sounded much too old. 'I want to speak to Mrs Waugh,' it said.

'She's asleep. She's had an extremely tiring day. Can I help? I'm with her.'

176

'I can only speak to Mrs Waugh.'

Who would call so late and be so secretive? 'My name is Ted Crichton,' he said. 'Barbara has asked me to speak to anyone who calls while she's asleep.' Before he was sure it was wise to go on he said, 'Including her daughter.'

There was a silence. He'd given away Barbara's secret, and he didn't even know to whom. Then the voice said, 'Do you know who I am?'

'Yes, I think I do.' He wasn't even sure who she was supposed to be. 'What do you want?'

'I wanted to see my mummy.'

If that was meant to convince him, it achieved the opposite: she sounded grotesquely self-conscious to him, an actress who might be able to convince a distraught mother but who didn't impress him at all. His cold rage was growing. 'If you come here I'll take you to her.'

'I can't. I wanted to meet her somewhere.'

'Then perhaps you'd better meet me instead.'

This time her silence was much longer. He mustn't have sounded sufficiently convinced by this voice that was trying to pretend it was thirteen years old. Perhaps it was the lopsided woman, who hadn't caught a train at all but had dodged out through another station exit. He was cursing himself – she had been almost within reach, if only he hadn't sounded too eager – when she said, 'All right.'

'You'll meet me? Now?' His delight was so extreme that he was sure she wouldn't be able to tell how cold it was.

'As soon as you can get there. Come as quickly as you can.' She gave him directions; it didn't sound far. 'You've got to come alone,' she said, 'and don't tell anyone you're coming.'

'You needn't worry about that.'

She rang off immediately. Smiling tightly, he hurried

177

upstairs for his coat. He hesitated only a moment outside Barbara's door before striding downstairs. Even if she weren't asleep, she would be the last person he would tell where he was going. At last he had the chance to find out for himself what kind of game her persecutors were playing.

25

Chasing the woman from Broomielaw must have taken more out of him than he'd thought. Halfway up the steep road he had to stop, for the raindrops felt like acid on his skin. The black sky squatted over the dripping roofs; a plane or a gust of wind passed overhead. Somewhere a flagpole's cord tapped like an impatient finger. When Ted had taken a few deep breaths he recommenced climbing.

The road was deserted, and so was Sauchiehall Street at the bottom. The sloping tarmac was streaming, the pavements looked oily beneath a couple of street lamps; cars with their tails in the air were parked on blurred impressions of themselves. He climbed past a college that was locked up behind bent spikes and reached Hill Street, where he'd been directed to turn.

Hill Street consisted of terraces with bulging bay windows. Roads plunged from it towards a motorway; graffiti glimmered through the rain on walls, seemed to jerk and writhe; one huge long-legged scrawl looked flattened like a spider against the side of a house. Ted unbuttoned his coat – the rain was lessening, humidity crawled over his skin – as he strode along the terraces. Beyond the porches, flat-dwellers stood talking in lit halls or even sat at tables; people sat on front steps between pillars that were peeling like wallpaper. If the phone call was a trick, as he'd begun to suspect at once, then whoever was responsible wouldn't find it so easy to get him alone.

Soon the houses grew less welcoming. Their stone balconies looked drowned, eroded by the rain. Patches pale as grass beneath a stone gleamed beside porches, where name-

179

plates had been removed. The gardens were a mass of drooling weeds. The empty sockets of street lamps dripped in the dark.

He wasn't nervous, he told himself. He looked daunting enough to deter most attackers, and there was certainly enough of him to take them on, if necessary. Nevertheless it unnerved him to feel watched, though a touch of paranoia was hardly surprising under the circumstances. The scuttling in the gardens behind him was rain. He didn't glance back, for that would have been absurd. In any case, the scuttling was now ahead of him.

A stray headlight beam showed him where he was to turn, at the next side street down to the motorway. A spidery caricature clung to the wall at the corner, amid a web of graffiti. As he reached the street the headlights groped along the terrace and lingered on the wall. It was a mass of graffiti, but he couldn't disentangle from it anything like the long-legged glimmer that he'd seen a few moments ago. Of course it had been only a glimpse, a trick of light and rain.

This street was even steeper than the one he'd climbed. As he went down between a high wall and a building that glistened like tar, he had to stamp to prevent himself from going too fast. He was dazzled by the floodlights high on stalks above the main road, beyond which the windows of tower blocks were feeble candle-flames, but he could make out that the entire sloping street was covered with graffiti. Down at the bottom the caricature with spindly limbs and elongated head must be an after-image, for when he arrived at the foot of the slope, there was nothing like it on the wall.

His knees felt bruised, dislocated by the slope. He stood for a moment and stared along the road, which led over a motorway and two other main roads. At least it was bright as lightning, though that showed him how deserted the pavements were. Only a drunk was picking his way along the thin concrete island between the traffic lanes.

Ted walked quickly to the top of the pedestrian walkway beside which he was meant to wait. Soon the drunk vanished among the grey houses piled on the hills above the road, and the desolation was complete except for cars sweeping by. A flicker of pale movement near the walkway must have been rain in headlights.

The lanes of the road had split into two flyovers which bridged the Inner Ring Road, a four-lane motorway sandwiched between two other roads. Traffic passed constantly on all of them; the noise was appalling. Bushes and shrubs and weeds, white as mould beneath the floodlights, hemmed in the concrete ramp of the walkway. Would whoever met him come up the ramp?

For a while he gazed down there. Leaves twitched with rain, but nothing else moved. He stared at each car that went by, spraying rain, though it was unlikely that whoever was coming would arrive by car; that wouldn't look convincing. There was nothing else to watch. He felt like Cary Grant, waiting in the middle of the desert in the Hitchcock film. Certainly the Inner Ring Road was as desolate.

He'd begun to march back and forth along the pavement, patrolling for lack of anything else to do, before he became suspicious. Suppose it really had been Angela on the phone and they had prevented her from coming? He was unwilling to believe that – he still didn't believe in Angela – but the likely alternative wasn't encouraging. Had he been lured out here so that they could have Barbara to themselves?

They couldn't harm her. If they called they wouldn't be put through to her room, if they dared to go to the hotel they wouldn't be told what room she was in or allowed to go up. Still, he wondered uneasily how soon he could go back to her. Another quarter of an hour – it was one in the morning now. He was patrolling, and arguing mutely with himself, when a face peered up at him from the bushes.

No, it couldn't have been a face. It must have been a

scrap of litter which had caught momentarily in the branches and then had blown away. He had already explained to himself why he felt watched. Even so, when he glimpsed the long pale thing again, gleaming whiter through the whitish leaves – perhaps headlights on the motorway were catching part of the foliage – he went down, to prove to himself there was nothing.

The walkway was much darker than the roads. Foliage made the concrete ramp narrower, fragments of floodlight blinked through the leaves. The undersides of the flyovers swarmed with graffiti. He leaned over the railings and peered into the bushes, but as far as he could tell, they concealed nothing. He hurried down the ramp, to see where it led – to see if anyone was hiding there, watching him.

Halfway down it divided, beside metal arrows whose directions had been scratched out by graffiti. A ramp led down to a pavement at the edge of the Inner Ring Road; a concrete path led above the motorway, parallel to the lanes. He could see there was nobody at the bottom of the ramp. He went along the path between the jerking bushes.

Once he rounded a curve he was surrounded by concrete. The two branches of the road where he'd been waiting led above him, the motorway glared below. Noise pressed in from all sides; he couldn't hear his own footsteps. He could see nothing but roads and slivers of wasteland between them.

Beyond a cobbled slope which led down from the gap between the flyovers, the path curved again between bushes. He stepped forward, though he was sure there would be nothing to see. The thin pale limbs beyond the foliage were stalks, of course, shifting in a humid breeze. When he reached the spot he couldn't even see them. Another empty ramp led up to the pavement opposite the place where he'd waited.

He'd had enough. The desertion was beginning to look

like a joke at his expense. Perhaps that was why they'd brought him here, to teach him not to try to get the better of them. In any case, he'd left Barbara alone long enough: suppose she woke and couldn't find him? He hurried back through the crowd of concrete pillars above the motorway, and round the curve. There he halted. Between him and the ramps, beside the erased metal arrows, two blank-faced men were waiting.

As soon as they saw him their faces grew even blanker. When they stepped forward he turned at once and strode beneath the flyovers. He didn't know if the men were a trap that had been set for him, but he wasn't about to find out here, not while he had a means of escape. He hurried along the stretch of concrete above the motorway – if they caught him there, nobody would hear – to the curve between the shifting bushes. Once he reached the main road he might turn on the men – except that two more, their faces identically blank, were marching down the other ramp towards him.

When he turned, the first two were almost upon him. One of them, a starved youth with monkish hair, he thought he'd seen before. Ted ran at them, looking as fierce as he could, but they blocked his way. A random glare of floodlight through the restless foliage made their faces seem even more like masks.

As soon as the monkish youth was close enough, Ted hit him. His chin felt like a sharp rock inside a thin padding of stubbly flesh. He sat down against the railings above the motorway and clutched his face, but clambered to his feet at once. Though Ted's knuckles felt as if he'd hit them squarely with a hammer, the youth seemed to feel nothing.

The diversion gave Ted the chance to run, though not very far. Two of them caught him by the cobbled slope between the flyovers. When they pinioned his arms he tried to kick one of them in the groin, but lost his balance on the

183

wet concrete. They threw him backward on the slope. Cobbles dug into him, grit and shards of glass stung his hands.

He could still struggle and curse them, even though he couldn't hear himself. It took three of them a while to immobilize him sufficiently for the largest of them to punch him viciously on the back of the neck. At once his head felt like a half-deflated balloon; he grew dizzy and hideously sick. The glare of a lorry above him seemed to burst in his eyes. He felt so dislocated that when the old woman appeared round the curve she meant nothing at all.

But she was a passer-by, an old woman whose hair was white except for a wide silver streak, and she'd seen what they were doing to him. They hadn't noticed her yet, and she was limping away from them as fast as she could. He tried to struggle in order to distract them, though that made his nausea worse. He was willing her to be quick, to get out of sight before they saw her, to call the police or anyone who could help.

She was almost round the curve when she fell. Perhaps that was all – she tripped and fell through a gap between the railings. Headlights flickered through the leaves, everything was oozing through his brain, and he couldn't be sure that a figure had been clinging amid the graffiti beneath the flyover. Perhaps it was only a flurry of branches. Surely nothing with a long whitish head could have scuttled down to drag the old woman into the bushes.

The men heaved him to his feet and rushed him down the path, though his legs were melting. His thoughts were all he could control, and it occurred to him that if any of the drivers saw him they would take him for a drunk who had to be supported home. For a moment he was afraid that his captors were about to fling him on to the motorway. Instead they shoved him into the bushes, twigs clawing at his hands, an undergrowth of litter tripping him. Beyond all this, a ramp composed of rubble led down to a house.

It seemed impossible that a house was there, on an island of waste land beneath the flyovers. It must have been allowed to remain until it was beyond demolishing. He was speculating to convince himself he could at least think clearly, for he was helpless to prevent himself from being carried forward to the house. A grubby curtain parted like a reptile's eyelid; he was expected. The front door opened as he was dragged to it, his heels catching on rubble. The men threw him into the dark hall, and the noise closed in.

26

Barbara couldn't tell if she was dreaming. Sunlight streamed between the curtains and spotlighted her empty rumpled bed, or was she lying there invisible to herself and dreaming that she was looking down at it? If not, was Arthur really somewhere close to her?

He was there, but he was shrinking. If she didn't find him soon he would have gone, and she sensed how anxious he was. She hurried to the window, but none of the heads bobbing by in the street was his. She was on her way to look in the bathroom when she realized how absurdly she was behaving. Her sense of him dwindled at once; his face receded into the darkness of her mind, grew smaller than an atom, and she was fully awake.

And there was nothing to distract her from her fears – from the worst of them, which she hadn't mentioned to Ted because she was afraid to admit it to herself. If the cult had stolen Angela because they feared her power for good, that meant it was too strong for them: Angela's calls proved that her sense of herself had survived – but what might they have done to her, or be planning to do, to break her down?

Nothing too bad, to judge from the tone of her calls – or was she too trusting to realize what they were doing? Suddenly Barbara didn't want to be alone. She pulled on clothes and hurried out to knock on Ted's door. There was no reply.

She knocked more loudly and stared along the corridor. On a tray outside a room one coffee cup was trying clumsily to mount another. Bedroom radios played relentlessly cheerful tunes. When a trolley full of linen nudged open the fire doors she called out to the chambermaid 'What's the time?'

'Nearly ten.'

Her watch wasn't wrong, after all. He'd said he would meet her for breakfast, but he must have decided to let her sleep. She washed hastily and hurried downstairs. A few people were scattered about the spacious restaurant, beneath yellowed chandeliers; an old lady waited to be wheeled away, a man with a silver moustache lowered his newspaper and bade Barbara good morning. The loudest sounds were the rattle of a spoon in a cup, the scrape of a knife on toast. None of the breakfasters was Ted.

One of the waiters thought that Mr Crichton might have breakfasted, though he clearly wasn't sure. She ordered breakfast and tried to be patient; no doubt he'd gone out for a walk. Or could he be searching on her behalf? The last breakfasters strolled away, waiters began to set tables for lunch. All at once her nerves couldn't stand their discreetly muted sounds. She hurried out to the foyer to see if he'd left a message for her.

There was no message, the girl said, but his key was at the desk. She was turning away – an impatient tweedy woman was banging the nipple of the bell on the counter – before Barbara thought to ask when he had left the key. 'I'm afraid I don't know,' the girl said over her shoulder. 'It must have been left before I came on.'

'When was that?'

'Half past six.'

Surely that must have been addressed to the tweedy woman – but when Barbara reflected, that didn't seem an unlikely time for the day staff to begin work. Where could he have gone so early? Even if he'd been unable to sleep – sometimes he was – wouldn't he have left a message unless he had meant to return before now?

When the girl had dealt with the impatient woman she

looked faintly annoyed to find Barbara still waiting. 'Are you absolutely sure that Mr Crichton left no message?' Barbara said.

'Well, if he did it's certainly not here.'

Could the message have been lost? Perhaps that was a reassuring possibility, though not reassuring enough to let Barbara eat breakfast. 'I'm sorry,' she said to the waiter who headed for the kitchen as soon as she appeared, 'I've had some bad news,' and wished at once that she hadn't said so, however guilty he had made her feel.

For a while she waited in the foyer. Guests passed her in slow motion, tapping their walking-sticks, gazing from wheelchairs. The gleam of the revolving doors snagged the edge of her vision, pestered her constantly to glance across and make sure it wasn't Ted. She ought to be glad that he didn't feel tied to her, that he felt free to go out for a walk. His message for her must have gone astray.

Eventually she forced her way through the revolving doors – they juddered for a moment, trapping her in the smeared glass cage with a ghost of pipe tobacco – and waited outside the hotel. Now and then a head rose above the chaos of faces, but it was never Ted's. Wasn't it enough that she couldn't find Angela? She wished she could look for him, but she had no idea where to start. If he returned while she was looking he wouldn't know where she was.

She ventured as far as the opposite pavement and gazed along Sauchiehall Street. One direction led to the Inner Ring Road, where the buildings looked grey as fumes. At the opposite end was a pedestrian precinct, the roadway paved over. People bunched outside the shops, workmen climbed scaffolding outside Charles Rennie Mackintosh's tearoom like spiders rebuilding a web, a board outside a doorway announced the viewing before an auction of books. Ted had wondered what they might be auctioning.

Before she knew she meant to, she was heading for the

auction rooms. She could be there and back in ten minutes or less. It didn't matter where he'd been, only where he was now, only that he was safe. Of course he was, why shouldn't he be? She knew how books could engross him. She wouldn't be surprised if he'd been browsing for an hour or more without realizing.

As she hurried past an enclosed shopping centre a fanfare was sounding. A dangling clock like a toy castle painted gold opened its doors to let out its knights and struck six. She stared at it, past a short-sleeved security officer with hairy tattoos on his forearms, but the face said eleven o'clock. She struggled through the crowd and ran up the steps to Straub, Tessier & King.

At the top of the second flight of steps was a long bare room the size of a bungalow. Ranks of chairs sat before a podium and waited for the auction. Bookcases and trestle tables, dwarfed by the space, displayed books. Booksellers with notebooks glanced at spines, a middle-aged couple with expensive suntans idled, pouting at illustrations. She saw at once that Ted was not there.

She stepped aside as two men carried in a tea-chest piled with books. There wasn't an author's name she knew. A spine said *The Psychic Stream*, but she'd had enough of red herrings. She went dispiritedly back towards the hotel.

A smell of hot bread made her glance into the shopping centre. The figures which had sprouted from the castle while it struck six had withdrawn. Security men wandered about, murmuring to each other with radios. At the end of the hall of shops, beyond a red and yellow cart full of a rock garden whose plants were too large for the rocks, was Ted.

Or perhaps it was someone who looked like him. He was standing before the bread counter, and she could see only his back. She ran down the hall beneath the strip lighting, green and mauve and pink and yellow and blue. The glittering floor looked tiled with Lurex. Shops were singing

189

pop songs, some so faint they might have been hallucinations. Nothing was real except the smell of bread – but when she reached Ted, he looked real enough.

She was so relieved that she had to sit down, on a slippery chair of chocolate plastic. As soon as she had a chance to look at him more closely she cried, 'You've hurt yourself.'

He glanced at his scratched knuckles as if they weren't his. 'It's nothing. Just a cat that wasn't very friendly.'

Even he had never looked so dishevelled before; no doubt that came of getting up so early. 'Where have you been?'

'I was tracing the Undying Light people for you. They're just a fringe religious group like a hundred others. They don't know anything about the kind of thing you're looking for. They'd be scared to know.'

His mood was odd, almost elated: perhaps that was insomnia. Despite her relief she couldn't share his mood, even though he seemed to believe her now, more than he had last night. Her elbows slid from the arms of the chair, which felt thin and hollow. 'What can we do now?' she said.

'Well, we mustn't tell the police about the woman we saw. Now that you've seen her, the nameless will be even more on guard.'

She had already thought of that, but the confirmation made her all the more apprehensive. 'Do you think they'll do something to Angela?'

'No, I shouldn't think so. They've no reason to.'

'Then all we can do,' she said in despair, 'is hope that Gerry managed to find them.'

'I wouldn't be surprised if you saw something of her soon. But no, I think we can do more than hope. Last night I thought that woman might have gone into the station to throw us off the scent, but when I thought about it later I realized that she had a ticket in her hand.'

'I didn't see that. Are you sure?'

'I can see it as clearly as I see you now.'

'Then we're back where we started. They could be anywhere.'

'Well, not quite. I checked the trains that would have been leaving just after we lost her. I've got a list of their destinations. That's where we ought to look.'

It didn't seem much of a lead, but his urgency was infectious. 'We should start with the largest,' he said. 'That must be Edinburgh. We ought to get started at once.'

He stood up quickly, and seemed impatient for her to follow. It was a relief to be led for a change; she felt too exhausted to lead. The smell of bread faded, a rush of faces which she hardly glimpsed carried her away. 'I'm sure of one thing,' he said. 'You'll find nothing in Glasgow.'

27

When Barbara found she was driving downhill she went down to the roundabout and drove back to her starting point, alongside the canal. Beneath a sky that looked sunbleached, Hemel Hempstead was a single monotonous blaze, possessed by the sun. On the canal ripples were slow lightning, swans on the banks were almost blinding. Windows and windscreens charred spots on her vision, as if looking weren't already difficult enough.

She turned left near Sarah-Boo the dressmaker's and drove uphill again. Above the rock gardens and pebble-dashed houses, the maze of cramped boxy houses closed in. She'd driven through once and had come straight back, yet the sloping streets were just as indistinguishable. She didn't know Iris's last name, for they couldn't find the cutting at the *Other News*; she couldn't recall the name of the street or the number of the house. She knew only that it was on a slope, which was true of most of them.

The doors paraded by like samples of paint in a book. Iris's mother had opened the green front door. Iris's mother opened the front door, which was painted red. Beyond the blue front door was Iris's mother. Barbara was appalled that she couldn't remember such a simple detail, but she hadn't realized at the time that she would need to do so.

Somewhere a lawnmower was whirring, children were throwing a striped ball across the driveways and meagre fenceless lawns, but these details seemed too real for the houses, the terraces flat as a street at the back of a stage. Perhaps some of that was the effect of her tension, but not very much. She was going down towards the roundabout before she realized that she'd missed the house again, and all she could do was go round once more. There was nowhere else for her to go.

She had found nothing in Scotland. In Stirling, Dunfermline, Kirkcaldy, Perth, Dundee, Montrose, Aberdeen and the narrow alleys that led behind the wide streets of Edinburgh, there had seemed to be nothing to find. She suspected that her encounter with the lopsided woman had scared them off to another part of the country. Barbara had gone back to her office to find none of the messages she'd hoped for, only a great deal of interest in Cherry Newton-Brown.

In more than one way that made her feel worse. The interest in the Newton-Brown novel was considerably greater than she had anticipated, which meant that her judgement was slipping. That was hardly surprising under the circumstances, but she couldn't make excuses to herself. She had been hoping to conduct the Paul Gregory auction from London – though it would be less difficult to conduct it in New York, she didn't think she could bear to leave the country as things were – but now she would have to go to New York to show the Newton-Brown to publishers, for it was too important a novel just to send. She was booked to leave in less than a week, but she couldn't make up her mind to leave until she'd tried to question the one person she knew had seen Angela.

The glaring shadowless houses trundled by. Television aerials were gleaming cracks in the blue gloss of the sky. Doors said yellow, orange, purple, and meant nothing. The children were still catching the ball, a striped cut-out which somehow was bouncing. Perhaps she could ask them where Iris lived, except that there was no reason why they should know. Their parents might, but why should their parents tell Barbara? They had no reason not to be suspicious of her. They would back into their shells, beyond the glossy doors, the neatly gathered curtains. In some of the impeccably symmetrical gaps between curtains, dolls were standing. All at once she remembered, and was searching.

She had to make a fourth circuit before she saw the purple gleam. Until she was at the end of the lawn she couldn't be sure – the gleam was bright as a knife – but yes, it was the lustre ballerina. She turned off the ignition and sat for a few minutes. Did she really want to know what the cult might be doing to Angela? Could she bear not to know?

As she ventured along the path towards the house she wobbled; Ted caught her by the elbow. She thought someone peered out of an upstairs window, but when she glanced up, there was nobody. Perhaps it had been Iris's mother, dodging out of sight of the unwelcome visitors, for they had to ring three times before Maisie came to the door. She frowned up at Ted to let him know she wasn't daunted. 'What do you want?' she said to Barbara.

'I wondered if I could have a word with you.'

'I'm afraid it isn't convenient. I'm very busy. Looking after my daughter,' she said with heavy emphasis. Perhaps she felt that was cruel, for she said more gently, 'was it only me you wanted to speak to?'

There was no point in lying. 'I really wanted to speak to Iris.'

'Well, you know I sympathize with you, but I'm afraid that isn't possible. For one thing, my husband wouldn't want you to.'

'He works near home, doesn't he?' Ted said. 'Shall I go and get him? Perhaps he would change his mind.'

Barbara wished he had kept quiet, however helpful he meant to be; after what she'd told him of George on the way, he ought to realize he was making it more difficult for her. He had distracted Maisie, who said, 'Are you another reporter?'

'No, he's just a friend of mine. The reporter you met is trying to infiltrate the group that stole your daughter, and we've been searching as well. We've come close, we traced them up to Scotland, but now I have to go to America without even knowing where they've taken my child.'

'If it upsets you so much you shouldn't go.'

'It isn't as simple as that,' Ted interrupted. 'People depend on her for their living. If she doesn't go she might just as well give up her job.'

'I think she's all right, she keeps phoning me. I only want to know what they might do to her,' Barbara said, and felt ready to weep.

Perhaps Maisie was afraid that Barbara would faint or break down outside her house. Several children were watching from the doorstep opposite. 'Come in and sit down for a few minutes,' Maisie said. 'At least I can give you a cup of tea before you go.'

Nothing had changed in the pinstriped front room. Only Ted made it seem shrunken. Maisie was murmuring upstairs; Barbara thought she heard, 'Don't come down.' She must already have made the tea for herself and Iris, for almost at once she wheeled in a trolley with cups and a pot. She seemed wary of Ted, and Barbara could understand why: she was small beside Barbara – Ted could have picked her up with one hand. Still, the idea of fearing Ted was laughable. 'How is Iris?' Barbara said.

'Better than she was. Some days she's quite chatty. I want to keep her that way.'

'We've found out more about the people who stole her.' Ted was gulping his tea as if he couldn't feel how hot it was; the cup was a small fragile shell in his hand. 'We know what one of them looks like. If we described her, that might shock your daughter into remembering.'

'I don't want her shocked at all.' Maisie couldn't be more dismayed than Barbara; what on earth did he think he was

195

doing? Before Barbara could interrupt, Maisie said, 'How do you know what this person looks like?'

'Because she followed us in Glasgow,' Ted said.

'Followed you?' The cup in Maisie's hand jerked, spitting. 'But then they could have followed you here!'

'Well,' Ted began, and seemed in such an insensitive mood that he might even have agreed with her if Barbara hadn't intervened. 'The woman knows we saw her,' she said. 'In fact, we nearly caught her. I'm sure they won't dare follow us again.'

'How do you know? There could be someone you haven't noticed.'

'I'm sure there isn't,' Barbara said, and wondered if there was. 'But look, we'll leave as soon as we can if our being here makes you nervous. Surely you could let me have five minutes with Iris? Of course I won't shock her, I only want to talk to her. Ted will stay downstairs, won't you, Ted?'

Maisie didn't look at him, which was just as well, for he seemed unwilling to comply. 'You've already seen her once,' she said.

'But there's something I didn't think to ask her.' All at once Barbara was happy to continue arguing, in fact anxious to keep the conversation going, for she and Ted were nearer the hall than Maisie was, and Barbara could hear what the mother was missing: someone was coming downstairs. 'I should have asked her if there was a child who kept mentioning her mother. I don't know if Gerry Martin told you – she was the reporter who brought me here – but Angela, that's my daughter, keeps phoning me. If she trusted your daughter more than the others she might have mentioned me.'

She was babbling, not even sure if she believed all of what she was saying, but the footsteps were descending, padded no doubt by carpet and slippers, and Maisie didn't

196

hear. 'I've shown her the photograph you left,' Maisie said. 'She would have said if your daughter had mentioned you.'

'Not if she didn't recognize the photograph. Presumably she wouldn't know Angela by name, presumably as far as Iris was concerned she didn't have one. If I could ask her directly she might remember,' Barbara said, and made a grab for Ted. She was too late; he stood up quickly and opened the door as the footsteps reached the hall. 'Hello, Iris,' he said.

Barbara could have kicked him. No doubt he meant to catch Iris before her mother hid her safely away, but what must the already disturbed girl be seeing? A door had opened in her home, a burly stranger was waiting for her – it was no wonder that she flinched back, staring up at him.

Maisie ushered her into the room, well away from him. 'You know this lady. She brought the picture of her little girl to show you. This gentleman is a friend of hers,' she said, glaring at Ted.

When Iris was settled – she sat as if she were made of china, afraid of breaking – Barbara tried to question her gently, despite her mother's open disapproval. But the girl seemed unable to look away from Ted, and the longer she stared the more visibly nervous she grew. Barbara wanted to hear that the cult hadn't tried to destroy Angela, that having captured her was enough, but how could she frame her question so that Iris wouldn't be reminded of whatever had made her break down? Ted must be growing restless as Iris gazed at him, for he stood up and leaned beside the window. That only distracted Iris more, made her shrink further into herself. She hadn't said a word. 'Ted,' Barbara said as calmly as she could, 'will you wait for me outside?'

'He needn't wait for you. You can both go.' Maisie was watching her daughter's hands crawling over each other in search of comfort, crawling more and more desperately. 'I'm sorry, I won't listen to any more. I'll ask her your

197

questions as soon as I think I can. I've still got your address.'

Halfway round the two-way roundabout Barbara's head began swimming. Ted stopped the car beyond the roundabout just in time for her to stagger to the grass verge and vomit her cup of tea. Eventually he got out of the car and stood by her, watching her so calmly he must mean to be reassuring. When she felt able to return to the car he drove more slowly through the sluggish waves of heat towards the motorway. 'I know I ruined that for you,' he said, then he smiled at the unstable landscape. 'But I've thought of something else I can do.'

28

As Iris glanced at the mirror on the dressing-table she saw movement behind her in the sunlit bed, a grub-like writhing beneath the sheets. It was about to nudge the sheets aside, and then she would see what it was. For a moment she felt as she'd felt yesterday – her limbs wanted to clasp her so tightly that she would be squeezed too small for anything to reach – then she realized that the movement was only the shadow of the curtain that was trailing over the bed. She was home now. Nothing could harm her. The bad wasn't here, even though it had come visiting.

When she reached for the top drawer her hand faltered. In the street a small boy was singing a song, blurring the words like a radio whose batteries were failing; down the hill someone was clipping a hedge, the sound tinier than scissors; inside her room the sunlight kept everything still, and yet she was afraid it might not be able to do so for long, not now that the bad had seen where she was.

But that was why she had to search. The thought jerked her into motion, made her open the drawer. There was nothing but her father's underwear, nothing lay in wait for her as she leafed hastily through. Of course the address wouldn't be in there; the woman had given it to Iris's mother. She knelt down and pulled out the next drawer. She had to be quick, before her mother found out what she was doing. Her mother wouldn't let her if she knew.

Perhaps her mother was right sometimes. Yesterday she had told Iris to stay upstairs until the visitors had gone. Iris had crept downstairs – she wasn't a child to be told to stay in her room, she felt as if she never had been, she was piecing herself together out of the present, having forgotten almost the whole of her past – and then the door had opened, and the huge bearded man was there.

As soon as she saw his eyes she had known what he was. All the nameless had that hidden look that nobody else could recognize, that look as if something had eaten them away from within until they were shells of themselves. She'd begun to shrink into herself at once. The worst of it was that he'd called her by her name, which she had only just started to believe was hers. The nameless wouldn't even let her have her name to cling to, to drag herself out of their reach.

She had to tell the woman what he was, the woman who was looking for her daughter. She could think of nobody else to tell; certainly her mother wouldn't want to know. 'You're home now, Iris. Don't think about those things.' She wanted to believe that Iris had forgotten, and perhaps one day Iris would.

Could her mother have thrown the woman's address away? She hadn't bothered to write it in her address book. But yesterday she'd told the woman that she still had her address, and her mother wouldn't lie. It had to be somewhere in here.

Perhaps it was in one of her mother's dresses in the wardrobe. She was hurrying across the room, past the bed where the fat writhing lump was nothing but a pillow troubled by shadows, when she heard her mother on the stairs. 'Where are you, Iris?'

'In here.' She was able to talk quite easily now; it was only when the subject turned to things she didn't want to remember that her lips began to feel like worms. She had to look as if she had a reason to be in her mother's room. She snatched up her mother's photograph album and sat on the bed.

'That's right, Iris. You sit in here if you want to.' As soon as she'd assured herself that Iris seemed all right, her mother went downstairs. Iris had the feeling that her mother had always been like that, wanting to believe that nothing was troubling Iris, constantly checking and pretending not to do so. For a moment, as she gazed at the photograph of herself and her parents beneath the pointed bulbs of Brighton Pavilion, Iris felt close to remembering – but she had to find the address. She stood up, careful not to disturb the bulge under the sheets, and went to the wardrobe.

The card was in the third dress she searched. *Barbara Waugh: Literary Agent*, it said. It must have been dry-cleaned with the dress, for the handwriting on the back was almost too faint to read; she could just make out an address in the Barbican. She closed the wardrobe hastily, because she was almost remembering a dim room where the object dangling in a wardrobe had not been clothes at all, for it had started writhing like a worm on a hook. Perhaps that was only a nightmare that felt like a memory because she had so few memories. She hurried to her room.

Now she had to be quick. She laid out her notepaper. It smelled years old, which it was. She had no stamp, but she thought she knew where she could get one. Above the hum of the town a clock was chiming five. Her father would arrive at the station before six. If she weren't there well before then, her plan would fail.

As soon as she picked up the pen it twitched out of her hand. She couldn't write about the nameless any more than she could speak about them. That trace of the bad was left in her, and she was close to remembering things she'd helped to do, remembering the time she'd fallen in the dark of one of the bricked-up rooms and tried to tell herself that she had touched a coil of slimy rope. The threat of memory blanked out her mind at once, to her relief. At least the memories were no longer tempting.

She could write about the bearded man. He had come later than her memories; the nameless couldn't stop her telling about him. She had to tell someone, so that they would catch the nameless before the nameless got to her. She could write, though her hand was shaking. But the clock was chiming the quarter, and she had written nothing.

Suddenly she thought she knew what to do. She wrote the address on the envelope. She had to write the whole address in large capitals, for her hand was shaking so badly that anything else would have been illegible; there was barely room for a stamp. Then, as if it was part of the same action, she wrote THE MAN YOU BROUGHT TO SEE ME IS A NAMELESS, THEY CAN MAKE HIM DO ANYTHING THEY WANT. IRIS and stuffed the page into the envelope. She licked the flap so hurriedly that she cut her tongue, then she went downstairs as quickly as she could, hiding the letter in a pocket of her dress. She was afraid her hands would retrieve the letter in spite of her and tear it up. 'Shall we go and meet Daddy?' she said.

'Yes, if you like.' At least this part of the plan was easy; her mother looked surprised and pleased. Sometimes they took Iris for an evening stroll, when there was less traffic. It must look as if Iris was improving.

Her mother took her time in getting ready. As far as she knew they had plenty of time. She would have strolled down the hill to the road, except that Iris hurried. No doubt her mother was pleased that Iris wasn't holding back from the traffic.

Down by the Whip & Collar, on the road beside the canal, the noise of traffic was an invisible wall. Iris braced herself to shoulder through it, but it was growing louder every second, jerking her nerves. Suddenly there was a gap in the traffic, and her mother ushered her across to the footpath which led down to the canal.

By the canal it was much quieter. Reflections of trees

drifted like waterweed. In the football field on the opposite bank, horses and cows munched grass between the goal-posts. A barge was waiting for the lock to fill; several young men with bare varnished torsos watched from the deck as Iris passed. Of course they were on a canal holiday, they were nothing to do with the nameless.

When the clock chimed the half hour she made herself walk faster, even though the road bridge was ahead. On both sides of the canal the noise of traffic was kept at bay by wide fields, except where the bridge crossed the canal. As she hurried underneath the water grew dark, metallic; she was trapped in a concrete box by noise that was closing off both ends – but she broke through the noise and pushed open the squeaking gate that gave on to the avenue.

Nothing could stop her now. The horse chestnuts closed over the path, where she'd gathered conkers as a child. Metal claws encircled the tree trunks, to discourage climbing. There was the steeple next to the gasworks, which had used to remind her of Laurel and Hardy. In the lush grass by the canal, horses stood by their reclining foals. It wasn't yet a quarter to six when the women reached the pub by the station and Iris said, 'I've got to go to the toilet. You don't need to come in with me. I won't be long.'

'All right, dear.' Her mother looked a little anxious, but pleased that Iris felt able to venture into the pub by herself.

A few early drinkers stood at the sharply curved bar. Above the toilet door a car's number plate said 4U2P, but that wasn't really what she wanted. She went straight to the woman behind the bar. 'I've got to post a letter urgently,' she said; she had been practising silently for hours. 'Can you sell me a stamp?'

'Just a minute and I'll see.' She rummaged in her bag for more than a minute; the quarter-chime drifted in the window. Iris's mother must be wondering what had happened: suppose she came in to make sure that Iris hadn't sneaked in for a drink?

The woman looked up from her handbag. 'No, I'm sorry. I thought I had.'

When Iris turned dejectedly from the bar – she had been utterly unprepared for her plan to go wrong – a small face packed with features and red veins was waiting just beneath her. She cringed into herself, but he was only a pensioner, a head shorter than she was. 'Is it very urgent?' he said.

'Yes.' She couldn't say more, for her lips felt as if they were swelling.

'I was keeping this because I liked the picture.' He gave her a stamp on which Peter Rabbit towered over Queen Elizabeth's bodiless head. 'I suppose I can get another,' he said wistfully.

She stuck the stamp on her envelope before he could change his mind. As soon as she'd given him the money she ran out, stuffing the letter out of sight. Her mother started up the ramp towards the station at once.

Embedded in the wall just outside the station was a postbox. Iris hadn't time to hesitate, in case her mother looked back to see why she was lagging. Here was the mouth in the wall, and she could only snatch out the letter and push it into the dark. For a moment she felt apprehensive, but how else could she have protected herself? She hurried to catch up with her mother.

A train rushed through with a shrill hollow roar. A glazed face peered at her through the ticket window. Everything felt withheld from her: the small two-platform station, the sunlight so relentless it was unconvincing. The letter was locked away. Nothing could stop it now.

Soon a train brought her father. He didn't seem entirely pleased to see her, and stared at her mother, whom he hadn't yet forgiven for letting Barbara Waugh in yesterday. 'Are you better today?' he asked Iris.

'Yes.' Both her parents were here to protect her now, nothing could harm her. Then she saw the Post Office van driving away from the postbox, on to the main road and swiftly out of sight, and all at once she was terrified. She had been too preoccupied with tricking her mother to realize what she was doing. She would have been safe if she hadn't written the letter – the bearded man had seen she was no threat. Now she had betrayed the nameless, and she could feel that they knew.

All at once she remembered the day she had left them, the day she'd been so stunned by what she had just helped to do that she'd wandered out of their house without thinking. She had been so unaware of herself that perhaps they and their power hadn't even noticed her leaving. Somehow she'd caught a train home, and she had been halfway there when something had found her. Without any warning she had no longer been alone in the deserted sunlit railway carriage. After that she remembered nothing for weeks, until one day she'd found herself back in her room at home, apparently safe – safe until now.

She followed her parents into the sunlight, as if that was any help. Now they were leading her on to the avenue. Couldn't they see how dark it was beneath the trees, how their metal claws gleamed? Didn't they realize that anything might drop from the low foliage or crawl out of the long grass? The nameless had once told her that she would never be able to betray them, but that if she ever tried, they would know. She remembered that now, too late. All the way along the avenue a horse paced her, staring. When her parents saw that it was troubling her they attempted to shoo it away.

The gate squealed, and they were waiting for her to go under the bridge. Her mother was in front of her, her father was behind, but they couldn't stop the noise from closing in. Now she remembered why it frightened her: it was like the noise in the decrepit houses where she'd had to live. Could the bad get into it too? The nameless must be more powerful now. They'd felt they were close to their goal, whatever it might be; the things they did – the things she'd helped to do – had brought them closer still.

'Go on, Iris,' her father said impatiently. She was so frightened that he might push her that she stepped forward at once. As soon as she was beneath the bridge the noise walled up both ends of the passage; the water was slowing, congealing into a grey corrugated strip. The noise was closing around her, a thick dim medium, impalpable yet obstructive. She could feel her movements slowing.

Her parents didn't notice. They marched onward, taking her with them, and somehow she was out of the trap of the bridge. Sunlight seized her, but at least that was neutral. Trees stood on their heads in the water, drowning. Across the canal a ball clicked against a cricket bat. A train squealed along the distant line like a fingernail along a blackboard. At least she was in the open now, and close to home, but how safe was her home? There was nothing in sight to harm her; nothing moved except the small shape above her. She glanced up.

It was a bird, which dropped at once. She flinched back, but it wasn't attacking her. It fell on the path at her feet. Though it was still moving, it was covered with blood.

'Dear God,' her father said, and blocked her view as they hurried her past. Did he think someone had shot the bird, or that a predator had dropped it? More likely he didn't think about it at all, for he certainly would not have believed what he was seeing. But when she glanced uncontrollably back she saw that it was true enough. The twitching bird had been turned inside out like a glove.

They were telling her that they knew what she'd done,

and that they could do anything. She would be no safer at home. She remembered the writing beneath the sheets, and what else would be waiting for her? She sat down on the bank of the canal. Dry grass pricked her legs and arms, her parents were calling her and then calling louder, but these distractions were already fading. Her limbs had folded tight around her, pressing her down into the dark inside herself where nothing could reach.

29

When the girls came chattering out of the school by the lake, their hair and their wine-red uniforms streaming in the wind, Barbara realized it was noon. Ted should have been here by now. She leaned out of her window and peered through her struggling hair, but could see nobody except a postman on the Barbican walkways. She wished Ted would hurry, for he was giving her doubts time to revive.

When she called his number there was no reply, yet she could see that he was at home; figures were moving beyond his window. Had something happened which would prevent him from helping her? But it was too late to hope. She was too heavily committed by now.

The September wind was unexpectedly chilly. The willows groped about the brick plateau, the inverted church was shivering. The postman was on his way to her flat, but she hadn't time to accost him; she was too busy fighting the gusts along the walkways, the wind which flapped her clothes and tousled her hair into her eyes. The chatter of schoolgirls kept rushing across the water like waves.

She was on the steps to the balcony which ran outside Ted's flat when someone took hold of her shoulder. Only a grab at the railing saved her from a fall. It must have been the wind, but for a moment she'd thought someone had tugged at her shoulder to stop her from climbing the steps. For that moment she had thought of Arthur.

She rang Ted's doorbell, rang again. Wind came floundering along the balcony. She was about to knock as well as ring when the door was opened, but not by Ted. It was a woman who looked older than she was, a headscarf knotted tightly around her tired face. Her eyes grew more pinched as she said, 'You're Barbara Waugh.'

Only one woman could greet her so coldly. 'You're – '

'Yes, I used to be his wife. You know, I often meant to confront you, but I'm glad I didn't bother. You're just about what I expected.' Ted appeared behind her in the hall, and she stepped out on to the balcony. 'I only wonder if you know how much you've changed him,' she said bitterly. 'Even his own child doesn't recognize him now. I expect you'll be satisfied now that you have him all to yourself.'

She stalked away along the balcony, her headscarf quivering. Barbara followed Ted into the flat while he found his keys. Her encounter with Helen had been too quick and unexpected to upset her, but it raised questions, none of which she particularly wanted to ask. Before she could say anything she noticed the typescript in a folder on the couch. 'Have you finished your novel?' she said.

'It looks like it. Take it with you if you like.'

'Yes, I will. I'll read it on the plane.' She felt he needed encouraging; he sounded utterly indifferent to the novel, as if it was nothing to do with him. Perhaps that was because of Helen. 'What was that scene all about just now?' she had to ask.

He was rushing her out of the flat. 'Oh, just something about Judy. She hasn't been the same towards me since I went to Scotland.'

'Do you mean she was jealous because you went with me? Tell me the truth.'

A crosswind dragged his voice out of shape; he couldn't really be laughing. 'You could be right,' he said.

He was hurrying her so fast she could hardly think. 'But is that all? It seems so little reason for her mother to come to see you.'

'Helen exaggerates, I've told you that before. This was just an excuse.'

'An excuse for what? She doesn't mean to try to stop you from seeing Judy, does she?'

'I don't know. Anyway, it doesn't matter now. We've got to make sure you don't miss your plane.'

He must be stunned by Helen's visit, or pretending to be unconcerned. As soon as she unlocked her door he hurried past her. 'I'll get your luggage if you'll tell me where it is.'

He stopped at once, for he'd stumbled over several letters, kicking them along the hall. He stooped quickly and picked them up. He peered closely at one, then slipped it into his pocket. 'That isn't for you. I'll deliver it later. No time now.'

It hadn't looked like anything for Barbara: it had been addressed in large straggly capitals that hardly left room for the stamp. The other letters were negligible. Ted was already striding back along the hall with her luggage. He was so eager to send her on her way that she almost forgot to give him the spare set of keys.

On the way to Heathrow Airport neither of them said much. Beyond Hounslow the fields looked frozen by the blue ice of the sky. At times Ted seemed hardly conscious of driving. He must be preoccupied with Judy, and that was Barbara's fault.

When he noticed her worried glance at him, he misinterpreted it. 'It'll be all right,' he said. 'Everything's under control. I'll be in your flat at the times you would be. If there are any calls you can be sure they'll be answered.'

She knew all that – he'd spent the whole of the drive back from Hemel Hempstead in persuading her – yet when it was time to check in for her flight she wasn't sure that she could go through with it. He would stay in her flat every night she was in New York, she had told him things that only Angela could know, she would be able to check with him as she couldn't with Gerry, but was all that enough? It was too late to doubt that it was; Ted had put her cases on the belt and they were sailing away, like coffins into a crematorium. 'Don't worry,' he said, gripping her arm so hard that it hurt. 'If Angela calls I'll know exactly what to do.'

30

The Gregory auction lasted two days, and when it was over Barbara felt as though nothing existed but her suite at the Algonquin, the Thurber cartoon of a huge puffy woman louring over a tiny victim, the monochrome view of West 44th through the high Victorian bay, the closet which seemed large enough to hide Woollcott and Benchley and Dorothy Parker and the rest of the old crowd. She called Paul to tell him that the bidding had ended in the millions, and got Sybil instead, who sounded grudgingly enthusiastic.

After the auction, Barbara couldn't relax. She might have given a party in her suite – she'd done so last time, and her bed had been spirited away at once – but she was too busy meeting editors in order to promote the Newton-Brown novel. Between meetings she tried to stroll. Invisible choirs sang Schoenberg in Bryant Park, jewellers' displays on East 47th glittered as if they were still crystallizing, reflections of skyscrapers sagged and melted on the giant curved slope of the Monsanto Building. She couldn't go very far from the hotel, for she was afraid that Ted might call.

Still, though she felt tired and edgy, her restlessness had paid off. The interest in the Newton-Brown book was intense, and she could conduct the auction from London. She had only to meet an editor to discuss Ted's novel, and then she could change her reservation to the next available flight home.

She was on her way to freshen up when the phone rang. It was Cathy Darnell, a friend and also the editor who had been looking at Ted's novel. 'Come up,' Barbara told her.

Was she early because she was anxious to buy the novel? Barbara had skimmed through it on the plane, but had been too worried to judge it properly; she had been wondering how Angela would react if she rang her flat and heard a man's voice. Suppose she thought that the cult had intercepted her call? Barbara could only hope that Ted would be able to persuade her to the contrary.

Soon Cathy appeared, in a long loose dress and a ponytail. The September mugginess looked to have condensed among the down on her upper lip. They kissed politely, then Barbara hurried to the bathroom, across whose threshold time leapt forward several decades.

She was halfway through washing, her eyes stinging with soap, when the phone rang again. 'I'll get it,' Cathy called.

Barbara rinsed her face quickly and turned off the water in time to hear Cathy say, 'I'm sorry, this line isn't too good. Could you repeat your name?'

All at once Barbara was apprehensive. She hurried out of the bathroom, rubbing her face with the towel. Before she could reach the phone Cathy said, 'Yes, I have it now. Could you just hold on one moment, please.'

She turned wide-eyed to Barbara, one hand deafening the phone. 'It's Laurence Dean,' she said, pronouncing it Law. 'He wants to speak to you.'

Of course Barbara knew who he was – he'd produced several phenomenally successful films – yet she felt wary; she had nearly finished her business in New York, she wanted to go home. 'What does he want, do you know?'

'You'd better ask him that yourself. He's very strong on doing things properly.'

His soft Californian voice sounded gentlemanly, but very quiet; Barbara had to strain her ears. 'I plan to be in New York early next week, Mrs Waugh,' he said, 'and I believe you will be there. I wonder if you would be free to meet.'

'Well, I was rather intending to go back to England

213

tomorrow.' Cathy was gaping at her, gesturing at her to change her approach. 'Did you want to discuss anything in particular? Sorry, hold on just a moment,' she said, for Cathy was gesturing wildly.

'He won't commit himself except face to face,' Cathy said when she was sure he couldn't hear. 'If you try to pump him he'll lose interest, but believe me, he never calls an agent unless he's very interested in one of her properties. You have to meet him, Barbara. It's got to be something big.'

'That's all very well, Cathy. I'm sorry, please go on,' she told the phone.

'I've been reading some books which I believe you handle,' the faint voice said patiently. 'I think it might be useful for us to meet.'

'Which books do you mean?'

Cathy clapped a hand to her forehead in dismay and closed her eyes. 'I believe you have a client by the name of Paul Gregory,' the faint voice said.

'Yes, that's right.' She felt helpless, trapped by his interest. When he suggested they meet on Tuesday she agreed, then opened her mouth to snatch back her agreement just as he rang off. Her dismay must have been visible, for Cathy said, 'Did he beg off? Oh, Barbara, I told you he would.'

Barbara told her what he'd said as they went downstairs, following the curlicued iron banisters into the leathery gloom of the lobby, where publishers sat talking. 'Barbara, that's terrific. I'm sure this is the first time he's ever committed himself to that extent. It sounds like a very big deal.'

Barbara tried to look pleased, but she was grateful for the gloom among the plants and dark panels. On the lobby newstand a small headline said CALIFORNIA CULTISTS CHARGED; there was always something to remind her, it seemed. 'We'll go out for a drink,' Cathy said firmly. 'You've been cooped up in here for a while.'

214

She took her to a bar on Sixth Avenue. Scraps of Bartók drifted through the traffic, from Bryant Park. A film crew had roped off several blocks of the Avenue, where Ricky Schroeder was emerging from Radio City Music Hall. Barbara found the self-assured professionalism of the eight-year-old face rather chilling.

The bar was small and dark. A few men sat drinking at the polished counter and watching a television set on which everyone looked raw as pork. Between the drinkers' elbows were dim smears, reflections of their faces. The women sat in a booth and ordered Black Russians. After a couple of sips Cathy said, 'Can I help?'

'I don't think so, Cathy. Thanks for asking. It's domestic, nothing to do with business.'

'So let's talk business. I liked Ted Crichton's novel a lot. It needs work, but I'll happily make you an offer.'

A blurred pink President of the United States snapped into the television frame. The newscaster's loud voice kept becoming entangled with Cathy's. 'That's good news,' Barbara said, trying to concentrate on her job. 'Are there particular areas of the book you think need work?'

'He'll have to work on the early chapters. It's the later scenes that really sold me on the book – you know, from where the private eye finds out her best friend is in league with the organization. But that's a bit too abrupt as it stands. He needs to leave a few clues early on. Right now it looks as if he thought of it late in the writing.'

'I'll tell him.' Several people smeared with television pink were being led into a courthouse, hiding their faces from the cameras. 'Or you could write to him care of me. He isn't officially a client of mine.'

'You'll agent him now, won't you?'

'I've always felt one shouldn't agent one's friends. It complicates the relationship in all sorts of ways.' She was trying to listen to the newscaster. When Cathy began to speak Barbara gestured her to keep quiet, and was dismayed by the violence of her own gesture. The courthouse and the furtive dishevelled figures had been swept away, the newscaster was chattering about pollution. 'What did he just say about not being able to find out someone's names?' Barbara demanded.

'I couldn't say. I wasn't listening.'

'Something about people being brought before a court which had to charge them without knowing all their names.'

'Oh, that would be those freaks in California. Didn't you hear about that? No, I guess you were too deep in your auction. Well, it was sort of a legal precedent – the police couldn't find out most of their names, and they had to give them aliases so that the court could charge them.'

Barbara's arms were beginning to stiffen with tension; she put down her glass. 'What else do you know about them, Cathy? Can you tell me everything you remember?'

'I didn't take much notice. It's a weird place, California. But these were a kind of colony of freaks, I believe, who were into some very bad things, black magic and torture and that sort of stuff. There kept being rumours about them, but nobody could track them down until just now. That's one thing I do remember. The police had the impression that some of them made sure they were found, because they were scared of the things they were getting into.'

Barbara found she was shivering, even before Cathy said, 'The part that upset me was that some of them had children. I mean, can you imagine how those kids are going to grow up?'

Barbara tried to pick up her drink, but had to leave it before she shook it over the side of the glass. 'Who could tell me more about them?' she managed to ask.

Cathy peered at her. 'This is important to you, isn't it? All right, stay here while I make a phone call. I've got a few contacts in broadcasting.'

Barbara was grateful that Cathy hadn't tried to question

216

her further. The heads of the men at the bar nodded forward as their right hands lifted their drinks; the rest of their bodies might have been paralyzed. Wrestlers grappled in the air, and she couldn't tell if the patches of red on the raw flesh were leaking colour or blood. Eventually Cathy beckoned her to the alcove at the far end of the bar. 'How badly do you want to know?' she said.

'Very badly.' Barbara had to hold on to the counter; her nails skidded on polished wood. 'Please let me speak to them,' she said urgently.

'This isn't the person you need.' To the phone she said, 'All right, have her call Barbara Waugh collect at the Algonquin Hotel.' She replaced the receiver and smiled as if Barbara should be happy. 'She'll call you in a couple of hours.'

That sounded like eternity. 'Can't I call her now?'

'Well, I don't think so. She's a contact of my contact. I mean, it's three hours earlier in California. She's most likely on her way to work.' She held Barbara's arm as though she could stop it from shaking. 'Try to relax. Tell me about it if it would help.'

'No, I can't.' She would only imagine worse things if she talked about it now. 'I can't,' she said dully.

'Never mind. Come and finish your drink.' But if someone was meant to call her at the hotel, Barbara had to go back there at once. When Cathy saw that she couldn't steer her into the booth she followed her on to the street. 'I'll walk with you as far as the Algonquin. We can talk about the Crichton deal next week if you'd rather, when you've dealt with this other thing. Don't let it get on top of you, all right? My mother used to say something I've always found to be worth remembering – nothing is ever as bad as you think it is.'

31

When Barbara hurried into the Algonquin the gloom settled on her eyes at once. The lobby was crowded; pale balloons of faces came bobbing in clusters out of a gloom that felt thickened by their hubbub. Her hand brushed the cold greasy leaf of a potted plant, her other hand touched a face at the level of her hip, a face that felt like dough. It must have been a child.

Barbara struggled to the news-stand, but couldn't find the headline that she'd seen. Perhaps it was on an inside page that had been exposed by mistake. She bought a copy of each newspaper and made for the stairs, which were often quicker than the lift. Though her eyes were adjusting, she still felt threatened by the crowd who could see her but whom she couldn't see.

She had almost passed the desk before the clerk saw her. 'Mrs Waugh, there was a call for you.'

Cathy had been wrong: her contact had called while Barbara was away from the hotel. No doubt now she had gone out reporting, and Barbara couldn't even find out who she was; Cathy wouldn't be home for hours. But the clerk consulted a note and said, 'A Mr Crichton called you from London about half an hour ago.'

Why couldn't he have left a message? Barbara ran along the corridor towards her suite, past glossy black doors, giant negatives set in the white walls. In each of them she looked close to developing, a running smudge with paler blurs for face and limbs. In one of the rooms a muffled phone was ringing. When she managed to unlock her door, after a flurry beneath the bulbous gaze of the peephole, the phone was still ringing, but it wasn't hers.

She threw the papers on the floor of the sitting-room and began to dial at once. Halfway through she faltered, muttering as though she were having a nightmare, for she had forgotten her home number. Six three eight, she muttered, six three eight, and was beginning to wonder how one called Directory Enquiries in England when she remembered the number. She dialled once and listened to what sounded like the jangling of rusty springs, dialled again and heard a phone ringing, presumably hers. There was no reply.

She remembered the number of Ted's flat without difficulty, but it was no use. Thousands of miles away but close against her ear, his phone rang on and on. Her watch showed nearly one o'clock, which meant the time was approaching six o'clock in London. She'd dialled Melwood-Nuttall fast and accurately, and the office phone had rung several times, before she remembered this was Saturday: nobody would be there.

She replaced the receiver gently, to help herself not to lose control, then she gazed at it as though it was a bomb. It glinted back at her, a black lump of silence. By now the time in California was ten o'clock, and perhaps the reporter had been given the message to call her. What had Ted wanted to tell her? Whichever of them called first might stop the other from calling.

She began to search the newspapers, to prevent herself brooding. Soon the floor around her was covered with shootings, bombings, kidnappings. At last she found the headline on a back page, but the report said far less about the cult than about its leader, a man whose name was now known to be Jasper Gance.

Or perhaps it was Kaspar Ganz. That was the name under which he had posed as a psychiatrist in order to visit Death Row on the pretext of doing research. The more atrocious the crime, the more anxious he had been to interview the murderer. After he had been exposed he'd been examined by a psychiatrist himself, who had diagnosed a morbid fascination with sadism and mutilation. Ganz or Gance had been imprisoned shortly before the Second World War, but after the attack on Pearl Harbor he had been drafted. Since then nothing had been heard of him until now.

Here was a fuller version of the psychiatrist's report than had been published at the time, and Barbara was appalled that Ganz had ever been released. He believed that the worst murders were inexplicable in terms of the psychology of the criminals. One of the criminals he'd interviewed had described a sense of being either close to something or part of something which the act of torturing had never quite allowed him to glimpse – a sense that he was trying to assuage a hunger which was larger than he was. Ganz had argued that he and all the rest – Gilles de Rais, Jack the Ripper, Peter Kürten – had been driven to experience the worst crimes they could on behalf of something outside themselves. Perhaps the crimes formed a pattern over the centuries, or perhaps they were stages in a search for the ultimate atrocity. The psychiatrist had assumed that all this was Ganz's method of justifying his own fascination, an elaborate fantasy as unlikely to be acted out as de Sade's had been – but now, the newspaper report continued, it was clear that Ganz had managed to convince others of his ideas.

Surely this could have nothing to do with Angela, surely she couldn't be involved in anything like this, and yet Barbara was growing desperate to hear her voice again, to be reassured by how normal she sounded. The newspaper said nothing about children, but it mentioned that Ganz was supposed to have sent disciples abroad to spread his word and his practices, in order to make it more difficult to stop them entirely. What had Ted been so anxious to tell her? Why couldn't he phone?

The television! Its news would be more up to date than the papers – she ought to have switched it on at once. She hurried to it, papers tearing underfoot, and began to switch channels. Here were the victims of a game show, a middle-aged couple emoting nervously and leaking colour. Here was Godzilla treading on a factory, here were commercials in Spanish, but she was hurrying back to the phone through a rustling of newspapers, for she had realized where Ted might be.

Her inspiration dulled at once: she had to persuade herself to finish dialling. Ted might be there, but it seemed most unlikely that he was. Nevertheless he had the key to her office in the set she'd given him. Suppose he'd found Angela and had decided that the office was the safest place to hide her over the week-end?

When the distant phone began ringing, drifting in and out of focus, she imagined it resounding through her empty office, except that the receiver was picked up at once. 'Er, Mrs Waugh's agency,' a faint voice said.

It was a female voice, a young voice, a young girl's voice. Barbara sat forward, closing her eyes as if that would project her wish more vividly. 'Who is that?' she said as loudly as she could.

The response was faint as a voice on the wind. Static engulfed it at once, and Barbara could hardly believe it had said 'Angela.' She was on the edge of her seat and bruising her face with the receiver. 'Angela,' she cried, 'is that you?'

But the young girl was no longer answering. Somewhere in the distance beyond the static, voices seemed to be arguing or conferring. Barbara clamped her free hand over her left ear, and heard what sounded like the rapid throbbing of a machine inside her skull. A blurred voice came through the static without warning. 'Who's speaking, please?'

'I'm Barbara Waugh and you are in my office.' At least

221

she was able to translate her trembling into cold rage. 'You had better tell me who you are at once.'

'I'm sorry, Barbara. It's Louise. I've been clearing some correspondence. Hannah wasn't very well last week.'

Her voice grew momentarily recognizable. Of course the young girl had said Hannah, not Angela. Presumably Louise had been falling behind with her work in Barbara's absence, but it seemed not to matter now. Barbara thought of a question to ask her. 'Have we heard from Ted Crichton lately?'

'Yes, he called yesterday. He wanted to know if you were coming back earlier than you'd said. I expect he's hoping for news of his book.'

And no doubt that was why he had phoned the Algonquin. She said goodbye to Louise and sat wondering what to do. Shadows crept over the buildings outside the bay window, the face of a Puerto Rican newsreader jerked on to the screen, newspapers rustled whenever Barbara moved. Perhaps she could phone one of the papers, perhaps someone there could tell her more about the cult. She could instruct the hotel switchboard to interrupt if anyone called her. She reached wearily for the phone.

But there were the members of the cult, trooping yet again into the courthouse, hiding their faces. If the newsreader had fresh information it was no use, since she didn't understand a word. She stared at the screen in the hope of glimpsing the faces of the cultists, and Kaspar Ganz looked straight at her.

It was only for a moment. Had the cameraman been moved on by police, or had those eyes daunted him? As they gazed out of the long sharp face, which looked dry and hard as an insect's, they seemed to swim forward out of their sockets. She could only pray that those famished eyes had never seen Angela.

At once he was gone, ousted by the newsreader. No

doubt 'magia negra' meant what it sounded like, but those were the only words she understood. She began changing channels, to give herself no chance to imagine what he was saying. Audiences were roaring, contestants grimaced desperately, reassuring monsters tramped about the small cage of the screen, the phone was ringing.

Her feet were tangled in the newspapers. The entire room seemed to be rustling. She kicked the papers aside and grabbed the receiver. 'Will you accept the charges for a call from Janet Lieberman in San Francisco?' the switchboard operator said.

'Yes, I will.' Her voice was firm, even if her legs were shaking.

Janet Lieberman was brisk almost to the point of rudeness. 'Mrs Waugh, I understand you want information about Kaspar Ganz. Why?'

'Because – ' Surely it couldn't matter if she gave away the secret so far from home. 'Because I'm afraid my daughter may be involved with his people in Britain.'

'I hope you're wrong.' At once she was sympathetic. 'What do you want to know?'

'Everything. As much as you can tell me.'

'In that case, maybe I should write to you.'

'No, please, I have to know now.' Barbara was afraid that the reporter would cut her off briskly now that she'd undertaken to write. 'I've read about Kaspar Ganz. I want to know what he influenced people to do.'

'Well, he got them to swallow his whole theory – you know, that apparently unmotivated killings are committed by the killers on behalf of something else. The purpose of the killings will only be apparent when the pattern is complete. Of course in a way that's a flawless theory, since it explains away all objections before they're even raised, and I guess the people who embraced it found that reassuring. Some people need that kind of reassurance.'

223

Barbara sensed she was reluctant to continue. 'You're telling me what they believed,' she made herself say, 'but what did they do?'

'I imagine you've heard that they gave up their names. That was supposed to show that they were only the tools of what they were doing.' She couldn't prevaricate any longer. 'What they did, well, they kidnapped people and tortured them to death. They believed in reincarnation, so they could tell themselves the sufferings of their victims were insignificant, because they said you never remember what you've suffered in your other lives. Well, that's California, that kind of garbage, and Ganz used to make his followers take drugs with him, which must have warped their minds that much more. It doesn't have to mean that his people in Britain went in for everything he did.'

Barbara wished she could feel reassured, but she was too aware of avoiding the question she had to ask. 'I can't understand how it took so long for them to be caught,' she said.

'Well, there weren't so many kidnappings. They made their victims last a long time.' She clearly regretted having said that, for she hurried on: 'It looks as though some of his people deliberately gave themselves away because they were close enough to achieving their goal to have an idea what it was. Or maybe it was their people somewhere else who were close, because the arrests don't seem to have worried Ganz at all. The way I hear it, his people here would like to see the others arrested, only they're literally unable to say anything about them.' After a token pause she said, 'Does that cover what you wanted to know?'

'No, not quite.' Barbara wished that it did. 'I heard that some of his people had children. How deeply were they involved?'

There was a longer silence. 'How old is your daughter?' Janet Lieberman said.

'She's just a child. They stole her.'

'I assumed she was grown up.' Perhaps Janet Lieberman was hesitating in order to break the news more gently, or perhaps she hoped it would give Barbara cause to hope. 'The children are initiated in their thirteenth year,' she said.

The hotel room grew flat as the television screen. The colours shivered, seemed on the point of leaking beyond their outlines. The floor sounded like a mass of static. 'Do you need to know anything else?' Janet Lieberman said.

'No.' It was less an answer than a plea. 'Thank you for calling,' Barbara said automatically, and replaced the receiver, only to cling to it while she tried to think what she could do.

She should never have left England. Everything was fitting together now, yet she had already known that Angela would be initiated, if she had only realized. She had almost known it that night at the Gregorys', when Sybil had mentioned how her daughter was going through the rituals of becoming a Girl Guide. Angela must have begun calling because she was afraid of the initiation – and now, if she called her mother's flat while it was occupied, she would hear a strange man's voice. Perhaps that would scare her away for good.

Barbara was still clutching the phone when it rang. Though she felt as if it had given her an electric shock, she managed to hang on to the receiver while she saved the body of the phone from falling off the table. 'Mr Ted Crichton calling from London,' the switchboard operator said.

Couldn't he wait for news of his novel? 'What do you want?' she demanded as soon as they were connected. 'What's wrong? Why do you keep calling me?'

'Because I know where Angela is,' he said.

32

When Glasgow went by for the third time she felt she was trapped on a merry-go-round. The captain's voice announced that the runway was still not available, and nobody seemed worried except Barbara; the stewardess patrolled imperturbably, the passengers shrugged and smiled. She was hanging thousands of feet in the air, she was crying out to be let off but nobody could hear. She managed to quell her silent cry; it wouldn't bring her destination any closer. At least she was on her way to the Glasgow house.

Glasgow had come round once more when the landscape tilted abruptly. The merry-go-round had fallen from its axis. She closed her eyes, for though the horizon was steep as a mountain now, she couldn't feel the tilt. She felt unreal, suspended in a dream by jet lag, even though it was true at last: Ted had convinced her she was going to the place where the cult was hiding.

At first she hadn't dared believe him. Suppose the cult had tricked him? Was he sure that he'd spoken to Angela? Eventually he had persuaded her that he was. Angela must have found him persuasive too, for she had told him the address.

Barbara couldn't help resenting that a little, guiltily. It was hardly surprising if Angela needed a father as well, and Ted must have seemed an acceptable substitute. Could he be, in time? She mustn't dream. Angela couldn't have trusted him entirely, or he would have gone up to Glasgow at once, by himself. He had told Barbara that she would have to go with him to the house.

The airport sailed up, growing all at once. A whisper of

muzak celebrated touchdown. People stood up around her, hemming her in while they reached for their hand-luggage, and she was still trapped. The plane hadn't even finished taxiing. She would be lucky to leave the airport in less than an hour.

Ted had insisted that she let him know as soon as possible which flight she would take, so that he could meet her at Glasgow. Eventually she'd managed to book herself on to a flight which reached Glasgow via London on Sunday morning. When she'd called him back at her flat it had taken him a while to answer, long enough to make her afraid that something was wrong. No, he'd said, everything was perfect. He would be waiting.

The resurrection of her luggage seemed to take forever. Her cases were almost the last on the belt. While she waited she couldn't help thinking of Laurence Dean, and how she'd had to send him a telegram to cancel their meeting. Perhaps that had killed his interest in *A Torrent of Lives*, perhaps now the film would never be made. Sybil had been right to sound grudging.

She thought she had nothing to declare at Customs, but the officer wasn't so sure. He was young and visibly determined to prove himself. She opened her cases and waited while he pawed through her underwear. Red spots of embarrassment or frustration burned on his cheeks. He glared at her before he chalked the cases and let her go.

In the main hall amplified chimes rang like giant door-bells, a large clear voice announced flights. People were meeting friends from her flight, but there was no sign of Ted. Of course there wasn't, since he was expecting her to arrive at Glasgow Airport on a later flight, not here at Prestwick. She wished she had been able to reach him to let him know what she was doing.

She had begun packing as soon as she'd spoken to him, and before she had finished she'd known that she wouldn't

227

be able to bear the delay. While she was detouring via London, what might be happening to Angela? Out of desperation rather than hope she had called the airline again, and there had been a cancellation on a direct flight to Prestwick.

And so she was on her own. By the time she'd thought of sending Ted a telegram, she had been rushing to Kennedy Airport, barely in time to catch her plane. At least she knew where she was going; she'd made him tell her the address of the Glasgow house, to convince her that he knew. She would rescue Angela by herself – she couldn't bear to wait for Ted, in case they were too late.

Outside the hall the Glasgow bus was ready to leave. Sliding doors slipped out of her way. She dumped her luggage beside the bus and rummaged in her bag as the driver waited patiently. She hadn't even found her purse when panic began to squirm in her belly. She had been so intent on planning what she would do in Glasgow that she had forgotten about money. She had almost no sterling at all.

She was clutching the handful of small change she had found, and wondering if she could ask the driver to trust her, when she discovered another coin in the lining of her purse. She paid him and dragged her luggage on board. All the banks were shut on Sunday, but she could get money from the Barclaybank machine on Sauchiehall Street, if she had the time.

The bus sped towards Glasgow. Fields sparkled in the early morning light, long unbaked loaves of cloud piled above the hills, in the cold sky of late September. In front of Barbara a man whose neck looked composed of diced raw beef was reading a Sunday newspaper. WHERE IS GRANNY WHO ALL THE CHILDREN LOVED? There she was, in a photograph beneath the headline, an old lady whose white hair was interrupted by a streak of silver.

The local children had adored her. She hadn't been seen for weeks. Police were concentrating their search in the Glasgow area, but Barbara had problems of her own. She closed her eyes and tried to doze; she'd had little sleep on the plane.

She woke at the Glasgow bus terminal. A few people waited among the silent buses beneath the low concrete roof. The journey had taken longer than she had expected, for it was nearly eight o'clock. Was there time for her to do whatever had to be done, or should she go to Glasgow Airport to meet Ted? She was tempted to wait until he arrived, but she mustn't lose her nerve. If she went to the house as early as this she ought to have the advantage of surprise.

She left her cases in the terminal, then she hurried uphill into Glasgow, past a car park that resembled a squat grey helter-skelter full of darkness. She was alone in a dead city, she was surrounded by tombs for Chicago businessmen, a multitude of windows blank as ice. A neon hyphen glimmered in a fourth-floor window, as if the office was refusing to die. Everything was oppressively close to her, the clang of her heels on the anvil of the pavement, the new-pencilled lines between bricks and paving-stones. Birds that sounded large as blankets flapped beneath eaves.

At the top of the hill a web of street lamp cables had caught a bird. It fell as she reached the crossroads. It was only a grey piece of litter, paper or cloth, which fluttered clumsily downhill. Nevertheless she felt unbalanced by the blackened castle above her, the YMCA building whose top-heavy turrets looked closer to her than the lower storeys. That was the architecture's fault, not hers. She turned left towards the Inner Ring Road.

She heard it as soon as she passed the Albany, a hotel whose windows resembled squares of tissue paper pasted on the chocolate walls. A stub of a street, derelict shops patched with notices, led her to the road itself.

Flaking terraces stood on its brink. Some were propped up

by ground-floor shops and bars, but the upper windows looked half-blind. Beyond the unpaved far edge of the road, the motorway underpass magnified the shrill roar of lorries. As she crossed the road bridge to the terraces, she felt as though a circular saw had got into her head.

She hurried past the Mitchell Library with its green stone skullcap. A stone woman sat above the entrance, waiting for the library to open. Further on, pillars held up an abandoned section of motorway, both ends in the air, as if the concrete was already falling into ruin. Traffic waited at lights, engines pounding like a factory. In a factory she would have been given earmuffs.

She must be close by now to where she had to go. On the far side of the lights the pavement was broken; she could feel sweet-papers sticking to her shoes. The day was growing hotter as it crept towards nine o'clock. Cars sprayed her with dust, which seeped into her throat.

The doors of the Dreamland Cinema were nailed shut beneath graffiti; the plastic letters of its name were entangled on the marquee. The narrow pavement led past a few discoloured shops to a service station, and all at once there was a sharp lump of apprehension in her stomach. That must be the service station at West Graham Street, close to the point from which, Ted had told her, she would be able to see the house.

When she reached the service station she paced slowly past the gleaming carapaces of cars for sale, and stared across the road. Above the motorway underpass, concrete pillars stepped out from behind one another as she paced. How could there be room for a house in the maze of concrete that was the edge of the motorway? Ted had been tricked. She had come all this way for nothing.

The pale concrete planes dragged across one another as she paced, to the sound of the roaring of traffic – but one of them was darker than the rest, and moved less. Another pace, then she could see the sunlight on a window, blazing through the grime. She halted with only the road and the confusion of concrete separating her from the house. She'd been wrong to doubt Ted's efficiency. He had brought her where she had to go.

33

As soon as she crossed to the pillars, she saw that she would be in view of the house well before she reached it. Between the concrete and the front door was a patch of waste ground at least twenty yards wide. She dodged between the pillars, which concealed her from the house but not from the roar of the motorway, for a closer look.

It was a nondescript house with a pair of bay windows one above the other, the kind of house that would go unnoticed in the midst of thousands of terraces. Perhaps it had once been the last house of a terrace; now it stood alone on the brink of the motorway. Whatever colour it had been originally, it looked like the back of a fireplace now. Above the greasy grey tiles of the roof the uneven chimney-pots were splintered sticks.

Both windows were heavily curtained. No doubt any windows at the back were curtained too. What were the curtains hiding? She turned uneasily, for she'd realized that the noise of the motorway made her unable to hear if anyone was behind her, sneaking between the pillars. The longer she stood here, the more nervous she would grow. There was no way she could dodge unseen around the house. Giving herself no time to think, she headed straight for the front door.

A bald doll with its head and limbs twisted back to front stared at her with a socket and one eye. She was watching the curtains to see if they moved, but she glimpsed the garbage all around her, a driving-mirror half-buried in the clay, a mosaic of broken glass, a sodden jacket or a piece of carpet, a giant blue and white chrysalis which was a shoe, a greenish length of copper pipe. Without breaking her stride she grabbed the pipe, which felt reassuringly heavy. Would she really be able to use it as a weapon, when she had never in her life encountered violence? The way she felt now, she was sure that she would.

The curtains were absolutely still. She was so intent on watching them that she had almost reached the front door before she realized it was open. Was it a trap? Cars roared by above and below her, isolating her with the house; none of the drivers could help her, she doubted that they even noticed her; if they saw her in trouble they wouldn't be able to stop. She lifted the pipe above her head and kicked the door wide open.

The interior was as soulless as the facade, but dimmer. A narrow hallway led past two open doors to a kitchen discoloured with fat and rust. Grimy light hovered between browning walls above the blackened shiny carpet, the cracked footprints of dried clay. Somewhere the plumbing had burst, for water glistened like a snail's track on the left-hall wall, over the stairs. It seemed clear that nobody had lived here for months.

Ted had been wrong, after all. Angela couldn't have trusted him entirely, this unfamiliar voice at her mother's flat. She had given him an old address, to teach him a lesson, perhaps. She was out of reach again, and the only reason Barbara restrained herself from weeping was that if she began she might never stop.

At last she stepped forward. She was still gripping the length of pipe, though there seemed to be nothing to fear. She had to see the kind of place where Angela had been forced to live. She stepped into the hall, and was afraid at once.

It wasn't only the dimness and the sudden chill. The air felt cold and soft, almost like walking into mould. Or perhaps it was her mind rather than her body that was being

233

hemmed in, suffocating her thoughts. She managed to persuade herself that it was only her fears that were closing in, her dread of what she might find, and jet lag was doing the rest. Nothing could harm her in an empty house. She could see that the doors on the upper floor were open too.

Nevertheless she found she was creeping along the hall, until she realized that however heavily she trod she couldn't hear her footsteps. She began to walk quickly, to be through the house and out again as soon as she could, for the hallway felt as if the walls were closer than they looked. That was only apprehension and jet lag and the dimness, and she mustn't let them cramp her thoughts.

The first of the ground-floor rooms was bare except for several mattresses lying on the floorboards. Lumps of stuffing protruded like worms from the mattresses. She hurried past, and was almost in the kitchen before she realized that she'd suffered a momentary blackout, a jerk of consciousness like dozing. There was no point in searching the kitchen: the oven and cupboard were open – their dark interiors looked unpleasantly like spiders' nests. She turned aside to the second room.

Here was nothing but a gathering of half a dozen armchairs that faced a hearth blurred by soot. She had a grotesque image of the cultists settling down before the fire in the evenings, chatting or reading newspapers, for a newspaper was protruding from beneath the arm of the farthest chair. Though the dimness felt as if the walls were padded, she went into the room.

When she peered at the newspaper she couldn't believe the date. She must be misreading it in the dimness. She made to draw back the curtains, but as soon as she touched them her hand recoiled; they felt more like a mass of cobwebs, grimy and clinging. Was it only her touch that had made them stir slightly? Suppose there was something behind them or in them? Furious with herself – she was growing as fearful as Iris – she wrenched them back with the length of pipe, then she turned to the newspaper.

She hadn't been mistaken. It was yesterday's newspaper. POLICE SEARCH GLASGOW FOR MISSING PEN-SIONER, a headline said. All at once the headline seemed ominously relevant, but she couldn't quite pick up the newspaper, not from the three-legged armchair whose leather had sprouted a kind of whitish fur. She had never seen leather look so recognizably animal. In fact, the way the deformed chair leaned towards her, it looked not quite dead.

So the cult had been here until yesterday. These were the conditions in which they had forced Angela to live. She stormed out of the room – it was all she could do in order to act out her appalled helpless fury – and was almost in the kitchen again before she jerked back to herself. Though her blackouts must be caused by tension and jet lag, they were deeply unnerving. Enough tricks had been played on her without her own body's joining in.

She tramped upstairs. A few crooked scraps of carpet squelched underfoot; dark moisture welled up around her shoes. A loft entrance gaped above the stairwell, out of reach. At the top of the stairs the linoleum was shiny with water, a rusty trickle from a clogged washbowl in the bathroom.

She lost her footing almost at once. Her palm slapped the wall, which felt fattened and hairy. It must be mould. Wiping her hand violently on her sleeve, she glanced into the rooms.

One must have been the main dormitory, for it was full of mattresses. If these and the mattresses downstairs had all been occupied, there must have been at least two dozen people in the house. She had to peer before she was certain that they were unoccupied now, that none of the huddles of worn blankets was stirring. The traffic noise was pounding into her head, the walls were growing fatter. She hurried to the other room.

Except for a blackened filing-cabinet, it was almost empty. She was halfway to the cabinet before she noticed that the fireplace was choked with the remains of books. When she poked them the charred pages spilled on to the floor, crumbling into oily flakes that made her cough. They made the room darker than ever, so dark that she ran to the filing-cabinet, in the hope that it contained nothing that would require her to stay. Nor did it, for when she pulled out the drawers she found it was gutted. Everything within had been burned.

Now that she had her wish it was not reassuring. On the contrary, it seemed terribly final. She was trying to think what it could mean, but the air in the room was fluttering darkly, her brain felt as clogged as her nostrils. She ran out, skidding on the wet linoleum, and down the stairs. Only the dimness made the walls look swollen. The crawling which she glimpsed above her on the wall was nothing but the stream of water. She was downstairs now. In a moment she would be out of the house. At least, she would have been, except that the back door was locked.

She'd had another blackout. That was how she'd returned to the kitchen without even knowing. She could admit to herself that the blackouts were frightening, for the fear would help her run down the hall and out of the front door instead of stepping forward into the kitchen. But it was not a blackout that was making her take several paces into the kitchen before turning to see what had been out of sight beyond the doorway all the time: the cellar door.

They had never been blackouts at all. It was her will that had been suffocated, not her consciousness. She was helpless to prevent her hand from reaching out to the cellar door. She was aware how the doorknob felt – a lump of dust or cobwebs clung to it, and now to her fingers – but she couldn't flinch away. As the door squealed open amid a sudden random silence of traffic, she couldn't even raise the length of pipe.

Beyond the doorway, rough steps led down into darkness. She stepped forward at once. The softness of the house had filled her brain, and she was unable to stop herself. Even though the dark at the foot of the steps smelled like an abattoir, and felt as though a crowd was waiting breathlessly for her, she could only close the door behind her, go down the steps and wait in the dark. She couldn't even make a grab for the light-switch.

As she turned to the door, to close out the meagre light, she slipped. She was falling into the dark. Perhaps some part of her mind was alert for the chance, for as she clutched at the wall to steady herself, her free hand struck the switch. The light went on below her, and she saw where she was going.

Though the cellar was not large, the light was too dim to illuminate the corners. Were they full of shadows or of something else? Certainly the place still felt crowded, however bare it looked. On the floor beneath the light was a makeshift cage of iron railings bound together with thick cables. The railings were driven into the floor. Between the bars of the cage, which was hardly big enough to hold a child, a mass of hair was caught, white except for a silver streak.

Perhaps the shock of her fall on the steps had given her back something of herself. The horror of what she was seeing jarred her momentarily out of her helplessness, and she staggered against the door to hold it open. Her heels were skidding on the steps, it was as though the hungry dimness had tripped her in order to drag her down, but she struggled out into the kitchen and ran towards the hall.

The swollen dimness was crushing her thoughts, her will was giving way, but the front door was wide open, the sunlight was almost in reach. Yet she was hardly out of the kitchen when she lurched to a halt. In the lull of the traffic she heard a quick stumbling, softer than bare feet yet heavy enough to make the uncarpeted stairs creak. Between her and the front door, something was coming downstairs.

34

There was only the back door. She mustn't be afraid to go back into the kitchen; at least it was brighter than the hall, and she still had the length of pipe. She could smash the window in the door – it was lower than the window above the sink – and clamber out that way. Her legs felt dislocated by fear, but she could run. She hadn't time to think.

As soon as she fled into the kitchen she forgot which door she wanted. It was the nearer one, of course, the one beyond which steps led down; she could hide there. The soft tread had reached the hall now, and was approaching slowly but relentlessly. One limb sounded considerably larger than the other, and the body seemed to be slithering along both walls at once.

Suddenly she could hear nothing for the traffic, not even her own sobs of panic as she realized where she had almost gone. She ran at the locked door, raising the pipe in both hands. She didn't dare look back as she slammed the pipe against the window with all her strength.

Perhaps the window was toughened to ward off burglars. The end of the pipe bent slightly, but the glass was unmarked. Something was growing closer and clearer in the dimness of the hall, and she was battering wildly at the glass with the length of pipe. Her inability to hear the blows emphasized their uselessness.

Suddenly a crack which resembled a very small twig appeared in the window. She smashed at it with the pipe, and shards fell outwards, glittering in the sunlight that seemed utterly beyond her reach. She grabbed the door frame and balanced on one shaking leg as she pulled off her shoe. With the heel she knocked out fragments of glass. Now the gap was large enough for her to crawl through – larger, for a fragment the size of her head dropped out of the top of the frame, narrowly missing her – if she were able to climb.

She had never been athletic. If she had been able to raise her leg as high as the window she would have kicked out the glass rather than take off her shoe. She tried to grab the empty frame, but sharp edges of glass were embedded wherever she tried to get hold. She could see movement in the hall, movement that looked almost as large as the doorway, yet her hands were flinching back from the glass.

Then she saw the cooker. It was almost close enough to the door. She dragged it closer, and felt something rip loose from the wall. At once there was a smell of gas, and perhaps it was the gas that was closing softly over her thoughts, making her wonder why she was going to so much trouble when a door was already open and waiting for her.

She hauled herself up wildly, one foot inside the oven. Her shoe slipped in grease, she had a glimpse of the dark clogged interior, and then she had pushed herself half out of the broken window. Glass clawed at her shoulders. Her palms were shoving against the gritty bricks on both sides of the door, her feet were thrusting at the top of the cooker, and then she was falling face down on the ground outside the door.

The fall bruised her forearms and wrenched her right shoulder. The copper pipe flew from her hand. She struggled to her feet at once and ran towards the concrete pillars. Even though she was free of the house, back in the everyday, she was terrified that something would be waiting for her on the far side of the house. Nothing stirred except scraps of litter, nothing was hiding among the pillars. Nevertheless, even when she had crossed the road and reached the service station she didn't dare stop running.

Eventually she slowed enough to be able to think. Pedestrians were crossing a thin bridge to Sauchiehall Street; church bells were just audible amid the traffic, where they sounded distorted as faults in the engines. At least there were people who seemed ordinary, and she followed them across the bridge. Those of them who met her eyes frowned or looked quickly away.

Did she look as desperate as she felt? The cult must have had to find another hiding place because the police were searching for the old woman they had captured. Far worse than their having cheated Barbara of her child yet again was the thought that perhaps they had involved Angela in whatever they had done in the cellar. No, she had still to be initiated, surely. Barbara must cling to that conviction, for she had nothing else to cling to.

She'd followed the pedestrians halfway down Sauchiehall Street before she was conscious of where she was going. She had to get some money so that she could take the bus to the airport. She needed to see Ted, to be with him. She felt as if he was all the stability she had.

Though she could hardly believe the time, it wasn't yet ten o'clock. Ted would be expecting her to emerge from Customs around half past eleven. She slipped her plastic card into the slot in the wall outside the bank and waited for the metal cover to lift from the keyboard so that she could type her code number.

Nothing happened. She tried to push at the cover in case it was stuck, but it was firm as a limpet. It took her a while to notice the feeble electric letters that were flickering above the slot: UNABLE TO ACCEPT YOUR CARD. Then why hadn't the card emerged from the reject slot? In a moment she saw why, for a red metal tag clicked into place over the glimmering letters. NOT IN USE, it said.

The cover gleamed at her with a blankness so innocent it seemed idiotic. The slot was too narrow for her to reach in;

besides, no doubt her card was deep in the machine. She was close to screaming, but what would that achieve? Though the nightmare she was living seemed to have turned into a farce, it was just as unbearable.

She was going to have to walk. She had seen a route sign as she left the Inner Ring Road: Glasgow Airport was several miles away, on the far side of the river. She could never be there in time. Suppose she went to the bus station and pleaded with one of the drivers, with anyone who could help? The chances were that she would only be wasting time.

She started for the river. People stared at her as if she had forgotten this was a day of rest. Eventually she found a bridge at the feet of the hilly streets, among a flock of unmanned cranes. It took her ten minutes to cross the river. The water oozed by, a sly reminder of her sluggishness.

Once she left the bridge she lost the airport route. Minutes later she found the sign, which pointed her through residential streets. Churches made the neat pale houses sound like music-boxes. Babies pushed jingling rollers in small square front gardens, children rode in plastic cars, swooped in garden swings. There was more than twenty minutes of the placid streets.

Beyond the streets the road led her among fields, beneath a sky that looked patched together out of steam and smoke, and seemed not to move at all. Her shoulder ached dully, her dress felt infested with humidity. The pavement had turned into grit, which was biting into her feet through her shoes.

Thumbing a lift made her shoulder worse. A couple of drivers slowed until they saw her face. In the spaces between cars the route smelled of grass, but her head was full of the stench of the cellar, the sight of the cage. What were they doing now wherever they had taken Angela?

By eleven o'clock there was no pavement. She had to

trudge through fields and keep as close to the road as she could. Lush grass hindered every step. Butterflies flickered away, scraps of colour that vanished momentarily as they flew, as though her vision was growing irregular. Distant cars shimmered like fountains. Her throat felt cracked as the soil at the edge of the road.

Sometimes she had to detour widely, keeping the road in sight. Sometimes she climbed barbed wire. Sometimes she crossed industrial land – one field was owned by Rolls-Royce – but nobody seemed to notice. By now she was too exhausted to walk straight. She slumped on the grass for a few minutes. It was twenty past eleven, and there was no sign of the airport.

Several minutes further on she began to see the planes, glinting miniatures that rose or glided down on invisible threads, but it was almost noon before the airport came into view. She had to go back to the road in order to cross a small canal, and by the time the traffic let her on to the bridge she was sobbing dryly with rage.

Once she was across she began to run. The airport building staggered from side to side, but kept its distance. The drivers of cars must have thought she was drunk, for they stayed well away from her; some halted until she was past. Her ears were deafened by a hollow roaring. Perhaps it was planes in the sky.

A bus stood outside the airport building, one of the buses she could have caught if she'd had any money. She stumbled all round the bus to stare at the passengers, but none of them was Ted. She staggered towards the building, and would have leaned against the doors for support if they hadn't slipped out of her way.

It was cooler inside, but she was beyond noticing. A digital clock showed 12.37. Everything swarmed at her – hundreds of people talking in groups and queueing at desks and listening to amplified voices in the air and riding upwards two abreast on an escalator. The animals went up two by two, the voice was a computer that had to speak in numbers, an oracle translating its own code aloud. Luggage sailed away behind the scenes, never to be seen again, just like Angela. People were turning, smiling, smiling because she was desperate enough to hope that one of them might be Ted when she would have noticed him at once. Turn, turn, turn, she was doing it now in search of him, turn had been the first three words of a song she'd heard when she was carrying Angela. She should have carried her with her always, never let her go. Faces turned, you turned up a card and hoped to win, but every one was a loser. Her mind felt close to caving in.

At last she saw the Enquiries sign. She managed to reach the escalator, and rode upwards in the midst of a stepped crowd towards giant shining brand names. It felt like being trapped in a window display, among mannequins. The girl at the Enquiries desk smiled efficiently at her. The flight from New York via London? It had been delayed at Heathrow. No, the girl said as Barbara experienced a twinge of hope, it wasn't still there, it had arrived a while ago. The passengers must be out of the airport by now. If any were still waiting, they would be over there. Just over there, madam, where you see the lady in the pink and mauve trousers.

Barbara stumbled over to the group of people. Somebody met most of them before she did, and ushered them away. Beyond the few who were still waiting she glimpsed a thin young woman talking quietly to someone who was sitting next to her on a plastic bench. Barbara limped around several New Yorkers, who were complaining loudly that maybe the couriers were on strike too like half this goddamn country, and saw that the other person on the bench was Ted.

She didn't dare speak immediately. She sat beside him –

244

there was just enough room on the bench – and clung to his arm for a while. Eventually she said, 'Thank God you're here. I was afraid you would have gone.'

When he'd gazed at her for a while without speaking she realized that something was wrong. He got abruptly to his feet, and she began to tell him she would like to sit for a few minutes, though perhaps he could bring her a drink. Then she saw that he was moving out of her way, out of the way of the underfed girl with the cropped strawy hair at the other end of the bench. The girl had something to tell her, and all at once Barbara was utterly depressed: it was another lead, another false trail, another move in the interminable game that she could never win.

Then the girl looked straight into her eyes. 'Hello, Mummy,' she said.

35

The airliners rose massively in silence. They grew tiny in order to merge with the clouds. Down in the airport hall, travellers were hurrying about in search of friends or information, but Barbara could sit still at last. The Coca-Cola had quenched her thirst, the rum was mellowing the presence of the airport until it seemed unreal enough for her dream to have come true.

At first she'd thought it was a trick. This self-assured young woman with her hair like ragged straw couldn't be Angela, couldn't be the child who had needed her mother so much. Yet her face was like Barbara's, it was very much like the sketch she had glimpsed after Margery's death. The young woman had risen from the plastic bench, her deep blue eyes gazing steadily at Barbara, and Barbara had seen the purple clover-leaf on her bare left shoulder. She'd stumbled to her feet and crushed Angela to her, weeping.

Now Angela was smiling calmly at her across the table in the airport bar, reassuring her that her edginess was natural, that everything would work out in time. It was hardly surprising that Barbara felt awkward when she had lost a four-year-old child and found a teenager older than her years. Perhaps she had never really believed as she'd searched that they would meet again. However distressing Angela's maturity was – nobody in the bar had questioned her age – it was also reassuring, for it meant she had survived the last nine years.

All at once she smiled at Angela. Of course, Angela was confident now because she was with her mother. Of course she hadn't sounded confident when she was in the hands of the cult, when she'd had no idea what might happen to her. But that reminded Barbara of questions to be asked, however anxious she was not to disturb Angela.

She held her daughter's hand to anchor her in the present. 'How did you get away? When I went to the address Ted gave me,' (she began to realize how many things she must never refer to, or at least not for a very long time), 'the house was empty.'

'When I knew they were going to have to move again I called him. I just walked out as soon as I saw him. Then we came here and waited for you.'

The police search must have made her captors careless. In that case, Barbara thought wryly, she could have called the police months ago. The end of her search had proved almost anticlimatic: Barbara seemed unaware how dangerous her plight had been, how terrified her mother had felt for her. That was all to the good, but the thought of the cult made Barbara nervous. 'Do you know where they've gone?'

Angela shrugged. 'They must be far away by now.'

How could she know? Suddenly Barbara was as nervous as she had ever been. They were surrounded by strangers, any of whom could be watching. If any of them were waiting for a chance to recapture Angela then presumably the girl would recognize them, but suppose she didn't notice them in time? Weren't the women at the table by the exit dressed too shabbily for air travellers? Was the large man opposite Barbara glancing sidelong at Angela only because he suspected her of being under age? 'We'd better make a start,' Barbara said abruptly. 'I feel all right now.'

And she did, once Ted rose to his feet. He could deal with anyone who tried to take Angela away from him. Angela was safe between him and her mother. When the crowd at the foot of the escalator closed around them Barbara was watchful but not afraid.

He led them to his car, which was parked close to the

building. 'Do you mind driving all the way to London?' Barbara said. 'I don't think I can be trusted to drive just now.'

'I don't mind at all.' He gazed blankly at her. 'In fact, I insist.'

He drove into Glasgow to collect her luggage, then he insisted that they eat before the long drive home. They found a hamburger place opposite the railway station, and Barbara remembered the night she had chased the lopsided woman. The cult had been here in Glasgow, despite what Ted had told her, but it didn't matter now. She felt safe in the restaurant, for there was no window to the street. Young Doris Day and Marilyn Monroe sparkled on the walls. Angela picked up her hamburger in both hands, and Barbara felt a surge of love at the glimpse of her child.

When they joined the motorway outside Carlisle the time was close to four o'clock. At last Barbara was able to notice that autumn had begun; the sun was a smudge of light above the rusty flaking trees, leaves swarmed beneath the cars. She sat in the back with Angela while Ted drove and played the car radio. She kept wanting to hug Angela to her, but she sensed that Angela wasn't ready to give herself. Of course they were strangers to each other after nine years, and Angela was all at once in a different world. After nine years of confinement, perhaps she might even find freedom unnerving.

For a while Barbara was content to sit quietly beside her. It felt like a hint of the peace they would share. Orderly ranks of pines marched over the horizon, a few cars cruised along the motorway. Ted had found a local station, American pop with Scottish interruptions. Here was the travel news; trains to London suffering from the aftermath of a strike, sudden fogs on the M6 between Penrith and Kendal, part of the Glasgow Inner Ring Road closed temporarily. A house had been destroyed by an explosion, scattering rubble across three lanes. Police suspected a broken gas main. 'My God, I did that,' she cried. 'That's the house.'

When Angela smiled fleetingly she regretted having spoken. Even if the house and its influence had been destroyed – even if that helped her forget her own experience there, it seemed already years ago – that was no reason to remind Angela of her life there. Surely Angela had other memories.

'Do you remember our house in Otford? There was the stream you used to like, just across the field by the Archbishop's palace. And the ducks on the roundabout always used to make you laugh.' She was talking down to Angela, but she couldn't think how else to talk; she had yet to adjust to the fact that Angela was no longer a child.

Nevertheless Angela was responding. 'I remember some things. Auntie Jan used to live next door. You used to leave me with her.' For a moment Barbara thought she was about to remind her of the kidnapping, perhaps to accuse her, then Angela went on: 'And you used to listen to me with an intercom when I was in my room.'

'That's right.' All at once she recalled what she'd used to hear Angela saying. 'Do you remember your father?' she blurted.

'How could I?' She sounded bitter. 'He went away.'

Was that a childish way of saying that he'd died before she was born, or did she mean something else? Barbara didn't like to ask. 'It seems so long ago, Otford. Almost as if it was another life,' she said, making the effort to address her as an equal. 'I've become more successful since then. I'm doing pretty well, I think. Only I didn't have anyone to share my success with until now.'

Angela responded when Barbara squeezed her hand, yet Barbara felt self-conscious: to be overheard by Ted made her feel she was uttering clichés, and perhaps they were disloyal to a vague secret dream of sharing her life with him

– perhaps he had dreamed of that too. Still, he seemed to be too possessed by his driving even to hear.

At half-past four a mist came flooding down the Lakeland fells. Ted had turned off the radio; the only sound was the hum of the engine. As the rocky slopes dissolved and the grey softness closed about the car, Barbara felt the swollen walls of the house closing in. She needed sleep, that was all. She could sleep now that she had Angela, now that Ted was here to keep an eye on her.

As they reached the Kendal junction the fog drifted away. Ted accelerated past several hitch-hikers who were displaying signs for Glasgow. Most of them were teenagers – Barbara wondered uneasily if the cult had ever captured hitch-hikers – but one man was considerably older. For a moment she thought it was Arthur, until she saw his face.

Beyond Kendal the landscape flattened. The featureless road looked unreal as a simulation in a slot machine, the same strip of road unrolling endlessly. Her glimpse of Arthur had made her feel suddenly exhausted, unable to hold back her dreams until she slept, but she tried to stay awake. 'I know,' she said to Angela. 'Would you like to go away for a holiday? I meant to go to Italy this year and I think I will, to celebrate. I have to auction a book for one of my authors but as soon as that's over, we'll go.'

That reminded her. 'Oh, Ted, I didn't tell you the good news! I found a buyer for your novel. You do understand why I forgot to tell you, don't you? Cathy Darnell will be writing to you.'

'All right.' He seemed hardly to have taken in the news. Really, she must try to sleep: she felt she was sharing the car with a couple of strangers. Of course Angela would be a stranger for a while, and no doubt Ted was still adjusting to the situation. Nevertheless their strangeness made her uneasy, and the best thing she could do was sleep.

The roaring of lorries woke her. She was surrounded by

lorries and concrete. The noise was closing in, closing over her mind. The house had been destroyed, but not its power. It had brought them all back here, into the concrete cage.

Then she saw that it wasn't the Inner Ring Road at all. She was on the motorway outside Birmingham, in the midst of a skein of roads. She relaxed, though her heart was scurrying, and then she realized that Ted was in the wrong lane. He was driving them to Birmingham.

When she pointed out his mistake he glared savagely into the mirror. That must be meant for the traffic behind them, not for her. Of course he had been driving for four hours without a break, and how long must he have been awake to have reached the Glasgow house before her? She wished she could offer to drive, but she still felt half asleep.

As they neared the motorway café at Corley she insisted that they halt. The long canteen was crowded with families, tired children picking at their food and wailing. Her sleep had done her no good, for everyone who came in made her nervous, even when the new arrivals looked like families: the cultists had children, after all.

Shouldn't she feel peaceful now that she was with Angela? But after nine years of confinement it was hardly surprising if Angela no longer radiated peace. Perhaps she still had her powers, perhaps they would become apparent in time. It was all to the good that she didn't make her mother feel too peaceful. Still, was Barbara able to be sufficently cautious when she seemed in danger of hallucinating? Arthur had appeared at the exit, beckoning urgently, but of course when she looked it wasn't Arthur at all.

By the time they left the café, night was falling. Ted had seemed reluctant to leave. When she asked if he felt happy to drive he snapped, 'Yes, of course.' She wondered if he was irritable partly because he felt excluded from the reunion.

As they drove the last hundred miles to London the landscape grew soft and blurred and grey. The fields were turning into foreshortened spreads of fog, the bushes at the edge of the motorway were lumps of stuffing that quivered in breezes, the horizon was closing in. Twin wedges of light roared by, again and again. An unlit caravan rocked close to the car, and Barbara thought a face was pressed against its rear window. Faces seemed to stare back at her from every passing car, especially those cars which swung into Ted's path. She must be hallucinating, for at the edge of the road a scrawny stooping figure seemed to pace the car, loping greyly behind the bushes, peering jerkily over the blotches of foliage.

They reached Hendon about ten o'clock. Ted seemed to have difficulty in following the route into London; at one point he began to head back on to the motorway, until he saw the two of them staring at him. Barbara insisted that he must stay with them overnight, and he seemed beyond protesting. She wanted him to be there, just in case the cult should try any tricks. Tomorrow she would think about tomorrow.

Before they reached St John's Wood they had to stop at several traffic lights. Barbara kept checking that the car doors were locked. Suppose someone wrenched them open while the car was halted and seized Angela! On the Euston Road pedestrians crossed in front of the car, and each of them made her more tense, even the sad-faced man who looked like Arthur. Was this how the rest of her life with Angela would be?

Even the Barbican didn't feel safe. The underground garage seemed very dim, its corners dark and clogged. It was only the jittery fluorescent tubes which made the darkness in the corners restless. Nevertheless the ceiling felt lower than ever. She was hemmed in by cars and vans, any of which might conceal an ambush.

Ted was lifting out her cases. She told Angela to stay with him while she went ahead to unlock the flat. That allowed her to hurry through the broken ranks of vehicles and see that nobody was lurking. She climbed the steps to the balcony, and found she was still nervous. Long dark fingers groped from beneath the willow towards the church, wind muttered behind the squat concrete pillars. Her shadow followed her up from the car park and seemed to dodge into all the darkest areas. Of course it was only her shadow.

She had no cause to be nervous now, she told herself. Angela was safe with Ted, and there was no reason why the cult should want Barbara. Still, she felt relieved when she arrived at her flat. Her key was already in her hand. She unlocked the door quickly and switched on the light.

Here was familiarity at last – the dark green carpet, the silvery wallpaper whose pattern shifted discreetly as you passed, the Escher lithograph which turned perspective inside out, even the smell of her perfume, though she had never realized that it could linger so strongly – but the first thing she noticed was the letter just inside the doorway. She left the door unlatched and made her way with the letter along the hall.

The letter was from Hemel Hempstead. The Kodak address had been crossed out on the envelope. In a minute she would see what news Iris's parents had for her, but first she wanted to get out of the hall, which felt narrower than it should. That must be an after-effect of her experience in Glasgow. She hoped it would fade once she turned on all the lights.

She switched on the main light in the living-room and stepped forward, inserting a fingernail under the flap of the envelope. Ted must have knocked over a bottle of perfume in his rush to collect her luggage for New York – the smell was overwhelming. She'd taken several steps before she glanced up to see what else was wrong.

The letter dropped from her hand at once, but it seemed to take seconds to fall. It was as though her shock had slowed it down, freezing it in flight as shock had frozen her thoughts. Books and records were scattered over the floor. All the furniture had been dragged out of shape, and looked stickily soiled. Her photograph album lay on the carpet in front of her. Most of the photographs had been torn up.

She was reaching desperately for the switch for the wall lamps – the cultists must have broken in and had vented their frustration on her flat when they hadn't found Angela, she needed more light to help her see how much damage they'd done, to stop the room from feeling so shrunken – when two children, a boy and a girl about eight years old, stepped out from behind the bookcases. They watched brightly as a man's arm closed tight around her throat.

When her vision started blackening, the stranglehold eased. Apparently they wanted her alive. She could see them all now, two dozen or more of them, emerging from the other rooms. When she saw the lopsided woman she began to struggle furiously but uselessly, choking. So they had found another hiding place. She wondered dully if their powers allowed them to open doors without keys.

She made herself seem to relax, as far as that was possible, so that her captor would let her breathe. Though the flat was sickly with her perfume she could smell him, stale sweat and cannabis. Presumably he realized that the flat was soundproof, which was why his grip had slackened enough to let her scream if she wanted. That was her chance. As soon as the door opened she would scream at Ted and Angela to run. She mustn't think what the cult might do to her, so long as Angela was safe.

When they heard the key in the lock, a large slack-faced man moved to stand just behind the door. The key fumbled for a moment against the latch, then the door edged inward. The arm tightened on her throat at once, and she could not make a sound.

But her captors had miscalculated. She realized that even as the iris of blackness shrank. He was holding her so that she was visible all the way down the hall. Ted would see her at once. Perhaps she could tell him with her eyes to save Angela, not to risk Angela in order to save her.

When the door opened, Angela was in the doorway. Ted loomed behind her, his face blank. Both of them came in quickly. As Ted slammed the door, Angela saw her mother and the rest of them. Her eyes widened, and their sudden power was so intense that it was sickening. She smiled triumphantly, the victor of a prolonged game. 'You'd better gag her before we take her down,' she said.

36

A sudden lurch threw Barbara against the side of the van. She managed to heave herself upright, her bound hands scrabbling behind her, her right shoulder throbbing, so that she could see out of the rear window. A smell of dust crawled in her nostrils, she tasted ink and paper from the letter which they'd stuffed into her mouth. She was afraid she was going to be sick. Perhaps that might dislodge the gag.

The van was speeding through dockland. Blank-faced warehouses loured over deserted streets, blocks of light hovered beneath the glaring street lamps. Was the cult looking for somewhere as deserted as this? She redoubled her efforts to break her bonds. She had to be free before the van stopped, before they came to get her.

Her struggles were having no effect that she could perceive. The tights which were strangling her wrists and ankles, flimsy though they always seemed as clothes, made unbreakable bonds. She had little room to struggle: luggage – suitcases and up-ended trunks – occupied most of the back of the van, which felt oppressively cramped. Even if she managed to break free, another of the vans was following; she would never be able to open the doors unnoticed. Nevertheless she wrenched at her bonds, tried to force her wrists apart as the tights cut into her skin. She had to keep trying while there was a chance of saving Angela.

But was there still a chance, when Barbara had already been so wrong about her – about the initiation? Of course that wasn't something that took place all at once when the children were thirteen; that was only when it was completed. No doubt Angela's initiation had begun as soon as they had captured her.

And her game with her mother, luring her from place to place, had been part of the initiation. Perhaps Angela would have continued playing her, confusing her and tiring her before the kill, if the cult hadn't needed to leave Glasgow hurriedly. Now that they had captured Barbara, what was the rest of the initiation?

She mustn't think about that. Above all, she mustn't brood over the hatred she had glimpsed in Angela's eyes. The cult had made Angela feel that way, whatever they had told her – perhaps that Barbara had taken her father away from her, to judge by her bitter remark in the car. No doubt they had poisoned her more thoroughly against Barbara, but for the moment it was more important to remember that they needed to corrupt her utterly. Shouldn't that mean that until the initiation was completed, she could be saved?

Perhaps it did, yet when Barbara remembered her eyes, there seemed no point in trying. The psychometer had been right, nine years ago: Angela had great power. But now that power was perverted beyond recognition in the service of the nameless. No wonder Ted was their puppet – presumably he had been since the day he'd disappeared in Glasgow – though one of the worst things had been his indifferent stare as he had tightened Barbara's bonds.

Angela's look was worse, for it was beyond indifference. When their eyes met, Barbara had felt destroyed, worthless, meaningful only as a victim. Angela's eyes looked unnaturally blue, polluted. Their gaze had held her mother absolutely still while she was being bound and gagged. Was Angela the reason why the cult was near its goal? Could her power have been what the cult had been awaiting?

Barbara mustn't think that, for it led to despair. She had already felt how the power of the cult seized on despair. Her

257

arms were throbbing and shaking as she tried to loosen the bonds at her wrists, her ankle-bones scraped together as she sawed her ankles back and forth. Surely her bonds could yield half an inch, even a quarter, to give her the extra surge of strength she needed.

By now the vans had left London behind. There was nothing beside the road for miles except distant floodlit factories, glaring across dark fields or marshes. Lorries roared by, their headlights tumbling shadows between the trunks that filled the van. A sack or a coat was slumped between two of the trunks.

Could she attract the attention of one of the lorry drivers? She tried to squirm towards the rear doors, to be able to press her face against the window while she thought how to communicate, but a jumble of suitcases blocked her way. She struggled to hoist herself over them – it didn't matter if she fell – but it was hopeless. In any case, the driver of the van behind hers would see her before any of the lorry drivers had the chance. Between the trunks next to the doors, the sack or the coat looked unpleasantly like a small figure with a collapsed head.

She searched the suitcases as best she could, for a metal edge with which she could saw through her bonds. There was none – no doubt her captors had made sure that none was within reach. Shadows staggered among the trunks as lorries passed. The van seemed to be growing smaller and dustier; certainly there was a harsh dry smell. As headlights rushed past the van, the shape between the trunks appeared to nod towards her, raising its caved-in face.

All at once the van lurched away from the lorries, on to an unlit road. She was thrown bodily on to the heap of suitcases, one of which snapped open. Now the only light came from the following van, a couple of dim scraps which jerked about near the roof and left the rest of the interior in darkness. Another lurch, and she was hurled back against

258

the wall. She heard an object thud out of the open suitcase and roll against her thigh.

After a struggle she succeeded in touching the object with her hand. Perhaps it was an ornament, or something equally fragile, for it was wrapped in cloth that felt stiff with stains. Parts of it were soft, or was that the cloth? Perhaps it was a container of some kind, for it had fallen open within the wrapping. There was no reason for her to writhe away from it: why should the smell of earth be intrinsically horrible? Nevertheless she squirmed violently until she managed to kick the wrapped object across the van.

When the van stopped it was almost a relief. Then the headlights of the van behind went out, and it was no relief at all. She was alone in the dark with the smells of earth and dust, with a faint dry stirring between her and the doors. Though she was choking on paper she held herself absolutely still, as if that would make her imperceptible. By the time they came to take her out she was shaking with the effort or with fear.

At first there seemed to be almost nothing outside the van, just darkness flattened by a hissing wind. When her eyes adjusted she saw that she was close to a small river which presumably led to the Thames. All around her, marshes glimmered spikily beneath a sky that glowed like fog. Gulls flaked away from the landscape, screaming. The smudges on the horizon might be hills or clouds. The lumps of darkness further up the river were houses, perhaps abandoned; all the windows were dark.

Angela came to where two of the men were holding Barbara. She stared at her mother for a while. Her dim face was unreadable as fog, but her eyes were gleaming. Eventually she glanced past Barbara, at the van in which she had been locked. Barbara couldn't understand why her captors grew tense, tightened their hold on her, until she heard something emerge from the van.

259

Ted saw it before she did. For a moment his face writhed, appalled, and then grew blank once more. In a few moments the dwarfish shape had stumbled to Angela. In the darkness Barbara might have mistaken it for a child, except that its unstable head was disproportionately small, its skin appeared to be flapping. It dropped the wrapped object that smelled of earth at Barbara's feet. When the wrappings fell open, Barbara closed her eyes.

'I thought you should see this,' Angela said. 'It belonged to your friend Gerry Martin.'

Barbara waited as long as she could before she opened her eyes, but when she did so Angela was holding up the unwrapped object by its hair for her to see. It wasn't as bad as she'd feared; it was so incomplete that she could pretend it was unrecognizable. Even so, she looked away, gagging on the wad of paper.

'It doesn't matter,' Angela said, shrugging. 'You'll be like that when we've finished. Only in your case it's going to take longer.'

She handed the object to the dwarfish thing, which floundered away at once, towards the marshes. Barbara was beyond reacting. All she could think of was the way that everyone had drawn back from the thing – everyone but Angela.

37

When the trunks and suitcases had been unloaded, the vans drove away into the dark. Once the engines faded there was no sound except for the scraping of marsh grasses, twitching in the wind. Even the children were silent, the children who smelled overpoweringly of Barbara's perfume.

If she managed to chew through the gag her cries for help would seem very loud. Surely they would wake someone in the nearby houses, if the houses were occupied. She was trying to move the gag forward surreptitiously, but it was lodged against the back of her mouth. If she fought it more violently her captors would notice; they must be able to see her face, since she could see theirs now – the lopsided woman, a large man whose bald head was dark with stubble, a small dumpy woman with a permanent defensive simper, a thick-lipped man whose tongue kept squeezing out between his lips. All of them seemed embarrassed by her presence as victim, for all of them avoided looking at her. No doubt when it came to torturing her they would be enthusiastic enough.

She seemed to fight to dislodge the gag for hours; it was impossible to judge the passage of time beneath the looming sky. The ink tasted like bile. Her captors seemed utterly indifferent to where they were, to the chill wind and the desolation – she might have deduced as much from the houses where they lived. No doubt that was one effect of their belief that they were only the tools of what they were doing. She had to believe that Angela was only a tool, unable to comprehend what she was doing – but of course she couldn't believe that at all.

Before she was able to shift the gag, the drivers of the vans came back. The cultists picked up the luggage and followed Angela stealthily towards the river. It seemed nightmarishly banal, a parody of a holiday outing that didn't dare take place in daylight. There were even a couple of stooped old people to make it more like a family party. At the end of the procession, one man carried nothing. She couldn't make out his face.

One of her captors had freed her legs. The two men marched her crabwise along the path, whose edges were sharp with grass. She was halfway there before she realized that the procession was heading directly for the houses. If the cult intended to hide in one of them, surely the neighbours would hear.

Angela led the procession into one of the long gardens, where a meagre stream glimmered beneath a pathless rustic bridge. The procession went straight past the bungalow, and Barbara saw that a powerboat was moored at the end of the garden, at a small landing-stage. She fought to cry out, to make any sound beyond a strangled moaning.

Half the luggage had been transferred to the boat when a light went on in the bungalow. Barbara grew tense as a spring while she made herself pretend to be limp and hopeless. Almost at once the back porch lit up. The door swung open, and a burly man stood there, staring at the people in his garden.

She managed to drag herself free of one of her captors and stagger a step towards the owner of the property – but it was no use. When he made out the people who were waiting in the dark, he switched out the porch light and strode to the boat where he waited in the wheelhouse for them. She ought to have seen he was dressed for a voyage.

There was hardly enough room on the deck for everyone. The children, the two who'd met her in her flat and a girl about six years old, were sent into the wheelhouse. They obeyed at once, though it was impossible to tell which of the cultists were their parents, and sat out of the way, against the wall of the open cabin. When Barbara was shoved on to the deck, into the midst of the crowd, the boat heeled alarmingly. She couldn't feel any more vulnerable.

As soon as everyone was aboard, the boat moved off with a roar. Surely the noise must wake someone in the houses – but the houses were falling behind now, and they were still dark. The faces of her captors had grown brighter, green towards the starboard side, red towards port. In the glow from the dials in the wheelhouse she could see some of them clearly, Angela and Ted both watching her emotionlessly, a raggedly tonsured youth whom she thought she'd seen before, a girl with hair like a cap of tar. Some of them were beginning to glance eagerly at Barbara now that they were on their way.

Soon the houses had sunk into the marshes. There was only the flat treeless glistening land, broken by wide strips of darkness that were ditches. Above the horizon, towards the North Sea, the clouds were the colour of ashen fire. Here and there pale blotches stirred, moved away lowing across the grass. They were the only signs of life.

When the boat reached the sea wall she began to shiver. Beyond the salt marshes and half-concealed gleams of their creeks, the Thames led to the open sea. That was where the boat was heading. Were the nameless bound for another country? How could they expect to make the crossing crammed into a small boat? Perhaps they were to meet a ship, or perhaps they didn't even care where they were bound now that they were so close to their goal.

And she was the victim who would enable them to achieve their goal at last. As the boat moved out into the Thames, her tongue was struggling more violently than ever, bruising itself against her teeth. Miles away along the bank, where orange flames danced above the metal desolation of an oil refinery, tankers were gathering. Even if she managed a cry it would never be heard over the engines, and in any case the boat was heading away from the bank.

Her tongue slipped, her cheek bulged, and Angela saw what she was doing. When she stepped forward Barbara shrank within herself, appalled to be afraid of her own child. But Angela thrust her fingers contemptuously into her mouth and pulled out the gag. Barbara could scream as loud as she wanted in this enormous emptiness.

At first Barbara dared not speak. She no longer knew Angela, she had no idea how to reach her, she was afraid to try. She must try. 'Thank you, Angela,' she said unevenly.

Angela was already turning away, and didn't even glance at her. Perhaps she no longer recognized her name. Barbara couldn't bear her indifference. 'Listen to me, Angela,' she said more loudly, trying to ignore her captors, all of whom looked ready to stop up her mouth.

When Angela halted, her face made it clear that was not because the words were meant for her. Barbara was shouting into the wind, her mouth was harsh with ink, but she had to go on. 'I don't know what they've told you about me, but I would have spent my whole life trying to find you except that they made me believe you were dead. They killed one of their own children to make me think that. I wouldn't have dared to dream you were still alive until the day you called me. You must know how I felt, even if you don't want them to think so. You remember how I loved you. You can remember how you loved me.'

Angela looked bored, and all at once Barbara thought she knew why: to judge from things she had referred to on the way from Glasgow, she remembered most clearly how Barbara had used to leave her all day, had left her to be stolen by the cult. She was right, of course; she had every reason to hate her mother. Whatever they did to Barbara would be a kind of justice.

She managed to push back her despair, for there was something else that Angela had said in the car. 'You think I took your father away from you,' Barbara said desperately. 'I suppose they told you so, but it wasn't like that at all. They took you away from him by taking you away from me.'

For a moment Angela showed her teeth. Was she jealous as only a child can be, or might she even blame her mother for his death? The deck was slippery, Barbara's legs felt crippled by having been tied, the boat was rocking. Surely that was why she fell helplessly at Angela's feet, not because Angela had glanced sharply at her.

There was one more insight Barbara was reluctant to put into words, even to stop Angela from turning indifferently away. 'I don't know what they want you to do to me, Angela, but don't you see that proves I still mean something to you? They realize that, and that's why they've tried to make you think the opposite. Otherwise they wouldn't have been so anxious for you to capture me.'

Angela gazed at her, and her eyes were blank as a clear sky. 'It wasn't their idea. I chose you. We've always used strangers before. That's the only reason I needed you.'

She sounded coolly reasonable, not at all defensive. She was telling the simple truth. She turned away, having dealt with her mother. The rest of them watched Barbara, and she could see they were impatient to begin on her. Only Ted's eyes were blank.

Hadn't she glimpsed pity in his eyes just now, when she had fallen? Certainly he had looked appalled when the thing had emerged from the van. His personality wasn't entirely destroyed, they couldn't have had enough time. Perhaps she could reach whatever was left of him, if only he would meet her eyes.

She lay on her throbbing shoulder and willed him to look at her, and at last he did so. She made herself smile at the person he had used to be, the person who was still inside him somewhere, at the mercy of his puppet body. She tried to put a sense of him into her mute appeal for help, a sense of the years they had known each other, the times they had shared. He was swaying back and forth but still watching her face, a faint bewildered look was growing in his eyes, as if he was beginning to waken and afraid to do so, and then the dumpy woman pointed at Barbara. Her simper had fallen awry. 'She's trying to make him help her!' she squealed.

'We've finished with him now. He won't be able to swim.' In fact he couldn't swim, but Angela seemed to mean that even if he had the skill, she would take it from him. 'He tried to trick me when he was driving down from Glasgow,' she said.

As soon as she looked at him he turned and made for the starboard rail. Hadn't Barbara wakened him sufficiently for him to be able to resist? Apparently not, for he trudged unfalteringly across the deck, through the aisle the others made for him. Their faces were green from the navigation light, and eager; the tongue of the thick-lipped man was crawling back and forth between his lips, the dumpy woman was rubbing her hands together. Their power, or the power which they served, was stronger. It had sensed the promise of a death.

Barbara could feel it now, for it had taken hold of her together with the rest of them. Ted didn't matter, he meant nothing. The enormous dark beyond the rail made him utterly insignificant. He could be meaningful only as an offering to it, to the darkness that it represented. Angela's corruption didn't matter. Barbara was meaningless, her whole life was. She was an offering, just like the rest of the world, and very soon that was what they would be. Soon the power would be able to claim its offerings for itself.

Her mind shrank back, for she'd had a glimpse of the source of all this, bloating impatiently in its own darkness, infinitely distant and perhaps infinitely huge yet as close as the depths of her mind. Now she was aware of the boat once more, but that was no help. Ted was nearly at the rail.

Angela must be having him take his time because she was enjoying herself, or because the dark power was. Angela was only a tool of the power after all, but Barbara saw no way to use that insight. Though it was true, it was meaningless. Only Ted's walk led to meaning, and even then his death would be unsatisfactory, too quick.

The dark was looming down at Ted, it seemed to close hungrily about the boat, to mock the microscopic lights of the deck and the wheelhouse. Ted was at the rail, and she could hear the water slopping like a huge loose mouth. She was resigned to his death, almost eager for its hint of meaning. But someone was stooping to her and taking hold of her shoulder as if to shake her out of her trance. It was the man whose face she hadn't been able to see.

She knew at once that it was Arthur. She hadn't dared to believe he was here, and she had been right not to hope; he wasn't even able to raise her to her feet. All he could do was make her feel his grief at her plight, grief so piercing that it broke through her indifference and restored her emotions. Now she could suffer as she watched Ted stepping out to his death, she could cry out to him, and her cry achieved nothing at all. The cultists glanced blankly at her while Ted gripped the rail and lowered himself beneath it. When she cried out more wildly he didn't even turn.

But Angela turned, and stared at Barbara. For the first time she looked uneasy. She must be wondering how Barbara had managed to cry out when she ought to be silenced by the power – but no, it was more than that. She was gazing in Barbara's direction, not at Barbara herself. Her face grew tightly hostile. 'Go away,' she said.

She was talking to her father. Perhaps she could feel his grief. Yes, she could, for her eyes were gleaming viciously, trying to bring him under her control. How could she grasp him with her power if she couldn't even see him? 'Leave me alone,' she said coldly, but her eyes were flickering; perhaps she was straining not to look at her memories. Was she remembering the days when she and her father had talked secretly, when he had waited by her cot until she went to sleep? Was he talking to her now?

The other cultists stared uneasily at her. The dark power seemed to be withdrawing now that she was distracted. She was swaying, perhaps not only with the motion of the boat. Though her eyes still gleamed, she was visibly struggling to ward off the onslaught of grief. 'Leave me alone,' she cried, and now her voice was trembling.

Suddenly there was a commotion in the wheelhouse. Ted had regained himself at least partially while her control was weakened. He'd rushed at the man at the helm and had knocked him down. Once he was sure that the man was unconscious he clung to the wheel and steered for the Kentish shore.

The cultists turned on him. He was easier to deal with than Angela's behaviour. 'Pull him to bits,' the dumpy woman squealed. Perhaps she felt that torturing him would recall the dark power, to keep its promise of meaning. They crowded into the wheelhouse, squashing the children against the wall. Their hands were claws.

Ted tried to keep hold of the wheel with his left hand and fight with the other. The thick-lipped man reeled back from the first punch; his lower lip was burst and streaming. But the boat was plunging from side to side, heading now for the tankers, now for the Kentish shore, and Ted lost his balance. At once half a dozen of them clung to his arms.

The girl with the tarry hair was bending the fingers of his right hand, trying to snap them. The dumpy woman had wrapped her arms around his legs and was biting deep into his thigh. Angela stared at her fellows, and all at once her

268

face filled with disgust. By the way her mouth was quivering Barbara could tell that some, perhaps most, of her disgust was for Angela herself.

As soon as her eyes widened, the cultists began to scream. They swarmed out of the wheelhouse like insects, tearing at themselves as though their innards had come alive. As faces were lit by the red light to port they looked raw, and perhaps they were. Certainly the cultists were trying to open themselves to reach whatever was torturing them. Some of them plunged blindly overboard as if that would drown what was inside them.

Barbara recalled how Iris had said that the bad got into them – yet Angela was making all this happen to them now. It was a child's exaggerated show of repentance, an acting out of her self-disgust, proof that she repudiated everything the cult stood for, perhaps in order to regain her father's love. Her victims were staggering about the cramped deck, stumbling over Barbara. The tonsured youth was clutching his face, and she thought she saw one of his eyes pushed out from within. She squeezed her own eyes shut and huddled into herself until the screaming had stopped and the boat felt empty.

When she opened her eyes at last she was alone but for Angela, Ted and the three children. The children huddled in the wheelhouse; they looked stunned, unable to grasp what was happening. Once she'd untied her mother's hands Angela made to retreat, looking sickened and ashamed. Barbara seized her hand and held tight, though the girl tried to squirm away from any contact. She was afraid that Angela might try to throw herself overboard for shame.

Ted had taken the wheel again. The Kentish coast seeped closer in the dark. Flooded meadows glimmered beyond groynes, caravans clustered like snails on a firmer stretch. On the horizon of the marshes, flames reddened the clouds above an oil refinery. Barbara wondered where the boat would be able to reach the shore.

All at once Ted began to groan. He sounded so dismayed that she went to him, taking Angela with her. As soon as she reached him he let go of the wheel and leaned shuddering against the cabin wall. 'Oh Christ,' he was muttering, over and over.

'It's all right, Ted.' She was glad when Angela took the wheel and seemed capable of handling the boat. 'It's over now.'

'It isn't all right. You don't know what I've done. Yes, you do know some of it, I did it to you.' When she tried to hold him he shuddered away from her. 'You mustn't let me touch you,' he cried.

'You were made to do those things. You couldn't help yourself.' His face was growing blank, as if he was trying to hide within himself, and she was afraid he would become like Iris. 'Whatever you've done, you can tell me. There's nobody else you can tell.'

She seemed to have trapped him. 'I was going to take Judy to them, except they wouldn't have wanted the police looking for her,' he said at last, and turned his face away.

'But you didn't. You didn't do anything that can't be mended. It's all right now,' she said.

Without warning the boat began to judder. She glanced nervously at Angela, until she saw that they had reached a landing-stage. Beyond it was only dark land and the distant flames, but it looked solid enough. Angela was trying to manoeuvre the boat alongside. 'You'll have to moor,' she said.

The stern was swinging in towards the landing-stage. Ted hurried back at once, glad to have a task to occupy him, and uncoiled the rope. 'He can't moor by himself,' Angela said urgently.

Barbara ran to join him, past the children who looked as if they no longer knew where they were. For a moment she hesitated at the rail, as the stern bumped the landing-stage, then she leapt into the dark. Wood slithered underfoot, but she kept her balance, weakened though she was. She stood up, ready to catch the rope – and then she saw Angela gazing at her.

At once she realized that there had been no need to moor the boat, that the boat was moving slowly enough to allow them to grab the children and make the leap. Had Angela prevented her from realizing? Perhaps Barbara was allowed to think now that it was too late.

As Ted leaned forward to throw the rope the boat jerked violently, hurling him over the rail. It was close enough to the landing-stage for him to fall at the very edge and clamber to safety. The boat roared out on to the vast dark water. 'Angela!' Barbara screamed.

Angela turned at the sound of her name. All at once she looked very small, a child afraid to be alone in the dark. She took one yearning step out of the wheelhouse, back towards Barbara. Then she must have remembered everything she had done, for she covered her face with her hands. Was there a shadow beside her, or could it be the figure of a man, one hand on her shoulder? If so, he could do nothing to prevent her. The next moment she burst into flame.

It was the last use of her power. She stood absolutely still as the flames rushed up her body. By the time Barbara stumbled to the edge of the river and reached out helplessly, the flames had streamed under the roof of the wheelhouse, towards the sky. The boat was on fire, it was drifting out of her field of vision, but she hardly noticed, even when it exploded. She was staring at the charred place on her vision where Angela had been.

Eventually she noticed that Ted was gripping her arm, so painfully that it wasn't clear if he meant to reassure her or himself. He sounded as if he was trying to understand or to believe. 'They couldn't kill her, they could only corrupt her. And they didn't manage that, not completely. She's given herself another chance.'

She had to believe that was true. As he managed to capture her hands, which were still reaching out to the charred darkness, and helped her turn away, she saw the distant flames streaming upwards beyond the marshes. Once Angela had seen something like that. The wind whined through the grasses, the river slopped against the wooden piles, the eastern sky began to grow paler. They slumped against a post on the landing-stage and clung to each other, unable for the moment to speak. She watched the undying flames and tried to believe while she waited through the chill grey time until dawn.